more on next page . . .

The Penetrators

"A THRILLING AND SUSPENSEFUL STORY."
— *Best Sellers*

"A PLOT THAT FLIES A STRAIGHT TAUT LINE . . .
A HAIR-RAISING FINAL EPISODE."
— *The New York Times*

The Big X

"TENSE." — *Kirkus Reviews*

"COMPELLING." — *The New York Times*

"ONCE YOU START READING IT, YOU MUST KNOW
HOW IT COMES OUT." — *Chicago Tribune*

Other Books by Hank Searls

ALTITUDE ZERO

HANK SEARLS

JOVE BOOKS, NEW YORK

This Jove Book contains the complete
text of the original hardcover edition.
It has been completely reset in a typeface
designed for easy reading and was printed
from new film.

ALTITUDE ZERO

A Jove Book / published by arrangement with
W. W. Norton & Company, Inc.

PRINTING HISTORY
W. W. Norton edition published June 1991
Jove edition / December 1993

ISBN: 0-515-11270-4

A JOVE BOOK®
Jove Books are published by The Berkley Publishing Group,
200 Madison Avenue, New York, New York 10016.
JOVE and the "J" design are trademarks
belonging to Jove Publications, Inc.

PRINTED IN THE UNITED STATES OF AMERICA

10 9 8 7 6 5 4 3 2 1

To Captain Tommy Carroll and Jeanie,
our dearest shipmates.
And to Captain Bob Duncan, too,
and Bob Pastore, for their help.
And to my editor, Starling Lawrence,
one of publishing's jewels.
And, as always, to Bunny . . .

Writing novels is not inherently dangerous,
but it is mercilessly unforgiving
of human error.

part one

BACKSIDE OF THE CLOCK

CHAPTER 1

She found herself nodding in the copilot seat. Startled, she jerked awake.

The ancient Boeing 747, sliding down through ten thousand feet toward a bright summer moon over Shannon Airport, rocked gently, nudged by an air current rising from one of the Aran Islands off Galway Bay.

From the cockpit on the top deck, three full stories above the belly of the enormous aircraft, Anne Woodhouse watched the moonlight etch faces on fat-bellied clouds over the River Fergus. Shannon lay forty miles ahead.

Half of Ireland seemed laid out for her pleasure below, but after the long great circle flight, she was too exhausted to care. She, the captain, and their flight engineer had been monitoring the progress of the 350-ton airliner from Los Angeles over the top of the earth all day long. She had returned from the identical flight only three days before, and she was groggy, barely able to stay awake.

The cockpit reeked of sweat, leather, and stale tobacco: over Iceland, the captain—ignoring company policy—had sneaked a cigarette.

She was certain that he would give her the landing, and she would somehow blow it. They had been delayed in L.A. on takeoff, and by headwinds south of Iceland, and now it was dark. She was too tired to think, and—though she had made night landings in the cockpit simulator—she had never landed a 747 after dark before. She rubbed her eyes. Her pupils felt as if they had been sandblasted.

She heard the second officer stirring at his flight engineer's panel behind her. His name was Barney Katz.

Like her, he had crossed the picket line and hired on— at B-scale wages, half of union pay—during the PacLant strike six years ago.

But unlike her, Katz seemed immune to the scorn of the union pilots who had returned. He was an investor in penny stocks and junk-bond funds, an entrepreneur, a speculator.

On the flight deck, he was a disaster. Over Canada, when she had tried to check their position with a cross bearing on the ADF navigational radio, she had found it tuned to a Chicago news station, while he checked pork-belly futures.

By Cape Farewell, off the tip of Greenland, he was tapping at his stock-market portfolio on a lap-top computer. South of Iceland he slept. Now he began to call out their fuel-remaining, tank by tank, though she had asked him not to, since it appeared on her instrument panel as well as his.

"Welcome aboard, Barney," she said grimly.

He was rotund, jovial, and impervious to sarcasm. "My pleasure! Hey, PacLant closed *up*, one and an eighth!"

She didn't give a damn. She was too broke to afford

PacLant stock, or any other. She was more worried about another PacLant pilots' strike than she was about the price of the corporate share.

For she would never have the guts to cross the picket line again. When the strike came, she would simply end up bankrupt, trying to teach surgeons to fly at John Wayne Airport, or selling glider rides to rubberneck tourists over the Mojave.

From a change in the cockpit noise level, she knew that the cabin door had opened. She glanced back.

Jeff Henlein, senior flight attendant on the hop, smiled at them from under a white fright wig. "Cabin ready for landing, guys," he reported. He shed the wig and regarded it with horror. "Oh dear! White? These *awful* Shannon runs . . ."

He was a sunny man from the old "Catch Our Smile" Pacific Southwest Airlines. He had curly gray hair, red cheeks, a small Herbert Hoover mouth and chin, and a bulbous forehead.

His eyes were brown, and when they fell on Anne, twinkled with affection. "Tired, sweetie?"

She nodded. She felt suffocated, trapped, imprisoned by her seat belt and her shoulder straps, which rubbed her breasts. She loosened them and flexed her back.

Jeff began to massage her neck. He was a wonderful masseur, with strong, tender fingers, but it was time to tidy up the cockpit for the approach. She shook her head and he left.

At dusk a half hour before, as their inertial navigation system guided them precisely over their next to last way point west of Ireland and the autopilot began their long descent to Shannon, she had picked up her mike for her last position report.

"Berna Radio, PacLant Six-one-eight at five-six north, two-zero west, on one-six-zero-zero-nine."

"Roger, good night." The dispatcher had a cold, Swiss-German accent. She felt unwelcome.

Neither she nor the captain, Oscar Plover, had touched the controls since they had passed over Las Vegas, eight hours ago.

She looked at him now in the amber glow of the panel. He was a fifty-nine-year-old veteran who—from decades of transoceanic jet lag—seemed seventy. He had a thin, lined face and a bulging blue-veined nose. He wore trifocal spectacles in order to see the instrument panel. He resembled a retired accountant.

She had been deliberately bidding his flights for weeks, because he seemed to have forgotten—if he ever knew— that she had hired on during the strike. Now he was glaring at the clouds ahead.

"My God," he said, "it'll be pouring at the terminal, time we land."

"Just a cool Hibernian mist," she said. "It'll wake us up, you'll see."

"I think I'll start bidding Mexico City." He stretched, unfastened his belt, studied the clouds, and drummed his fingers on the control pedestal between them.

She knew that he was weighing another trip to the john: his cruising range was even less than hers, and on every flight he seemed to go more often. And he stayed in the head forever.

He was squirming in his seat already. She winced: if he left his seat now, and she had to circle because he wasn't back in time for the landing, they would be burning unnecessary fuel: at least fifteen hundred gallons, at a buck and a quarter a gallon.

Flight Ops would notice the excess fuel consumption on its computers. Besides, the passengers would sense the delay and someone was bound to complain.

She touched his hand on the pedestal. "Not enough time, Skipper," she warned. "Just three minutes to touchdown."

"Yeah . . ." He refastened his safety belt, sat back, and yawned. "Who's at bat? You or me?"

He was giving her the landing. Damn . . .

She had a gut-deep feel for wind and shear and pockets in the air. At fourteen, she had soloed her father's fifteen-meter sail-plane and at sixteen won her first soaring competition at Tehachapi Pass.

She had two thousand hours in prop planes, and almost four thousand copilot hours in jets. But she had qualified in the 747 only six months before, from the smaller 737. She was awed and terrified by its mass and power and still searched fearfully for its enormous, by-the-numbers soul.

And, with the squall ahead, it would be gusty on the runway.

On the other hand, she coveted the left-hand seat with all her heart. If she was going to make captain in the next five years, she needed every landing she could get.

"My turn, I guess," she admitted.

He waved his hand at her control column. "Then be my guest. You're a better man than I am, Annie Woodhouse. Put her down nice and easy, or else I'll wet my pants."

Too smooth a landing on a rain-slicked runway was not good: when the surface was wet, your tires could hydro-plane; you should really forgo the applause of the passengers and set it down solidly. But if he needed an eggshell touchdown, she'd do her best.

She hid her nervousness and turned off the autopilot, setting up for landing.

It was raining hard when she turned final. She switched on the windshield wipers: *whap*-whap . . . *whap*-whap . . . *whap*-whap . . . With each swipe, the view smeared, cleared, and smeared again.

When they broke from the clouds she could see the corridor of runway lights. After the endless forests passing below, of Manitoba, Hudson Bay, Labrador, and then the vast gray North Atlantic, the runway seemed too close, too short, too cramped and narrow.

Tongue between her lips, she rolled in a touch of trim tab. Her left hand on the throttles reined 185,000 horsepower, and her right hand on the yoke guided the mass of hurtling flesh, fuel, and metal along invisible tracks at 150 knots.

With the tower warning her of turbulence and wind shear at the end of the strip, and a twelve-knot gust across the runway in a sudden vicious squall, she heard the captain begin to call off her radio altimeter readings. Because her eighteen massive wheels groped a full three stories below, hidden by the fuselage behind her, it was impossible to estimate their height above the ground by eye. She felt tiny in the seat, a surfer clutched by a monster wave.

"Fifty feet," chanted the captain. "Twenty-five feet . . ."

Let it be soft, let it be gentle . . .

"Touchdown!"

She heard her tires chirp lightly as she laid them perfectly on the silvery numbers glistening in the rain.

The coffee cup in the receptacle by her right knee hardly jiggled.

CHAPTER 2

Still glowing from her landing, she turned in her paperwork at the Operations Counter. The duty dispatcher handed her a message: *"F/O Woodhouse: Please call your mother at home."*

Her first thought was that her daughter Laurie had won a place on the swim team in the tryouts at the tennis club, and couldn't wait to tell her. She sped to the crew lounge. Captain Plover and Barney Katz were sprawled on leather chairs, waiting for the crew bus. She went to the pay phone on the wall and dialed home on her credit card. Over the transatlantic crackle, she heard her mother's voice. "Ann, he's here! McCann! In Newport Beach!"

She fumbled with the phone. "I don't believe it!"

"I think I saw him outside the tennis club, when I took Laurie to the meet. Sitting in a—"

"Did you call the sheriff's office?"

"No. Do you think I ought—"

The line went dead. She tried again. Now the circuits were busy. She tried once more, then slammed the phone into its cradle, trundled her navigation flight bag and suitcase into the ladies' room, and changed from the slacks she wore in flight to her navy-blue uniform skirt for the hotel, a company regulation.

She slipped into her uniform jacket, with the three gold stripes. Facing the mirror, she adjusted her gold-winged cap, modeled after the navy's female officer's hat. She looked tired and a little frightened. She put on lipstick and hurried back to the lounge.

Captain Plover, the flight attendants, and Barney Katz had left. A tall man in slacks, a sport jacket, and a striped school tie was pouring coffee at the Silex. Shakily, she tried the telephone again. Still busy. *"Damn* it!"

"Problems?"

"They cut me off!"

"Father's Day in the States," the tall man said in a soft Irish brogue. "I've been trying to get my grandad in Miami since half past one. A cup of coffee for you, then?"

"No thanks." She heard the hiss of a bus door closing outside and the squeal of tires on wet pavement. "Now I've missed the crew bus!"

He was broad-shouldered and rangy, with the wild curly hair of a black Irishman and sapphire-blue eyes behind glasses.

"Not to worry," he said. "Give the telephone another go, I've ten minutes more of work to do, then I'll drive you in the van. *You* made that landing tonight?"

"Yes."

"Then I've something to show you in my office, in any event."

"Your office?"

"I'm Ian Corello. Your station manager here."

To atone for her abruptness, she put out her hand. "I'm Anne Woodhouse." His palm felt as if it could crush coconuts.

She tried the phone twice more, then pulled her cart along the empty corridors, until she found the station manager's office. Corello was at his desk, signing cargo manifests.

"And did you get your call through?" he asked.

"No."

"Is everything all right?"

"I don't know."

He handed her a cup of coffee. "I've some passenger comments for you." He dug in his outgoing basket, found a paper, but paused, studying her.

"Now, where have I met you?" he asked softly. His brogue was delightful. "La Guardia? Rome International? O'Hare?"

She would have remembered meeting him, *any* woman would: he was taller than God, and the blue eyes were unforgettable.

He snapped his fingers suddenly. "I saw your picture in an American periodical last week. So you'd be a model, then, a model on the side?"

"No. You must have run across that thing in *People* magazine."

The *People* article had come out last week. Every pilot on the line had read it and had his stupid crack to make about it.

Three months ago, she'd done her best to kill the whole idea. Howie Ball, PacLant's public relations gnome, had suggested it. He had sped down to Newport Beach in a block-long white limo and sat with her in a patio chair on her deck, cantilevered over the Big Canyon Golf Course. She had poured him a beer.

Howie was a tiny, tidy Georgian. A shock of white hair was perfectly laid across his forehead. He had a knife-edge nose and enormous ears. His teeth were exquisitely capped. He smelled faintly of Calvin Klein's Obsession, which she had disliked ever since.

Sitting erectly, feet barely reaching the deck, he had gone to work on her.

According to Howie, the future of PacLant lay in her hands.

The Airline Pilots' Association was in full bay after Stanley Block, Jr., the company's president, alleging safety violations, scheduling delays, maintenance hazards, near midairs, racial discrimination in hiring. PacLant management was on the ropes.

"But you know all this, dear."

"They're *right*, Howie," she said coldly. "And if the Airline Pilots' Association would let me in, I'd join this minute. Management's cutting corners like there's no tomorrow. PacLant's an accident waiting to happen. Block hasn't learned a thing."

"That's very interesting," he said quietly. "You scabbed in '84. If our ALPA pilots walk, you're going, too?"

She flushed. She had been a good union stewardess, once, and she hated the word "scab."

"Maybe."

"Great," he said. "Wonderful!"

"Look, I 'scabbed' because my ex-husband wasn't sending child support! I 'scabbed' because nobody but PacLant would hire a copilot with a lousy two thousand hours! I 'scabbed' because I had a four-year-old daughter to feed!"

"Well, your paychecks haven't bounced, have they?"

"They're only half what an A-scale copilot gets!"

"But you knew that coming in. Unless you're the lead dog, the view never changes." He sipped his beer. "Anyway, we *did* hire you, and now we've got a half-dozen other women, and we *still* get a bad press!"

"You've only hired six women in two years! You have *no* female captains!"

"We don't like to buck seniority!"

"We're not senior enough because you'd never *hire* us!"

He shrugged and went on smoothly: he'd discovered last week that *People* magazine was ripe for the story of a lady airline pilot. Maybe she—Anne Woodhouse—could help patch PacLant's image?

"And maybe not," she said. "No way."

He ignored that. "But you have to decide now, or we're lost it. There are plenty of women pilots at Pan Am or United. They maybe aren't as *pretty* as you, but—"

"You're too sweet, Howie," she said. "But you're just saying that because if some other airline beats you to it, Junior's going to burn your butt."

His mouth tightened: " '*Mr. Block*,' OK?"

"No. 'Mr. Block' was his old man. 'Junior' is just 'Junior.' To *me* and every pilot on the line." She gazed out on the golf course, thinking. "Look, half the union pilots won't speak to B-scale pilots *now*, and suddenly there *I* am: full-page, living color, a symbol of the line! How *can* I?"

"As far as we're concerned," he said, "there *are* no union pilots. Our flight crews are nonunion, open shop, from A to Z! So don't let the bastards grind you down!"

"Why pick me?" She squirmed uncomfortably. "You have a flight engineer named Deborah Gregory. I'm sure you never heard of her, but she's black. You hired her after the strike, so everybody likes her: she *didn't* cross the picket line. Why not ask her, and kill two birds with one stone?"

His face turned hard. "One, I *have* heard of her. Two, she's just an engineer, she's not *flying* one of our airplanes, you are. Three—"

"Three, she's five-six and weighs one-eighty," finished Anne, "and wears her hair Rastafarian."

"No," Ball said, "*three* is, she's so junior that if we have to cut any more flights, she'll be furloughed before *People* goes to press!"

"Things won't get that bad."

"They *are* that bad, little lady."

"That's all BS, Howie," she said. "You rode down here in a limo. If we're going belly-up, why didn't you rent a Ford from Hertz?"

"We'd never met," he said simply. "The limo was to impress you. I can see it didn't work. That doesn't change the basics one damn bit. You don't *believe* we're in trouble, do you?"

She shook her head. "Junior's been crying 'wolf' too long. He did the same thing last time."

"You want to let the pilots bankrupt your company, fine," shrugged Howie. "But Legal's laying groundwork *now* to take us into Chapter Eleven. Did you know that?"

"No," she said. She wondered if Howie was leveling. Suppose the airline *did* go belly-up? What of her condo? The guard at the gate? Where else would they be as safe from McCann?

"We all have to pull together," Howie droned. "Every bit of good press helps."

"Assuming I *did* want to make a public fool of myself, and piss off half the pilots on the line," she warned, "there's a problem."

"Captain Fremont?"

She wasn't surprised that he knew: airline scandal spread at six hundred knots through the whole wide flying world.

She nodded. "Yes: Captain Fremont. Suppose they print *that*?"

"They won't."

"Why not? His wife was an actress. People remember her on 'Dallas.' The Hollywood press would eat it up. He's a lawyer, too, with corporate clients. I can't have people writing articles about *him*."

"Not a word about Gary, I guarantee."

"*You* can't guarantee a thing!"

"*People*'s not the *National Enquirer*. If *you* don't mention Fremont, how can they? Goddamn it, Anne, your company *needs* this from you."

"The trouble is, I *hate* my company!"

"Then think of your house payments! Look at this place! Hell, Sears is trying to garnishee your wages!"

"Where'd you hear *that?*" she demanded.

"Payroll, Security, Personnel? I don't remember."

"You really ran a brain scan, didn't you?" she asked fiercely.

"Yes. Because we *really* want you to do this!" He sat back. "I talked to Flight Training. Suppose I guaranteed you 400 Series transition?"

"Series 400?" she snorted. "Out of seniority? Some fifty-year-old copilot would probably slash my tires!"

"At least you could afford a spare."

Transition to the new, computerized 747 would mean the safety of new equipment. PacLant's older Boeings were coming unglued in the sky.

It would also mean more pay.

"You're making me drunk with power, Howie."

"Plus a cash kicker right away," he went on. "I can probably get a couple of hundred for you for overtime, out of my own budget."

"No. I'm a pilot, not a model."

"Think of it as company business. It's a one-day shoot. What do you make an hour?"

She had always thought herself a marshmallow, but now she found herself bargaining.

"*Hard* time?" she asked. Flying time—"hard time"—was $50 an hour. Eight hours was $400—nearly as much as she made on a Shannon flight, and enough to pay off Sears. "About four hundred bucks a day."

He nodded. "You got my word."

"*And* Series 400 transition?"

"Within a year. You could even mention that to *People*."

She gave in with a sigh. "Today *People* magazine, tomorrow the world. Where will it end, Howie Ball?"

"The centerfold of *Playboy*, y'all get lucky."

The closest *People* had got to centerfold nudity was a shot of her hurtling in under the curl of a monster, motherless wave at Zuma Beach, and another, full page, of her in a French-cut suit, emerging with her surfboard.

This was sedately balanced with her picture at the controls of a 747, another polishing the windshield of a glittering Nimbus sailplane, and a fifth helping Laurie finger her guitar.

People had found out that she was divorced, of course:

> "*When she split with McCann, a Viet Nam vet and himself a former PacLant copilot, she resumed her maiden name, Anne Woodhouse. ' "Anne McCann?" ' she laughs. 'It sounded as if I made it up anyway.'*

> *"Her ex, Cal McCann, led a wildcat faction of the pilots' union during the bitter strike six years ago. He left PacLant International when the strike was broken by Stanley C. Block, Jr., son of the founder."*

She had not mentioned McCann's problems, nor that the Airline Pilots' Association had expelled him, nor did *People* magazine. And if the writer had somehow learned of her affair with Gary Fremont, he did not print a word.

The bathing suit picture—truly spectacular—had given the line pilots something to chew on all week. Someone had tacked it up on the bulletin board in Los Angeles Flight Ops: now it was probably in every PacLant lounge from here to Hong Kong.

It reminded hardliners that she had hired on as a strike-breaker, and she'd heard locker-room cracks everywhere she flew.

The Shannon PA system crackled in French with an Air France departure. Corello handed her the passenger comment cards across his desk.

She scanned them quickly. Each complimented the pilot on the landing. One said: *"hardly knew he was down."* If she ever made captain, would they still say "he"? She thanked Corello: No one had ever shown her comment cards before.

"Quite welcome. Give me five minutes more, and we're off. I'll be taking in one of your stewardesses, as well."

Anne strolled to the operations van. Its ceiling light was on inside. The stewardess was a brittle brunette named Jackie Foley, a regular on the Shannon run. She was sitting next to the driver's seat, and not happy to see Anne. She had struck with the pilots in '84, and was no friend of anyone who had crossed the picket line.

Anne hefted in her bag. "Hi, Jackie. Miss the crew bus?"

"Yeah." She sounded annoyed. She glared at a lighted Flight Ops window, where they could see Corello locking his files. "Is Ian taking you to the Ballyduff, too?"

"Is there anyplace else?"

A silence. "How'd *you* miss the bus, Woodhouse? Get caught on the can?"

"Phone call." She was antsy herself. "Tell me everything, Jackie, your aims, frustrations, the pinches in the aisles. Above all, how *you* managed to miss the bus."

"Tallying up our cocktail receipts. I've been waiting here for the son of a bitch for about a half an hour." More silence. Then, angrily: "While, what? He sat in his office with you, slurping coffee?"

"He had something to show me," said Anne.

"I bet he did."

"Look, do you *go* with this guy?" asked Anne. "Or just *want* to?"

"We've had a drink or two," said Jackie. "Now and then."

"Good! Because, Jackie, I couldn't care less!"

Ian drove them through sleeping streets to their quarters in Limerick's Ballyduff Hotel. Jackie flounced in before Anne reached the pavement.

The Ballyduff Hotel had hosted PacLant International flight crews ever since corporate management, flushed with victory after winning the strike of '84, had decreed that flight crews would no longer billet at first-class hostelries overseas.

It was an old structure of whitewashed stone, with ivy

fingering its eaves. It lay on the river near Thomond Bridge, in the shadow of King John's castle. It was old and sometimes noisy, but quite restful. In the Ballyduff, unlike other hotels and motels on layovers, Anne often slept well despite her jet lag.

As Ian slung her bags down from the rack in the van, he said: "Fly over to Dublin and meet me for lunch tomorrow? It's my day off. I'll show you a pub or two and sure, you'll be back by six."

"Why don't you ask Jackie?"

He looked her dead in the eye. "Were I of a mind, I should. But now I'm asking you."

"I'm sorry, Ian. I get so whacked on these flights, I'll probably spend half the day in the sack. I really can't."

He smiled. She noticed that his cheeks were dimpled. He took her hand.

"Of course you can. You must!"

She'd brought no dress and couldn't be seen in a bar in uniform. On the other hand, in case she wanted to go walking, she'd packed jeans and her Ferragamo boots, which she'd bought on sale in a moment of madness.

"OK."

She was still feeling the heat of his fingers as she registered at the old oak desk. She kept the feeling all the way up the creaky lift, until she reached her floor.

They had booked her into the same barren, whitewashed room she had on her last flight. She called home as soon as the bellman left.

Her mother's voice came on the line, distant and strangely on guard: "Hello? Who is this?"

"Me, again. I got cut off, and the lines were busy. Go ahead. You thought you saw McCann?"

"On Eastbluff, watching the club."

The bellow of a DC-10 thrusting for altitude set the window to vibrating. It was thundering west, bound for New York, or L.A., or O'Hare. Despite her fatigue, she wished that she were in its cockpit, heading home.

She sagged on the bed. "You *think* you saw him? Mom! *Did* you or not?"

"Yes."

"Are you absolutely sure?"

"If he's wearing a moustache, I saw him. On Eastbluff, parked. In a white BMW."

"Did Laurie see him?"

"No."

Under a parole agreement with the county prosecutor, McCann had committed himself to the VA psychiatric ward in San Francisco. Perhaps he could *un*commit himself, by now. She didn't know.

Or could he, after all this time, just take off at will?

"What time was this?" she asked her mother.

"Around one."

She looked at her watch, set to L.A. time. It was quarter to four in California now.

"I'll call you back," she said.

She dialed San Francisco information, then the VA hospital in the Avenues, and finally got the psychiatric ward. She asked for Cal McCann. An attendant with an accent— Filipino or Chinese—said that he had just gone down for dinner. "You call back? No, wait! He right here."

She heard Cal's voice, strong and vibrant. "McCann speaking!" Quickly, she covered the mouthpiece, and heard him say: "Hello?"

She waited, to make sure. "*Hello*, goddamn it!" he yelled. "Who *is* this?"

Gently she replaced the phone. There was no way he

could have got safely back to the San Francisco VA in three hours. She called her mother and told her she'd been wrong. Then she had a chilling thought. "You didn't tell Laurie?"

"Of course not." Her mother's voice sounded cold. "Is that all?"

Good God, the swim team! "Did she win?"

"First in the backstroke, second in freestyle. She's at Kimiko's watching TV."

"Tell her I love her. Home Tuesday."

She'd spent seven bucks on phone calls, but at least she could sleep tonight.

And all day tomorrow, if she wanted!

Then she remembered Corello. Now, why had she made the stupid date, and blown a good day's rest?

Ridiculous. He was as full of BS as McCann and the rest, probably, only here they called it blarney.

She'd try to check him out before she went.

CHAPTER 3

Half asleep, she sensed that dawn had come. A departing jet was thundering over, out of Shannon. But she could not awaken. She drifted in limbo between the ancient bed and lonely darkness.

She was in the copilot seat of a 747, number two behind another, lumbering toward the takeoff runway in a driving San Francisco rain.

Through her earphones "White Christmas" trickled from the cabin PA system. Gary's voice was droning, responding to her checklist items. Then all was swallowed in the scream of the other PacLant aircraft's engine as it began its takeoff roll.

Amber runway lights behind the other plane shimmered through its jet blast, as if underwater. Its logo light shone on the leaping PacLant panther on its fuselage. In the glare, she suddenly saw the crease between its wing flaps and its trailing edge grow smaller. "Gary! Is he pulling up his *flaps*?"

He grinned at her and nodded. She grabbed for her mike. His hand clamped her wrist. She fought free. He slapped her, hard. "Flaps!" she screamed, blood trickling from her mouth.

She could hear the flight engineer howling with laughter behind her: "Too late, too late!"

"Flaps!" she screamed at the other plane. "Abort your take-off! Flaps! Flaps! *Flaps . . .*"

She sat up, trembling. In a few moments she calmed down. She'd had the dream before: already it was growing as faint in her memory as the truth.

Sunlight was shafting through a streaked blind and chintz curtains. She fumbled for her travel clock on the bedside table. She always left it set, like her watch, to California time, a trick she had learned from McCann to fight jet lag.

Midnight at home, but 9 A.M. here.

Despite the ploys with her timepieces, jet lag gripped her thoroughly. Flying against the sun from Los Angeles to Ireland was like breasting an incoming wave on a surfboard. Yesterday had passed quickly, like a breaker, and left her floating in time.

There was no use lying in bed, if she couldn't sleep. Time for breakfast, if she wanted any.

She showered and wandered down to the dining room. Its cuisine was infamous and its coffee almost undrinkable.

But she had bid Shannon on her last five flights and had grown used to the cramped dining room and the surly, farm-girl waitresses.

Jeff Henlein, in his PacLant steward's uniform, was sitting alone at a table by the window. He was her best friend on the airline, now that she had broken off with Gary. She sat down at his table and ordered.

"So," Jeff asked, buttering his crumpet. "Have we buried Gary Fremont, as Father Henlein told us to?"

"I am trying, Father Henlein," she nodded. "He just won't bury *me*."

The waitress slouched in with her breakfast and set it down, slopping her coffee on the tablecloth. Anne tasted her orange juice. It was sour.

"Jeff," she asked, "have you ever met our station manager here?"

"No."

But he was teasing her: as purser of flights continually coming into Shannon, of course he'd met him.

"*Ian*," she prompted. "His name is Ian—"

"Ian something Spanish? Or Italian?"

" 'Corello.' Probably Spanish, right? From the Armada?"

"But he's Irish?" he probed. He sat frowning, finger to forehead, as if trying to recollect. "Just as Irish as can be?"

"You got it. Coffee?"

He nodded. "He's about eight feet tall?"

"Well, six-four, anyway," she guessed.

"Broad shoulders?"

"Kind of," she said.

"Does he have blue eyes? You're *shaking*, Anne. Hey, you were a stewardess. Don't spill."

"Don't be an ass," she said. "Yes, blue eyes."

He chewed thoughtfully. "Eyes to kill for?"

"*Some* girls might."

"Some *guys* might," he said.

Surprised, she stared at him. "Oh, come on, Jeff!"

He held up a hand. "Oh, *he's* straight. I'm sure of that." He folded his napkin carefully, making a perfect swan. "Saddened, but sure."

She was damned if she'd pry any more. She pulled over the *International Herald Tribune* from his side of the table, and tried to read.

A ten-foot section of an AerLingus Boeing had peeled from its fuselage over Sicily at thirty thousand feet, sucking a stewardess to her death. The plane had landed safely at Palermo.

She winced. McCann, who had jumped with the Airborne and loved to dwell on terror, had once told her that in a free fall from cruising altitude you would have almost three minutes to reflect on your sins before the lights went out.

She skimmed the rest of the page. Someone had car-bombed an intersection in Belfast, killing three and mangling five more. There was a picture of three broken bodies. One was a child not much older than Laurie, with an arm twisted backward like a broken doll's. Anne turned quickly to page two.

"That all you wanted to know?" prodded Jeff. "About Ian?"

She shrugged. "What else is there?"

He grinned: "Efficient station manager. Food services here are outstanding. Cabin cleaning crew is tops. Kleenex in the dispensers, sanitary napkins topped off, toilet paper cartridges full. Terminal facilities are good. Security poor, but that's normal with us."

"Jeff, I don't want to *hire* him!"

He smiled at her innocently. "What *do* you want to do with him?"

"Nothing. I've got a kind of date with him today, in Dublin," she said, nibbling at the toast. She wanted the Belfast picture to go even further away, and turned another page. "Hey, Boeing's on a roll. They sold six more 747s to Cathay Pacific!"

"You want to know if he's married?" he prompted. "Would you like to know *that*?"

She dropped her eyes. "I don't care."

"Not married," he reported. "So far as we know."

"Why would that be?"

"*You* know, dear. Irishmen don't marry until they're forty. Sometimes they never do. He used to shack with some of our girls—"

"Jackie Foley?"

"Jackie, the Walking Orgasm? Maybe. Years ago. He seems to have quit all that."

"Why, I wonder?"

"Everybody's too damn tired, I guess. Anyway, your boy is free."

"Look, he's not *my* boy! He came on to me too fast."

"But you're smiling, child, and when you do, it's like the dawn. Poor me," he sighed, "now I'll have to shop alone. And poor old Captain Gary will have to make do with his wife."

"You're something else," she marveled. "A cup of coffee and a lift to the stupid hotel! And out of that you're writing me another soap?"

Anne sat with Ian Corello at an age-blackened table in O'Donoghue's pub on Merrion Row. She sipped at a bitter, creamy glass of Guinness stout.

Outside, a soft rain fell, smearing the amber windows. The place smelled of damp raincoats, and ale. She imagined trench-coated rebels planning the Irish Republic forty years before her birth.

The bar was jammed, and the back benches packed with students from Trinity College, artists, poets, would-be writers.

Near the door, a red-nosed youth in a cap of green piped a jig on a penny whistle, while a fiddler sawed beside him, tapping his hobnailed boot.

By the bar, a one-armed tenor sang a ballad:

> *St. Patrick was a gentleman*
> *Who came of decent people;*
> *He built a church in Dublin Town*
> *And on it put a steeple . . .*

"I found that *People* magazine again, and read it," said Ian.

"That's not fair. Now you know *me*, but I don't know *you*. Are you in a magazine, too?"

He smiled. "Once. I stroked a losing crew at Cambridge. It's dull reading."

"I wondered," she said. "You still row, too, I can tell. You have palms like a ditchdigger's."

"It's a *sport* for ditchdiggers. You want fourteen stone of meat, piled six feet or more high, with no mind at all. And it helps if one's a masochist."

She was still angry from the picture in the *Tribune*, the awkward, broken-doll arm on the figure of the little girl.

"*Ireland* is masochistic," she said. "Did you see this morning's *Tribune?*"

This he did not like.

"That's the bloody North," he said. "I've no love for the IRA, but *we* have no corner on violence, do we?"

She studied him. "Just what do you mean?"

"Violence." He smiled grimly. "He's out of your life, then? McCann?"

She almost spilled her Guinness. "*You* knew McCann?"

"No, but I heard he invaded Block's office, and scared hell out of Junior himself."

"Who *told* you that?" she asked.

He shrugged. "Sure, now, Shannon's a quiet posting, but it isn't Timbuktu!"

"Jackie Foley?" she guessed. "Right?"

"She mentioned it once, with considerable glee."

She should never have given *People* magazine her married name. "McCann is out of my life," she said, "and out of my daughter's, too."

"As the IRA bombers are damned well out of *ours*."

"Q.E.D.," she said. "I'm sorry I started this."

He grinned. "What else does one do in an Irish pub, but argue? Are you sure you aren't Irish, yourself?"

Her plane back to Shannon would leave at six tonight, and she was due to fly back to L.A. in the morning. They left the pub at five and strolled toward the alley where they'd parked his ancient Austin Healy.

Sauntering in a light drizzle across Halfpenny Bridge, they paused to gaze down at the Liffey, green as the parks around it.

She sniffed. "Even the rain smells green."

" ' . . . a faint incense rising upward through the mould of many hearts,' " he said.

"James Joyce?" she guessed. "I never liked him."

He crossed himself, grasped his heart, and staggered to the rail. " 'Oh gracious God!' " he moaned, " 'how far have we profaned thy heavenly gift of poesy!' Someone could hear you, lass!"

"I'm *sorry*. But I never did."

"Well," he said, "you're wrong." He looked into her face and then gazed out across the water. "Otherwise, you're perfect."

"Of course. Anyway, it's a beautiful smell, and a beautiful city, even in the rain."

He said: "It's ugly, too, reason enough to like Joyce, who told us this. There's poverty in this 'mould,' Anne, like I doubt you've seen before." He shrugged. "But it's not all just prehistoric barrooms. There's Stephen's Green, and Trinity College . . . And the Abbey Theatre, too! Will you come with me again, next trip?"

"Yes."

At least he hadn't asked her to call in sick and stay the night.

CHAPTER 4

She woke up long before dawn, in her room at the Ballyduff. The shower head was dripping in the bathroom: *plop . . . plop . . . plop . . .* A standard piece of Irish plumbing.

She squinted at her travel clock. Just past suppertime, home in Newport Beach, where her biological hourglass was set, but only a little after 2 A.M. here.

At least she hadn't had the Christmas dream tonight. Not yet . . .

She had used to take little blue Halcion sleeping pills to smooth out her sleep. But they were prohibited now, and showed up on PacLant's random drug tests, so her jet lag was chronic when she flew the east-west routes.

Until dawn, she would lie here nervous and jumpy, "working the back of the clock." Her normal West Coast bedtime would come just as the curtains began to lighten.

She lay wide-eyed, wondering if Cal McCann could have

flown to Newport and still returned to San Francisco in time
to take her call.

They had met ten years ago, on her first polar flight, east-
bound to Copenhagen. She was a TWA stewardess with a
sail-plane license, a private-pilot ticket, and an instrument
card, vaguely hoping some day to earn a transport rating
and a cockpit job.

The cabin slept. The flight was a TWA charter for the
Viking Club of Hollywood's Scandia Restaurant. Free booze
was part of the charter, and she and the other girls had poured
generously. The Vikings were festive, southern California
businessmen, and by Iceland, most of them had collapsed.

She was stuffing their smorgasbord trays into racks in
the rear galley when she glanced out the little porthole and
noticed the arctic moon, low in the southern sky. It threw
a highway of silver across the Atlantic to her window.

She paused. How could the spotlight follow her, when
they were tearing through the stratosphere so fast?

All at once she sensed someone behind her. She turned.

He was peering past her out the porthole. He wore the
navy-blue uniform of PacLant, with the leaping panther on
his white cap, gold wings and the three broad stripes of a
first officer on his sleeves. On his lapel was the tiny union
insignia of ALPA, worn, she was to find later, against his
company's regulations.

He was deadheading to Copenhagen to pick up a crippled
PacLant plane. He had been riding the cockpit jump seat as
a guest, so she had not seen him until now.

"What do you see out there?" he asked.

"The moon path. How can it keep up? Stupid question,
right?"

She noticed gold flecks in his eyes. He said unsmilingly:

"It keeps up because *I'm* here. When I go back to the flight deck, I'll have to take it with me."

"That's cruel."

"All right, I'll leave it, just for you."

He gave her a little-boy grin, erasing his arrogance. She watched him go. He moved with careless power.

In Copenhagen, within an hour of landing, he had her sitting under the stone arches of Hvild's Vinstue, a jammed, centuries-old wine cellar near the center of the city. They were drinking glogg, a hot spiced wine.

He studied her. "You're not married?"

"No."

"Can we fix that?"

"Sure," she said companionably. "Here? In Copenhagen?"

"How long's your layover?"

"Three days."

"Long enough. What's your last name, Anne?"

"Woodhouse."

" 'Annie Woodhouse McCann,' " he said. "Nice ring to that."

"I hate 'Annie.' And 'Annie McCann' is abominable."

"You'll grow to love it, believe me."

They were sitting on a scarred bench that he claimed had been there when Nelson bombarded the city in 1801. To her horror, he began to carve their initials into it with a penknife. "There will be five children," he decided abruptly.

"And just three hours ago we hadn't even met!"

"We will name our first one Calvin, after me."

"Of course."

"Then, our daughter," he mused. "She will be born *no less* than two years after Calvin. *That* daughter we'll name Annie, after you."

She shook her head. "No daughter of mine goes through life named 'Annie.' "

" 'Laurie,' then: you had your chance."

"OK."

"I had a baby sister named Laurie. She died."

"I'm sorry."

"Why? To check out at two, with no baggage? Not too bad."

"What a terrible thing to say!"

"She had a rich, drunken father. *And* a mother on Valium. And she'd lived in two countries before she was eighteen months old. And her only brother teased her all the time."

"I don't *care*! At *two*?"

"Umm . . ." He inspected his carving on the bench, found it satisfactory, and snapped shut the knife. "So, 'Laurie'? OK, then, that's it."

She sipped the glogg. A golden haze was descending over the noisy little bar. "This will be *my* child, too, I take it?"

"I wouldn't dream of having her with anybody else."

She said: "Sorry, no kids, no wedding. I like to fly too much. Some day I'll sit up there where you sit, wait and see!"

"Look," he said, "instead of the boy, the *girl* first. What do you think?"

She looked into his eyes. They were level on hers, patient and understanding, as if he was simply waiting for her to catch up.

Why was she sitting here, listening to a monologue? She should get up and go, but she was too lethargic.

"You're a *fatuous* bastard, you know?"

The words sounded fine, but her tongue felt thick and her mind seemed fuzzy.

"No, Anne. 'Fatuous' means silly. I'm twenty-six. I didn't

find you in college, I didn't find you in Nam, I found you on an airplane, at thirty thousand feet—"

"And tried to take my moombean!"

"Moonbeam." He patted her hand. "We're airline people, chaff in the wind. Who knows who's laying who? So I'm not about to let you go. If I *do*—"

"Stop it, McCann!" she said thickly.

"If I *do* we'll be a world apart this time next week. So what's so frigging silly about *marrying*?"

Then he flashed his grin, which could make her believe anything, and shifted a lock of her hair from her forehead, and kissed her hand.

That night they feasted at the smorgasbord in the Hotel d'Angleterre, where TWA billeted her, and danced at the Scarlet Pimpernel.

There, he charmed a bar full of Europeans. Incredibly, he seemed to speak understandable Danish, and when they met a honeymoon couple from Lyon, quite fluent French.

"Why are you so smart?" she asked.

"British public schools: they flog you. In France, my dear old daddy did. In Switzerland, they lock you in the study hall. After that, the army was a piece of cake."

By midnight they were in the Arab Bar at the Richmond Hotel, where PacLant, to save money, put its flight crews.

They finished the night in his room, exactly as if she were one of the "stewardae," as they called them in those days, with hinges on their heels.

She might indeed have married him by the third day, had it not been for a Danish law that required that banns be published two weeks before the wedding ceremony. Instead, they were married in Vegas, while phoney bells pealed from a stucco belfry, under a blast-furnace sun.

They bought a house in Turtle Rock, near Newport Beach,

with payments that required her still to fly. In a year Laurie was born, and she took a temporary leave. Laurie was a patient, tolerant baby, with McCann's gold-flecked eyes.

At three months, Anne—over Cal's objections—went back to her stewardess job. She was senior enough now to bid decent flights. By then, McCann had already displayed their daughter on the counter in PacLant Flight Ops: he hated PacLant's management, was running for the ALPA local executive committee, and wanted to project the image of a family man. He was too radical, and lost.

At eighteen months he put Laurie in the charge of a stewardess and took her on her first flight to Hawaii. Before she was two, she'd been to Hong Kong with him, too.

Cal had a blazing temper and confessed to Anne that he had been through a VA drug-rehab program after Viet Nam. But he was a doting father who saw almost as much of their baby as she. Flying for separate airlines, staggering their bids to take care of their child, they lived by calendar and clock. Anne's mother, who lived close by in Laguna Hills, filled in the holes as a baby-sitter.

The system worked beautifully, and Laurie thrived, until one night when everything came apart.

On that afternoon, he was due home at noon from a Honolulu flight. He should have been back at the house by two. Anne was scheduled for a six o'clock cabin-crew briefing and a London departure at eight. With the San Diego freeway jamming for the rush hour, she'd have to leave the house by four.

He wasn't home at two. At two-forty she called the PacLant Flight Information Coordinator. "They're turning final now."

He would be at least an hour on the freeway, maybe two. It would be close. At three-thirty, she put Laurie to bed with her stuffed giant panda. She kissed her. "See you Tuesday, Doodle. I love you!"

"*Pwa* . . ." Laurie blew her a kiss and punched the panda experimentally in the mouth.

Anne looked at the Donald Duck clock on the nursery wall. Three-fifty: where the hell *was* he?

She called PacLant's FIC again.

"He landed at two-thirty-two, ma'am, he's probably on his way."

Getting into uniform, she switched her bedside radio to KLAC: ". . . south of Artesia, bumper to bumper. Traffic slowing for a noninjury accident northbound on 405, near the Atlantic off-ramp. And bumper to bumper traffic, too, on—"

Things were getting very tight. She might have to try to cancel. She hated to face the decision. She had a cup of coffee, pacing the kitchen. Finally she slammed down the cup, and phoned TWA crew scheduling in New York.

"*Central crew scheduling, flight attendants' desk. Last name, first name, ID number?*" The woman on the phone had a quick, hard New York accent and no time for foolishness.

"McCann," she reported. "Anne McCann . . ." She gave her ID number. "Look, I'm scheduled out of LAX on Flight 222 to London. By any chance, is it departing late?"

While she prayed, she could hear the keyboard clacking. The woman came back. "Departing on time."

She swallowed. "Overstaffed?"

The keys clicked faintly. *Please, let it be, let it be* . . .

"*Under*staffed: we're barely legal. Why are you calling?"

"I have a problem."

"It's too late for a problem, McCann." The woman obviously heard this every day, from dawn to dusk. "You *got* to go."

She'd called in sick last month, because Laurie had a sniffle and her mother had the flu and couldn't baby-sit. She wasn't sure she could get away with it again. She steeled herself.

"I'm calling in sick."

Shocked silence. Then: "At four P.M. out *there*? On an international *night* flight? And your briefing time's, what, six? Well, you better get *well*, McCann, because, believe me, one less attendant, and they'll have to scrub the flight."

"I *am* sick! You've *got* to find somebody."

"There is nobody. And . . . Look at this! You were sick last month." The voice turned cold: "Shall I connect you with the flight attendant supervisor? At her home?"

They would dock her pay, at the least. If they actually had to delay the flight it could cost the company thousands and she'd lose her job.

"Never mind!"

She hung up. Much as she hated to do it, it must be done. She had risked life and license slaloming through traffic on the freeway. Finally she sat safely in the first row in the briefing room at Flight Operations, dutifully attentive, with the rest of the cabin crew.

A TWA first officer was finishing their briefing for the London flight. She felt virtuous as a child who had slid into her seat before the bell. By now, Cal would be home, for sure.

"Try to get the breakfast trays stowed away before we cross Ireland. If it's VFR at Heathrow—"

A dispatcher from the Flight Ops counter handed him a message. The copilot sighed. "Airplane's broke."

"Oh, *no*," Anne groaned to the world at large.

The copilot said: "It all counts toward twenty years,

Anne. One-hour delay. Break out the pinochle cards, ladies. Sorry."

"If you guys *knew* what I had to do to *get* here . . ." Her voice trailed off as she saw the copilot staring past her.

"Tell us, Annie." It was McCann's voice, calm and clear. She whirled. He was still in uniform. He loomed above the girls in the back row. He had Laurie on one arm. Her eyes were like golden pesos. "Go ahead, Annie," he said softly, walking toward her. "Tell us what you had to do!"

"Cal?" She left the chair and started toward them. "What are you doing *here*?"

His hand flashed out, catching her on the side of the face. She hurtled backward across the room. She crashed against the desk and slammed into the blackboard, but kept her feet.

The copilot, hands out, tried to stop him: McCann, without pausing, sliced him across the neck with the edge of his palm. The copilot dropped as if shot.

"Cal!" she screamed. "What—"

Stewardesses shrieked and bolted from the room. McCann slapped her again, hard, across the face, and knocked her down. Laurie howled and struggled to be freed. Anne stared up at him. "Have you gone *crazy*?"

He put down the child and squatted next to Anne. He took her cheeks in his hand, and squeezed until her jaw hurt and her lips pursed. His face turned diamond hard.

"Don't you *ever* leave my child alone! You got that, Annie? You got that *good*?"

He flung her away. Laurie clutched her, whimpering. A blonde stewardess peeked in the door, and disappeared again.

"She *wasn't* alone!" Anne choked. "Laurie? She wasn't alone at all!"

"Bullshit!"

The copilot bolted for the door, muttering something about airport police. Laurie's face was blank with shock. Anne hugged her close.

"She *wasn't*!" Anne cried again. "You *idiot*!"

He studied her, and his eyes narrowed slowly. "Your mother?" he muttered finally. "Where?"

"Lying on the guest room bed, when I left her! Waiting for *you*! Sick! Watching the news on TV! With the door closed, probably, so Laurie could nap!"

He stood up and stretched.

"Sorry. I blew it. I should have checked."

" *'Sorry, I blew it?'* " she yelled. "Is that all you've got to say?"

"No," he said. "You're quitting."

"I'm *what*?"

"You're quitting tomorrow. It's too tough on the kid."

She wouldn't take the London flight, because she wouldn't trust Cal alone with Laurie, even for the night; Flight Ops found a spare stewardess in the maintenance lunchroom. That night she slept with her mother in the guest room. The next morning McCann was gone by breakfast time. When her mother left, Anne studied the child in her high chair. The baby seemed perfectly happy.

Still too young to understand, thank God, although she was jabbering more every day, and already seemed to follow every nonsense word her father spoke.

Anne bent down and hugged her, close to tears. "I'm *not* quitting flying, you know."

Laurie smiled encouragingly.

"Just quitting TWA," said Anne. "I can't face *anybody* down there, now. They'll probably find a way to can me anyway."

The child seemed to agree.

"But before we actually leave him, we've got to find a way to make a decent living!"

Laurie jammed her hand in her applesauce and painted it carefully on her tray.

"You know why?" Anne asked her daughter sharply, through the tears.

Laurie pointed proudly to her work, and grinned. "Pwa?" she asked. "Pwa, pwa, pwa?"

"Because if he knows we have to depend on *him*, he'll eat us up alive, and spit us out, and then he'll leave *us*, in the end!"

That afternoon she took Laurie to the bank and drew $7,312.80—half the total—out of their checking account. She deposited it in the savings account she had kept from her single days.

This gave her over twelve thousand. It was nowhere near enough, but just the same, she drove to Top Flight Aviation at John Wayne.

Chief instructor Hasagawa was a tubby Japanese-American with a bald head. Photos of early Orange County aviators, in goggles and jodhpurs, hung everywhere in his office.

"I'm Anne McCann, and this is Laurie." The rug seemed clean, so she put Laurie on the floor to play. "I want to fly for the airlines."

"So do I." He regarded her benevolently.

"I'm a TWA flight attendant. I have to get a transport rating."

His eyes twinkled. "In case the cockpit crew's sucked out?"

"Mr. Hasagawa, I'm serious. I'm quitting TWA today. I want to get *out* of the cabin and into the cockpit."

"You got a license? Commercial?"

"Private. And glider, of course."

He looked doubtful. "How much time do you have?"

"To get a transport rating? I don't know: things are coming to a head."

"I don't mean how big a hurry you're in, I mean how much *flight* time do you have, *already*? *Stick* time. *Command* time?"

"Around eight hundred hours, single-engine props."

"No multi?"

"No."

"No instrument card?"

She shook her head and laid her logbooks—airplane and glider—onto his desk. He leafed through them. "You started young. Fourteen?"

"My dad ran a soaring school, over at Cherry Blossom. And we had an open-cockpit Stearman, too."

"But no jet time? No cockpit time with TWA?"

Meaning, did some horny pilot risk his job to let me sit in the seat?

"An hour in a 737 with no passengers, on a delivery."

"A whole *hour*?" He smiled. "He didn't let you land it, I take it?"

"Mr. Hasagawa, I don't need *discouragement* right now, I have a two-year-old baby to take care of, and I don't know if I have the money to swing this, and . . ."

She had to quit talking or else she would cry.

"How much *do* you have?"

"Twelve thousand dollars," she said and added recklessly: "Maybe more."

"You know that's not enough. You need fifteen hundred hours. You need multiengine, and you'll have to get into a Lear jet. It could run thirty, forty grand."

"Suppose I go for a plain commercial license?"

"It won't get you into a TWA cockpit, not a prayer."

"Not *TWA*, no. But my husband flies for PacLant. He claims they're hiring off the street. Look, suppose I get an instructor's rating, just to build up my hours?"

He shrugged. "You'll starve. I pay *my* instructors ten bucks an hour."

He reminded her that even if she did get the commercial ticket she'd be competing for a job against military-trained applicants. "What can we do here to match that? I don't think PacLant hires women, anyway."

"Look, I *know* the odds!" She felt Laurie's rear. It was wet. She took a deep breath and faced him. "But suppose the PacLant pilots strike?"

He hadn't thought of that. "Are they really going out?"

"If my husband's reading it right, next year."

"Then all bets would be off, I guess."

He got up, stepped to the wall, and studied an autographed picture. She recognized Jacqueline Cochran, organizer of the Air Corps' WASPs of World War II. She wore earphones and was sitting in the cockpit of a bomber.

"I met her at an air show once," he mused. "That's an early B-26 she's in. She ferried it to England in '41, across the North Atlantic. In winter!"

"Really?"

"Stubby little wings," he said. " 'No visible means of support,' people said. So they called it the 'Baltimore Prostitute.' Flew like a rock, until they enlarged the wings. On her advice."

"Pwa," marveled Laurie, staring up at him. "Pwa?"

"That's right," he told the child. "The army claimed a woman wouldn't have the strength to fly it, but she did. Right along the Arctic circle: Presque Isle, Maine, to Goose

Bay, Labrador; Goose to Bluie West One, in Greenland; Bluie to Reykjavík, Iceland—Even the names scare me."

"Yes," said Anne. She noticed that Laurie was rearranging the flight charts in his bookcase, and swiftly picked her up.

"And when she got there," Hasagawa said, "she was jumped by a German plane in the clouds and almost got shot down." He returned to his desk and sat down. "Anne?"

"Yes?"

"The PacLant pilots will shoot *you* down if you scab. So just how bad do you want this?"

"With all my heart."

"With all your heart . . ."

"I got married and sidetracked. But I *have* to fly. Like Cochran, I guess. OK?"

He slapped his desk. "OK. Next Monday. Basic air work, so I see how good you are, in a Cessna 150, to save you some dough. If I think you can do it, then we'll start."

"No. Tomorrow, instead?"

He sighed, and then said: "Hell, why not?"

She left a check for a thousand dollars, for cheap block time, in case she was tempted to change her mind. It would get her well into the curriculum and into an instrument course.

At home, as she was unbuckling Laurie from her car seat in the garage, the child reached toward her cheek. "Dirty," she said, wrinkling her face. "Dirty, dirty, dirty!"

Anne swung down the sun visor and peered at the mirror on its back. A purple bruise had grown on her chin, outlining the squeeze of Cal's fingers. Hasagawa must have seen it too. Last night, which had seemed a week ago, was all at once very close. She was scared.

Cal was due home at seven. She hid the bruise marks

with cover stick, fed Laurie, and put her to bed. She tried to read and couldn't. She grew more and more frightened as the hours went by. She waited for him in the den. By ten she had decided that he'd left her, and prayed that he had.

At ten-forty-five she heard the garage door open, then the strains of Neil Diamond. The music died with the engine of his Corvette. "I'm home!" he shouted from the kitchen.

She heard him pass through the dining room and climb the stairs. This was nothing unusual: he always checked on Laurie after a flight, kissed her goodnight if she was in bed; told her crazy, impossibly imaginative stories if she was up, stories she seemed to understand.

She poured him a scotch, straight; stupid, perhaps, but she needed one herself. Finally, he appeared, coatless, but wearing his uniform pants. He carried Laurie, in her pink snuggies.

"Cal," she said. "Put her back. We have to talk."

"OK," he said companionably, but made no move to take the child upstairs. "Did you quit TWA?"

"I called and gave them notice, yes."

"Good." He pressed his nose to Laurie's, and she giggled.

"Cal, we can't just sluff this off!"

"Come on! I screwed up, I'm an idiot. I told you I was sorry, Anne." He blew into his daughter's neck, and she writhed in ecstasy.

"I can't talk while she's down here," she protested.

"Why not?" He nuzzled the baby, nose to nose, and Laurie beamed.

Anne gave up and barged ahead: "OK. First, if you ever manhandle me again, we're leaving. Suppose she'd been older?" She touched her jaw. "She thought this was dirt."

"Dirty, dirty, dirty . . ." agreed Laurie, disgustedly.

"Did you hear that?" asked Cal. "She knows a dirty word!"

"Yes."

He got up and walked with the baby to the garden window. He flicked a switch, and the outside lights illuminated their pool, their myoporum trees, Laurie's slide. "Lawn needs mowing. I'll get it tomorrow."

She took a deep breath and told him she was taking flying lessons. "I'm starting right away. Mom will take care of Laurie—"

"You *have* a private license," he said coldly, "to hang up on the wall. Now all at once, you need a *commercial* ticket? And an instrument card? Why's that?"

"I just . . . *do*."

He grabbed her wrist, and she thought the bones would crack. Laurie, still clinging to his knee, whimpered.

"And if you get it, you think you'll split?" he said. "Get a cockpit job, grab her, and go?"

"I'll go *now* if you don't quit hurting me," she quavered. "Let go!"

He flung her arm away and shattered his glass against the wall.

"You'll never get the rating."

"Yes I will!"

"Well, sure as *hell* you'll never get my child."

After two weeks of frosty silence between them, Cal asked her to forgive his outburst. She believed him, wanted so much to believe him, when he said he was stressed from his union campaign and too much flying and PacLant politics, and would go to the Veterans Administration in Westwood for counseling.

The "counseling"—which, because it implied instability,

had to be kept secret from PacLant—went on for two years. But one afternoon when he was on reserve, the telephone rang. It was PacLant Scheduling, and they wanted him for a flight.

She couldn't tell them that it was his day for group therapy at the VA, so she phoned Westwood herself.

He was nowhere on their records, and never had been.

He was back at four—in time for the flight—and she confronted him.

"You've been lying to me for two *years*!"

"I'm a liar?" His eyes slitted, he gripped her arm, and hurled her across the bedroom. She slammed against the door jamb, her wrist doubled, and she heard it crack. She was holding it numbly when he slugged her in the jaw and everything went black.

She divorced McCann and got a court order enjoining him from approaching her, or her mother, or Laurie, closer than a hundred yards.

She took her FAA instrument check ride with her arm in a cast. She still had a wire in her jaw when she got her commercial ticket.

A month after the divorce, when the PacLant strike began, McCann attacked the company president in his office, and drew a year for assault.

To get his sentence suspended, his lawyer got him committed to the VA psychiatric ward in Westwood.

Anne had heard that he was in and out of the VA for years, always under the suspended sentence: smuggling arms in Honduras, flying dope, abalone diving. Just before Christmas last year, he had phoned, wanting to see Laurie: when Anne refused to let him, he had threatened her, and she had informed the Orange County court. He had simply gone to ground again, in the VA Hospital at Fort Miley, in San Francisco.

Over the years, she had told Laurie only that he was in Honduras, flying, and after a while, the questions stopped.

Her bedside alarm began to beep. She turned it off. A departing jet squeezed the room with sound. The window shade was turning to gold. She tossed her feet over the side of the bed. Where the hell was she? London? Honolulu?

Plop . . . plop . . . plop . . .

Ireland . . .

She stumbled to the loo.

On the PacLant 747 from Shannon back to L.A., she asked Plover if she could "rest her eyes," since sleeping in the cockpit was a violation of federal law.

He nodded and she put on shades, and slept for two full hours. He took the landing at L.A.

As she left the flight deck she glanced into the upper-deck galley. Jeff Henlein and Jackie Foley were snacking on business-class leftovers. Jeff slapped caviar onto a piece of toast and held it out.

"Caviar, Anne? Salmon mousse? All going to waste."

"No thanks, Father Henlein, I'm B-scale. I've got my daughter eating hot dogs. I can't have caviar on my breath."

"B-scale, that is really sad," said Foley. She studied the beverage cart, selected a Smirnoff miniature, and held it up coyly. " 'Breakage,' Jeff?"

Jeff shrugged and Foley slipped the bottle into her bag. Foley started down the spiral staircase and paused. "If scabbing got you into financial problems, Annie—"

" 'Anne,' OK? Or 'First Officer Woodhouse' would do."

"Whatever. Anyway, if you're going broke, maybe you should have hung in there with Cal."

When she was gone, Anne looked at Jeff. " 'Cal'? Now, that's real chummy. How well did she know *him*?"

"On layovers, Anne," said Henlein, "she knew him pretty well."

From the cargo deck two stories down, she heard luggage pallets sliding.

"That bitch!"

"Now, Anne . . ."

He sounded amused. She colored. "You *bastard*. You're thinking *me and Gary*? And his wife?"

"I didn't say it, *you* did."

"Gary and I were no roll in the hay!"

"It's not you, dear, it's the *airlines*. That's just the way it is."

McCann had said: "We're airline people, chaff in the wind. Who knows who's laying who?"

He'd somehow been with her, this whole damn trip, after all these years, and she wished he'd go away.

In the Los Angeles PacLant terminal, Anne stopped at the pilots' lounge to check her company mail.

There were two envelopes in the box. She knew from the handwriting on the first that it had been left by Gary Fremont. There was no return address on it; they had learned to be circumspect, toward the end.

She summoned her strength and put it into his own box, unopened.

The other envelope bore the letterhead of the National Transportation Safety Board. She ripped it open. Her eye dropped to the signature, a miracle of calligraphy, controlled and graceful. The name was Mike Ruble, Chief

Accident Investigator, Southwestern Region. Finally, reluctantly, she read the text above.

She was requested at his office at Los Angeles Airport tomorrow. ". . . in connection with the investigation of a fatal accident at San Francisco International Airport, December 24, 1989."

Damn it, she'd made her report! Her memory was a jumble: her own pre-takeoff checklist, glimpses from the cockpit window of the other 747, doomed to die, rumbling out to its takeoff spot, with its wing-tip light a blood-red eye, accusing her, blinking in the night.

Two-hundred-five dead . . .

And the awful, awful question: had she done all that she should?

She needed legal help. If she were an ALPA member, the union would provide it. But she wasn't. Gary Fremont was a lawyer, but obviously too closely involved with the Christmas crash himself to help her.

At the Flight Ops counter, she picked up a phone to call PacLant Legal.

Then she hesitated. If Junior's lawyers found themselves in a conflict of interest, they would throw her to the wolves. She was better off without them.

She'd just have to go it alone.

In the air-crew parking lot, hurrying toward her little red Mazda RX7, she saw the graffiti from ten feet off, scratched on her driver's door: SCAB. They had broken her side-view mirror.

Bastards! She held in her tears until she was safely inside, in case someone was watching, and cried half the way to Newport Beach.

CHAPTER 5

The barn-red stable with white trim stood high on the Rancho Palos Verdes Peninsula, overlooking the Pacific, the sweep of Redondo Beach, and the sprawl of Los Angeles International Airport ten miles north. A hundred feet from the stable prowled Sylvester III, PacLant's panther, in his cage.

Stanley C. Block, Jr., CEO and chairman of the board of PacLant International Airways, leaned against his tack-room door. He was breathing hard from his morning ride. He regarded his ungrateful stableman and gardener, Juan Hernandez.

Block reflected that the manure of his two Arabian horses covered some of the most valuable land in the world, and that Juan, who lived alone above them, had the best ocean view in Southern California.

But there was trouble in paradise. As usual, labor was its cause.

Block was a dumpy man of forty-two. He wore tight Levis, a pressed denim workshirt, and a western string tie with a silver bull's head pull. Embossed on his silver buckle was a horse's head of fourteen-carat gold encircled by a silver lariat. He wore a spotless tan Stetson and hand-stitched eel-skin boots.

Hernandez, who was supposed to groom the two horses and keep the stable clean, had just refused again to brush down Block's daughter's gelding. Now its hide was growing dull and lusterless.

"Why not?" demanded Block. *"Por qué no?"*

Juan gazed back at him sullenly. "He is dangerous, Señor Block," Juan said. "I have told the señorita. *Es muy peligroso.* He bites me!"

"He doesn't bite *me*! And he doesn't bite my daughter!"

"She does not ride him often, like before. So he is too much . . . *desocupado?*"

"Idle." *Like you, you son of a bitch.*

He had a payroll of almost a thousand pilots, mostly union; two thousand copilots and flight engineers, half union and half not; ten thousand union flight attendants; three thousand IAM machinists; and over two thousand nonunion operational, service, and clerical personnel. But his one Mexican gardener-groom had for the past week been giving him more trouble than any of them.

"OK, Juan, I don't want you bitten, you're right."

Juan's eyes widened. "I am right, señor?"

"Now, how long did you used to spend currying that horse, and brushing him every day? *¿Cuantas horas?*"

Juan shrugged. "Oh, señor . . . Maybe half of an hour, each day."

"Half an hour at five-fifty an hour, that's two and a quarter bucks." He wrote with a finger on the dust of the feed-bin rail. "You *were* getting $44 a day. Minus $2.25, that's $41.75 from now on. Right? *¿No es verdad?*"

The Mexican looked stricken. "But, señor, someone must brush the horse! It will have sores . . ."

"I'll *sell* the horse, you *said* she isn't riding it." He smiled and punched the Mexican companionably. "*Buenos días, amigo*, have a nice day."

Hernandez watched him walk along the flagstone pathways, which he also had to sweep, through the Monterey pine and Bougainvillea plants he was made to prune so carefully.

"Bastard," he said. "Shit!"

What could one expect of such a man? The cook—and she should know, for she had worked for him since he left west Texas—said he had overthrown his own father and stolen his company away.

Juan began to curry Block's horse. The animal was still panting. There had once been three Arabians, the cook said, and then one morning six years ago there were two in the stable and the mare—the most beautiful of them all—was gone forever.

The tale was horrible past all belief. Even the *pantera* had nearly died, shot in the flank and left for dead with a dart gun the intruders had found in the stable. The cook hinted to him that she had seen the men who did it, *¡Madre de Dios!,* but *el patrón* had sworn her to secrecy, and Juan must never, never tell.

Block's horse nuzzled him with a moist, hot nose and he looked into its soft brown eyes. "What did *you* see that night, *caballo*? Do you miss your *corazón*? Are you happy it wasn't you?"

He touched the sweating neck. *El patrón* always loped the gelding up the last grade home, tailed by a bodyguard on a snorting motor scooter.

"Puerco," he said, glancing after Block. "Pig!"

Stanley Block, Junior, strolled into his living room. His wife Dorothy was sitting on their couch. She was wearing lavender sweats with a starburst of spangles at her heart, and amethyst earrings bordered with diamonds.

She looked up at him and kissed the air. "Good morning, darling." She had a Panhandle drawl, softened many years ago in a Baltimore finishing school.

"Mornin', gorgeous."

She looked good, considering her mileage: tanned, skin taut, leggy. Since she had quit riding two years ago, she spent a half hour a day in their gym, pedaling and tread-milling, and was slimmer than their daughter.

She had been to their postbox and was reading their new *People* magazine.

"I had to cut Juan's pay," he announced. "He won't curry Marjorie's horse."

"I know, the poor thing looks like hell," she said.

"So does her horse."

"Ha ha." She frowned at the magazine. "My God, Stan, have you seen this? She's one of yours!"

She folded the magazine along its spine and handed it to him. He looked at the picture. A pretty woman in a PacLant uniform sat in the copilot's seat of a 747.

"Hadn't seen it, no, but I knew it was coming. Howie Ball set it up." He peered at her. "What's wrong?"

She strode to the bay window, and looked out at the sea. She strode very well. She whirled and faced him. "That's McCann's ex-wife!"

"*Cal* McCann's? How do you know?"

"Read the damn thing!"

He skimmed the article quickly. "My God, you're right!"

"You hired his ex-*wife*?"

"Come on, now, Dorothy," he said. "She changed her name. How would Personnel have known? You know how many pilots we took on during the strike? Damn near six hundred!"

"I don't care! If she's his wife—"

"*Former* wife, it says here."

"Well, then she knew what he planned to do!" she said.

"That depends on when they split, doesn't it?"

"If they really *did*!" she said. "They're probably laughing at us now! You *fire* that bimbo, damn it!"

"I cannot fire her," he explained, "without grounds." He clumped to the window and looked out. The sweep of the ocean and the lovely gardens leading to the edges of his cliff calmed him. "After all, it worked out mighty well."

"No! They should have locked him up and thrown away the key!"

During the strike six years ago, he'd been sitting in his enormous office when the striking copilot had burst in past two secretaries and a dozing security guard. The copilot was in uniform and wore a striker's "Scratch Junior" button on his lapel. He was brandishing the ALPA handout refusing the latest company offer.

"On your feet, you lard-assed bastard!"

Block had never seen the man before. "You fly for me?"

The man was within ten feet of his desk when Block fumbled for the loaded .44 his father had always kept in his top desk drawer. He yelled: "Hold it, buster!"

"The name's McCann."

Block had been hearing of him for years, too hot for the union to handle, running for office on their local committee and being soundly scrubbed. "How'd you get in? Bargaining committee?"

"I don't bargain. On your feet!"

Clumsily, Block cocked the gun. "Stay where you are!" His voice was rising uncontrollably.

"Put it down, Junior, or I'll jam it up your ass."

Where the hell was Security? He jabbed the red emergency button under his desk as McCann's arm, with the three gold stripes, whipped out and wrenched the gun from his grip.

He bolted for the corner of his office and whirled, at bay. He yelled in alarm as he saw the pistol leveled at his head. McCann laughed, let down the hammer of the weapon, and tossed it onto the desk. He jammed the wage offer into Block's face.

"Eat it."

"The hell I will!"

McCann reached out and grabbed the back of his neck. "Eat your fucking *offer*, Junior!"

He had hands of steel. Block found himself bent forward, the crumpled handout crushed into his face, ripping at his lips. He spluttered, gagged, and was still spitting and struggling when the security guards burst in.

"I'll fire you!" yelled Block.

"Then, Junior, I'll kill you," grinned McCann, and offered no resistance. Uncertainly, Block signed charges. McCann spent most of the night in jail because the union refused to bail him out, and he had to raise $5,000 on his own.

Block instantly purged McCann from the payroll. He fired the security guard and the receptionist on duty and hired bodyguards around the clock.

McCann was back on the picket line the next day, spreading the story. Pilots who had revered Block's old man were laughing at "Junior the Gunslinger."

Now he studied Anne Woodhouse's picture. "I wonder what happened to him?"

The last he had heard, McCann was hiding from his one-year sentence for assault with a deadly weapon—Block's own—under the VA's skirts.

He turned the page. Now McCann's ex-wife was emerging from the surf in a French-cut bathing suit, all gleaming thighs and golden hips.

"Maybe I'll have them send her up," he said, "and see if she knows where he is."

He had bodyguards, a dog outside, and a twenty-grand alarm system. Plus a .357 Magnum in his bedside table, and a shotgun beneath the bed.

But sometimes at night he could hear McCann's words clearly: *"Then, Junior, I'll kill you."*

CHAPTER 6

It was almost 2 P.M. before Anne turned off the jammed freeway at the Newport Beach exit. She swung her little red Mazda RX7 south on MacArthur, toward the water and her home.

She passed John Wayne Airport, only five minutes from her condo. A bigger-than-life bronze statue of the Duke—wearing chaps with a holstered Colt—had guarded the entrance to the terminal until they moved him inside. The statue had comforted her, as if Wayne were the town marshal, come back to life. She missed him now.

She swung the Mazda into Big Canyon Town Homes, a secluded enclave on a dead-end private road. She waved to Eduardo, the kingly, Buddha-faced day security guard.

As always, he seemed relieved to see her, and a little incredulous. She had seen him crossing himself in his little kiosk when she left on her last trip. She suspected that he didn't trust an airline that would hire a lady copilot.

Years ago, the police had given him a mug shot of McCann to hang inside, but he was afraid that Laurie would see it, and refused.

She sat on the big couch in the den, with Laurie trapped between her legs and Bonnie, their golden retriever, regarding them sadly. Anne was brushing her daughter's hair while *Ghost Busters II* rewound on the VCR.

Laurie wore cutoffs and a T-shirt: *"How can I love you when you ate my puppy?"* She still had baby fat under her apricot skin.

She had been subdued all evening. Brushing gently, tongue between her lips, Anne asked: "Did you feel bad because you beat Kimiko?"

Kimiko was her best friend and the second best swimmer on the team.

"No. She bugs me all the time about Kenny. And I don't even *like* him."

Kenny was her first suitor, son of a foreign-car dealer, precocious, sly, and very spoiled. Last Christmas he had tried to give her a thirty-dollar bottle of perfume. Anne had no idea what he had in mind, and made her give it back.

Anne hit a tangle and she squirmed.

"Sorry, Doodle," said Anne.

The fearless, golden eyes filled with tears. "I didn't mean to pull," Anne said quickly, easing the brush from her hair.

But now Laurie was weeping silently. Anne hugged her. "What is it? Honey, what's wrong?"

"Do you have to bid *Ireland* all the time?"

"Well . . . I make more on international flights. And we need the money, Laurie. Why?"

"I was lonely for you."

All Laurie's life she had accepted absences. If she was going to grieve about them now, they were both in trouble.

"Doodle, flying to Ireland, I'm home *more*. And longer! If I bid Dallas, or New York, I'd be in and out, and in and out—"

"OK. It's *OK*!" She pulled away impatiently.

"Laurie, what happened? Something! What?"

"It was on TV . . ."

"What?"

"About the bomb on the airplane. In Ireland. Air what's-its-name, the Irish one? And the stew fell out?"

"Now, wait a minute, Doodle! The bomb was on the ground, in Belfast. The plane was in the air, a million miles away!"

Laurie regarded her doubtfully. "It was?"

"Of course. Why didn't you ask Grandma, if it scared you?"

Laurie shook her head. "She had a block."

You were supposed to honor her mother's "writer's blocks," not add to her problems with complaints.

"You can *ask* her about things, though," Anne assured her. "I'll tell her that. You *have* to!"

"Why *did* the stewardess fall out, then?" asked Laurie softly.

Anne explained metal fatigue, and cabin pressurization, and what happened at thirty thousand feet when you popped an aging Pepsi can that weighed a hundred tons and made five hundred knots.

Then, in the honored airline tradition of lying to the innocent, she demonstrated how, with PacLant's superb maintenance, it could never happen to her mother's plane.

Laurie accepted it, but had another question: "Were you in that place? Belfast?"

"I *never* go to Belfast. It's not even the same country, really. Shannon and Dublin . . . Where we fly, it's beautiful. The Emerald Isle!"

"The Emerald City, in the Land of Oz?"

Cal had read her *The Wizard of Oz*, over and over again, when she was too young to understand, but she seemed to remember.

"Better than the Emerald City. Hey! Would you like to *go* to Ireland, while school's still out?"

"No. San Francisco. For your check ride? Can we, Mom? Like last summer?"

They had wandered Fisherman's Wharf, scarfed ice cream at Mama Maxwell's, ridden the cable car, taken a ferry ride.

"Why not, Doodle? It's all for free."

Laurie gave her a high-five and without any argument at all, trudged up to bed.

Anne patrolled the downstairs windows and drew the drapes. It was a warm night. She slid open the glass door to the patio, and leaned for a while on the railing, in a slant of light from the living room lamp. A drunken, lopsided moon rode above the Palos Verdes headland, thirty miles northwest: you couldn't see the ocean, just the bluffs.

The tropical smell was heavy out here. An owl hooted softly. She gazed across Big Canyon Golf Course. Far below, one of its sprinklers began to whirl, snaking a silver stream of water around the fairway, *tchuu, tchuu, tchuu* . . .

On the other side of the course, behind sandtraps and eucalyptus, big homes loomed in the moonlight. Despite gate security, a large, rawboned woman who played on the tennis club's Hill and Dale team had been raped in her home at knife-point, three years ago, while her husband worked late at his office.

The man had climbed through brush and bracken from the course, eased open a glass door, presumably like the one behind Anne, and attacked her in front of her TV.

It was so impossible a crime for Newport Beach that it still haunted everyone. You couldn't see the woman, pounding away on the tennis court, without thinking about it.

Anne felt Bonnie's head pressing her knee, and scratched her behind the ears.

"You wouldn't let that happen, would you, Bonnie? You'd bark, and snarl, and bite?"

The deck creaked as her mother stepped out. "Wouldn't let *what* happen, honey?"

Her mother was nervous enough already, if she was seeing McCann behind every bush. "Private conversation with my dog," said Anne.

Her mother lit a cigarette. In the flare of her lighter, her dark brown eyes were bloodshot. She had been a pretty woman, when her features were sharp. Now they were blurred, and her skin lined and wilting. Her mouth turned down and her body slumped.

She was trying to finish her twenty-seventh paperback— *Love Not the Wind*—in time to chair a panel at a Romance Writers of America convention in Houston in two weeks.

"American Express called again. They're dunning us pretty good."

"Why tell me at bedtime?"

"Sorry."

"I'll send them a check in the morning."

"Oh, and Gary Fremont! Three times, but I didn't pick up."

The Christmas crash . . . Damn!

"The calls are on the tape," her mother went on. "He left a number."

"I've got *her* number."

"Whose?"

"His wife's, and that's enough."

Her mother had loved Gary, married or not, and protected his memory still. "You're burning bridges you might want."

"They're burned."

Her mother ignored her and scratched Bonnie's ears. "What were you talking to Bonnie about? Bonnie wouldn't let *what* happen?"

"Wouldn't let anyone bother us," said Anne. "She'd bark, anyway."

"And you just wanted to remind yourself of this? So *you* think I saw McCann, too, way down deep?"

"No," said Anne, "I don't."

"Good. Because after the freestyle, somebody snuck into the ladies' locker room while Laurie was showering."

"What?"

"He stuck a red hibiscus in the pocket of her cutoffs," said her mother.

"I don't believe it!"

Her mother shrugged. "She heard him, whoever he was."

"Why 'he'? Maybe it was Kimiko, being noble: Laurie beat her."

"No. Kimiko was with me at the snack bar, drowning her sorrows in Coke."

"It didn't have to be a guy!" insisted Anne.

"A girl?" her mother scoffed. "Come on!"

"Kenny!" decided Anne. "That little creep!"

"My first thought," said her mother. "But Laurie says he wouldn't dare."

"Well, we know McCann was safe in San Francisco," said Anne, "because I heard him on the phone."

Her mother flicked her cigarette in a glowing arc toward the sprinkler down below.

"I'm glad," she said. "Good night."

Anne stretched in the moonlight. She was wide awake, and jumpy. To her body, it was time to get up. She roamed the condo, disconnecting the phone jacks.

Nothing must disturb her during the first night home. Laurie knew that she must move like a ghost if she awakened early, and make her own breakfast; Anne's mother was trained to creep to her desk and work silently.

Blinds drawn, phones disconnected, alarm set, Anne poured herself a glass of milk, to sleep on. She caught a glimpse of her face in the ebony glass front of her refrigerator.

She looked as tired as her mother did. According to airline lore, every year she flew the airways took three months off her life.

CHAPTER
7

Early the next morning, Anne attacked the northbound freeway savagely, angry at the summons and scared of what lay ahead.

Speeding in the fast lane under the approach path to Runway 25 at Los Angeles International, she glanced up at the procession of landing aircraft, drifting out of the creamy sky like howling ghosts, one after another, landing on alternate strips.

She dreaded the smog around the airport. When she was flying, descending into the murk, she would hike up her cockpit seat, to see better, and try to scan the haze ahead: down, up, right, left.

The captains she flew with scoffed. Their own eyes were on their instruments and their faith lay in air-traffic controllers at radar screens fifty miles away in Palmdale. But once every few months she would spot a little Cessna or a Beechcraft, illegal, uncontrolled on VFR and confused in the smog, flitting like a vision across their path, then swallowed into limbo as they flashed by.

The errors of amateur pilots weren't her problem today. The fatal error of a veteran pilot was, and her own false report: her lie.

Mike Ruble arose, shook hands, and indicated a chair. He was a stocky, rumpled man, with gray eyes. He had curly, pepper-and-salt hair. He was wearing a tan corduroy jacket with leathered elbows. A gold Star of David and a wedding ring dangled from a chain around his neck.

Sunlight, yellowish with the muck outside, slashed across the room and fell on the surface of his desk. On it she noticed a silver-framed photo of a pretty blond stewardess, in a page-boy hairdo from the fifties, wearing the cap of the old Braniff Airways. "To my darling—Kitty."

"Coffee?" he suggested. "Let's start our engines on full-rich." He pressed his intercom and ordered it from the black secretary outside.

In the silence while they waited for it, she looked around. The office was drab. Everything was painted a pale, government-issue green.

But on the wall behind his desk were two vivid oil paintings: a DC-10 skimming through thunderheads in a shaft of silver sunlight; and an ancient, camouflaged DC-3, rusting on a jungle strip, ablaze with splashes of crimson in the dusk.

Both works were signed in the lovely hand she had noticed on the letter.

She saw now that he was sketching her face. He slid the sheet across the desk. In a few strokes, he had caught her features: straight nose, square chin, rounded cheeks. She looked younger than she felt.

"I'm flattered."

"I don't often get a model out of *People* magazine."

The receptionist brought them coffee and left. Ruble opened a binder and found her report.

"Anne, you say here: 'We taxied to the holding area at 2018 hours local. I heard Flight Fourteen cleared to the runway for takeoff.' "

"Yes."

"You have here: 'light drizzle, ceiling eight hundred feet, visibility a quarter mile.' But San Francisco Aerology says a *half*-mile."

She found herself tugging at a strand of hair. "Why is the visibility a factor?"

"I'm trying to find *all* the factors. A quarter mile?"

"Let me think."

She closed her eyes and sent her mind back to Christmas Eve.

The impact of holiday traffic had shattered PacLant scheduling last year. Junior had lately bought Intercon Airways, with a hub at Dallas, and was trying to absorb feeders servicing Cincinnati, Detroit, and Minneapolis–St. Paul. It all climaxed on Christmas, when he apparently decided to ignore federal pilot time regulations and take his chances on the penalties.

She had fought Scheduling, trying to stay home for Christmas with Laurie, and failed. The only bright spot in the holiday was that she could bid Gary's flight to Hawaii: they had fallen in love months before, and flew together whenever they could.

She arrived in San Francisco after a New York flight at noon, grabbed three hours' sleep at the Holiday Inn where PacLant lodged its flight crews, and shuttle-bussed to San Francisco International, so tired that she could hardly trundle her bag to Flight Ops.

It was drizzling at SFO. The crowds in the terminal were sparse. Everyone flying home was already there, except for her and Gary and a few thousand other flight crews, spread across the world.

She spotted Gary walking through the entrance. His jaw was shadowed. He seemed as tired as she. He had just come in from Denver.

He had made reservations for them at the Royal Hawaiian Hotel, away from the rest of the crew.

A cretinous hulk at the PacLant security gate waved them through. Anne jabbed the three-digit PacLant security code into the lock on an unmarked door, and they rode down an escalator. Gary punched through another security door and they entered Flight Ops.

The girl behind the Flight Ops counter pulled out their pre-computed flight plan, their weather briefing for the central Pacific, and their "Notices to Airmen."

They stepped to the briefing counter and laid them out. As Gary rubbed his eyes, she read him the winds aloft: "Ninety knots from two-ten at thirty-four thousand feet. We could get Kona winds when we get there." She slid him the printout.

The aircraft was fueled with 150,000 pounds of jet-A now. That was plenty, if all went well. But if the headwinds increased, and the Kona winds came up in Honolulu, or if they lost an engine . . .

She hoped he wasn't too tired to notice.

"I want another twenty thousand pounds," he decided.

"Gotcha, Skipper," she said. He left to shave, and she moved down the counter and told the girl.

The girl didn't like it, nor did the dispatcher. There was ramp construction in the fueling area, and a Kennedy-bound flight, parked inboard of their plane, would have to be moved. The dispatcher emerged from his inner office. He looked as tired as Gary.

"Look, Woodhouse, the computer says you're *fine* on fuel!"

"Doug, we kind of hoped to get to Honolulu *nonstop*, see?"

He didn't even smile.

"Look at it this way," she continued. "Fuel's expensive in Hawaii. If we tanker some out there, we'll save Junior money coming home."

"We're jammed out there! I can't get a fuel truck to your plane!"

"Then maybe we better cancel out!"

He shuffled flight plans sourly. "OK. That Kennedy plane's almost topped off: I'll give it to *you* for Hawaii and give Danny Cable *yours* for Kennedy."

She accepted it. "Thank you. Sorry, Doug, and merry Christmas."

"Yeah." He stamped back into his office.

As they passed through the door to the ramp, Gary flicked a tiny airplane thrusting for altitude on the Flight Ops Christmas tree. On it gleamed the orange PacLant logo: "PACLANT: The Path of the Panther."

"He could have tried to clear that tree a little higher."

Later, bound for Hawaii, she wondered if he'd had a premonition.

Gary headed directly for the cockpit, but she pushed through the door to the ramp. Out here, she could smell the rain and fuel. She heard the howl of a taxiing jet.

Gusts off San Francisco Bay whipped the canvas covers on a baggage cart jolting toward the cargo bay. The wet tarmac glittered. In the glare of the terminal lights, their flight engineer, in a yellow slicker, was leaning over the nosewheel with a flashlight.

Gleaming white, shimmering with rain, the aircraft dwarfed him. High in its bulbous third deck, she saw Gary, tiny in the cockpit window. He stretched, yawned, and took the pilot's seat. He could have been starting an interplanetary voyage, to Mars, or Jupiter.

Some day the left-hand seat would be hers.

Below him, through the cabin windows, she saw first-class passengers passing down the aisles. Traffic was light, with only 189 passengers in their three cabins, which could take 400.

She had read in a Boeing handout that the Wright Brothers' first flight could have been made in the length of the 747's economy section. The vertical stabilizer on the tail, almost a football field away in the distant shadows, was as tall as a six-story building. The sharply angled wings, which always seemed placed half-again too far from the nose for flight, would stretch from home plate to deep center field at Candlestick Park.

The enormous engine air scoops, eight feet in diameter, could suck a careless mechanic from a scaffold and swallow him up.

The plane awed and frightened her now: too heavy, too long, too wide. But some day, she swore, she would ride its left-hand seat like a proud mahout on an elephant, and it would eat out of her hand.

Their flight engineer was making his way aft, under the fuselage. he was Chinook Showalter, an ex-mechanic from Alaska Airlines. He stepped away and peered up at an engine nacelle, then began to inspect the wheels.

When she joined him he looked up angrily. "Look, you

want to finish this walk-around yourself? Did you bid down to engineer?"

"No," she blushed. "Sorry, Chinook."

She retreated to shelter under the terminal's overhang and took a final look at the jetway. In its window, the profiles of their passengers were passing in review, bottlenecked at the entrance door. She glimpsed a woman nuzzling her baby's neck, and then they inched from sight.

She studied the lowering skies. The wind had shifted to the west: they would take off on Runway 28, over land instead of water. She could hardly see the runway lights, a quarter-mile away.

She walked aboard and climbed the spiral staircase to the flight deck. At the head of the stairs she glanced aft, idly counting the house in business class: an army general, in uniform; a tubby man already in an "aloha" shirt; a white-haired man in a business suit; a woman, vaguely familiar, jamming a suitcase into the overhead rack above the first seat on the aisle. Only four out of twelve seats filled: Junior would lose money on this flight.

The woman turned. She was someone Anne had seen on television, years ago. She smiled at Anne and held out her hand. Automatically, Anne took it, and suddenly knew.

It was Yvonne Fremont, Gary's wife. She had put on weight. She had heavy hips and bleary, wide green eyes.

The grip on her hand tightened. With her other hand the woman grabbed her wrist. Anne was trapped. The woman reeked of whiskey.

"Look," stammered Anne, "I'm late."

"By sixteen years, sweetheart," the woman said, in stage voice, clear and loud. "You goddamn little whore!"

The white-haired gentleman across the aisle glanced over. The man in the Hawaiian shirt became fascinated with his seat belt. The army general picked up a magazine and buried his nose in it, trying to hide a smile.

A stewardess bobbed from the galley, staring. Anne cringed: the story would be in Hawaii tomorrow, and in Hong Kong and Frankfurt, probably, next week.

She tried to pull away. "Listen, I have to—"

"Hold his hand? Sing to him? What *do* you do for him up there? Inflate his autopilot?"

"Let go of my arm!"

The cold green eyes flashed wickedly. "Just stay away from us in Hawaii, Woodhouse! And don't you ever, ever, *ever* bid my husband's flight again!"

Anne jerked loose and fled to the cockpit. She slammed the door and stumbled forward past the empty flight engineer's station. Gary was punching the latitude and longitude of en route way points into the inertial navigation system.

He looked up. "My God, what's wrong?"

"She's here! Aboard the plane!"

"Who?"

"Your wife!"

"Yvonne is *here*?"

"Business class, Seat 1A."

He looked sick. *"Drunk?"*

"Yes."

He unsnapped his belt and began to rise.

"Wait! What have you got in mind?" she asked savagely. "Throwing her off the plane?"

He sagged back into his seat. "That *bitch*!"

"*I'm* the bitch! A *whore*, she said."

"Anne, I'm sorry."

"She's right! Why the hell am I shacking up with a married man on Christmas Eve?"

"Because he loves you?" he suggested. "How's that?"

"It doesn't cut it, Gary! If I have to start bidding Anchorage, Alaska, this is *it*!" She slid into her seat and yanked at her seat belt. "I'll never go through that again, so help me God!"

Chinook walked in, dripping. He hung his slicker by the emergency door aft of his station, eased into his seat behind her, and began to check his fuel-loading sheet.

She jerked her Jeppesen Manual from her flight bag and found the San Francisco departure plate. "OK, Captain? Prestart checklist, now?"

Ruble was doodling impatiently behind his desk. "So you estimate a quarter-mile visibility?"

"If that's what my report says, yes."

"All right. You made that estimate from outside the cockpit, or in it?"

"Outside. On the ramp."

"OK. Let's jump to the cockpit, and just go on from there."

She was relieved not to have to tell him of the awful scene in business class. "Normal push-back. Normal start-up. We were cleared to taxi to two-eight right. Captain Fremont told me to taxi while he checked his way points. I just followed along behind Captain Cable in Flight One-four. Cable always taxied about five knots slower than anybody else. . . ."

"You'd *flown* with him?"

"*Everybody's* flown with Danny. My *dad* flew with him in the navy. And at United, too. . . ."

Damn! Why had she volunteered *that*?

She found that she was trembling. Danny Cable was a legend, a tall, white-haired captain with over thirty thousand hours. He lived on Lido Island, now, not far from her in Newport Beach.

She had got to fly with him only once. He had given her the landing at Narita, in Japan. To her mortification, she had got low on her final approach, and he had gently nudged the throttles forward.

Cheeks burning, she had taxied to the terminal. When they shut down the engines, he turned to her.

"Your daddy tried to teach me to surf once, on shore leave in Hawaii. He told me to stay ahead of the curl, *anticipate*."

"I know. I'm sorry."

"You'll be fine. You flew his gliders?"

"Yes sir: I instructed."

"You have a gentle hand on the controls."

Now Danny was an invalid with no memory of the crash, and she—and a missing "black" box painted orange—were apparently the only witnesses with the key.

Ruble was staring at her across his desk. "So you've flown with Captain Cable?"

"Yes. Why?"

"Are you particular friends?"

"Everybody likes him." She felt sweat oozing to her forehead, but was afraid to wipe it off.

He shifted impatiently. "OK. You're taxiing behind him, and . . . Then what?"

She rubbed her eyes, fighting for composure. "I'm sorry, Mr. Ruble. I got in from Shannon yesterday, I've been flying back-to-back since Christmas, I'm not quite glued together yet."

"You're doing fine. Then what?"

"I taxied behind Danny to the head of the runway, and—"

"Did he taxi with his landing lights on?"

"No."

"Logo light?"

"Yes. Company rule: advertising."

"Collision light? Rotating beacon?"

"Yes."

"Flaps down, taxiing?"

She chilled. "Yes, of course."

"How *far* down?"

"Well, ten degrees, I guess. They looked normal."

He tensed. "They looked normal *taxiing*, you mean?"

"Yes."

"OK. Go on."

"So on the way to the head of the runway, ground control passed us off to the tower, and I heard Danny cleared to the takeoff position, for a Gap Nine Departure, and . . ."

"Now wait. You're taxiing behind him, you and Captain Fremont. And SF ground control says, what?"

"SF *tower*, not ground control. By then Danny's on tower frequency. So are we. I *told* you that. Are you trying to trap me, or something?"

"I'm not a cop! Go on!"

"Don't you have the tapes from Air Traffic Control? Why are you asking *me*?"

"I'm trying to establish how good your memories of that particular night are."

"Not all that great," she said. "I mean, what the hell, we were bushed. And besides, you *want* to forget." Her voice rose: "Have you ever seen a crash? I mean, *happening*?"

"Not happening, no." He drummed his pencil. "But plenty afterwards, including this one. Come on, Anne, that's my *job*."

She was supposed to be a professional, but she found herself close to tears.

He noticed and sat back. "Anne, I'm sorry. I have to know what you saw. *Everything* you saw! And *did*." Quickly, he sketched the runway plan on his pad. He drew in the planes, neatly. "You're here, still taxiing at right angles to the runway. Flight Fourteen's waiting for takeoff. It's maybe two hundred feet away. And he starts to roll. And he's dead ahead, crossing from your own side to the captain's. Right?"

She felt a sudden nausea. "Yes."

"Did you *see* him start to roll? Did you watch his takeoff?"

She dropped her eyes, back in the cockpit again. Gary was busy with his radio. She had braked the plane to a gentle stop between the runways.

"PacLant One-four Heavy," the tower told Danny Cable. "Cleared for takeoff."

Danny's copilot's voice came back: "Rolling . . ."

The scream of the other aircraft's engines filled the cockpit. As always, it drew her attention like a magnet.

Cable's plane began to roll. His logo light, shining on the leaping PacLant panther, reflected brightly from his ailerons and tail. The crease between his flaps and the trailing edge of his wing began to narrow.

She saw a man peering from a business-class porthole, high in his fuselage. Her mind drifted to the cabin behind her. She wondered if Yvonne was still spilling bile to her captive audience. *Whore?*

Cable was rotating now, bringing up his nose. All at once he was swallowed by the slanting rain, and only the runway lights shimmering in his jet wash showed that the plane had existed at all.

She froze. In the afterimage of his disappearance, the gap between flaps and wing had disappeared!

His flaps!

"Gary! Did he pull up his *flaps*?"

"What?"

"His flaps!" She grabbed for her mike. "He pulled them up!"

His hand clamped her wrist. "Hold it! If he *did*, he knows it now."

For an eternity, they listened. No crash, no tower transmissions. His grip relaxed. "You saw wrong."

"I don't think so."

"He'd never have got off the ground," said Gary. He wiped his forehead and blew out his cheeks. "Jesus, suppose you'd made him try to abort, and he *couldn't*?"

"I'm sorry," she murmured. "OK, we're cleared to go."

Mortified, she sagged into her seat and cinched her shoulder straps for takeoff. Gary took over the controls and taxied slowly to the takeoff spot. When Cable's jet wash had blown from the runway Gary poured on his power, easily and smoothly. His hand, which could falter awkwardly on her body in bed, was always quite firm on the throttles.

Again, she thought disjointedly of Yvonne, not thirty feet behind them.

"Whore?"

Yvonne, she promised, *get off my case, and I won't touch him again.*

The engines thundered into her gut. The acceleration seized her as if she were mounting a shore-bound wave. Faster and faster, the runway lights shot by outside her window.

She was chanting their airspeeds, approaching their own V-1 point of no return, when she heard Danny Cable on the tower frequency, staccato, strained: "Got her off . . . But I can't *hold* her . . . Goin' in!" A sudden shout on the radio, from someone else on his flight deck, a roar of static, and then silence.

An awful cherry burst, far past the end of the runway, turned the hills of the coastal range red.

Their own takeoff became a jumble: her numb, automatic chant of airspeeds, Gary's instant decision that they were past V-1 and committed to a takeoff, rotation as their nose came up, momentarily blotting out the view of reddened hills. Then the terrible sight of the spreading flames below.

She heard the cabin stereo channel, leaking into her earphones: *"God rest ye merry gentlemen, let nothing you dismay . . ."*

Gary reported the crash location to the tower, but made no announcement to his passengers. He swung left to pass directly over the conflagration so that no one in the cabin could see it. She felt the jolt at a thousand feet as the first thermal, rising from the heat of the disaster, heaved them up and let them go.

"Remember Christ our Saviour was born on Christmas day . . ."

She stared at Gary blankly. He jerked his head back toward Chinook, busy at his panel, and touched a finger to his lips: they must not discuss it now.

An hour at sea, they switched their ADF radio to a San Francisco news station. First estimates were that there were fewer than fifty survivors. She found herself weeping silently.

Five hours after takeoff, she stood with Gary at the briefing counter in PacLant's Honolulu Flight Ops office. There were rumored to be over two hundred dead. Danny had survived, thank God.

Already the unspeakable gnawed at her: suppose her mind hadn't drifted in the cockpit? Suppose she'd called the other plane, the moment she sensed the gap?

Sagging with fatigue, they began to write their eye-witness report of Danny's takeoff for the NTSB.

"Don't mention what you *thought* you saw," muttered Gary. "If it *was* his flaps, they'll know it without any help from you."

She thought swiftly. The cockpit voice recorder was a continuous half-hour loop, so her pre-takeoff panic had been erased by the time they were three hundred miles to sea. Safe enough there, but . . .

"Chinook must have heard me!"

"Who's going to ask Chinook? He couldn't see the runway. Anyway, he was busy: he didn't hear a thing."

Her pencil hovered. "Gary, I don't know . . ."

"I do! Suppose you were wrong? It isn't fair to Danny, if he lives."

"It's like lying!"

"Who's the lawyer, here? You or me?"

Now her report was on Ruble's desk, and he was studying it. He shook his head and shoved it aside.

"Did he swerve on the runway, taking off?"

"No."

"And ten degrees flaps, you said?"

She heard voices in his outer office. On his desk, a blinker shone. His intercom crackled: "Mike, Captain Fremont's here."

Oh, God . . .

Ruble ignored the call. "Flaps ten degrees?"

She swallowed. "Taxiing, yes. I think so."

His brow wrinkled. " 'Taxiing . . . ' What do you mean? Did he lower them *further* on the runway?"

"No."

"Well, he certainly didn't *raise* them, did he? By mistake?"

She tried to bluff: "Do you realize who we're talking about? Danny Cable?"

"Yes." He was watching her curiously. "*Did* he raise them, Anne?"

She knew that Danny's cockpit voice recorder should have picked up his copilot's voice as he ran the checklist.

"Why are you asking *me* these things? Listen to their checklist! It's all on the CVR tape!"

"Blown fuse. The tape—it's a wire, actually—was blank. Not a word."

"What about their DDFR?"

The digital data flight recorder was installed in the tail to shield it from impact. It should have given them all the aerodynamic facts about the plane for twenty-five hours before it crashed.

"Gone."

"Burned?"

"They don't burn. Just . . . gone."

She couldn't believe it. "From where?"

"Stolen from the crash site. While everybody else was still schlepping bodies around, we think."

"Who'd steal it?"

He shrugged. "Kids? Rubbernecks? Souvenir hunters?"

"Why?"

"Because it's orange. Because it says to leave it alone. Because it looks important. Crowds come from miles around to airplane funerals, Anne. Tie up traffic, ambulances . . ."

"God!"

"We caught some idiot leaving with a size seven shoe, complete with one left foot."

"Oh, stop it!" She felt sick.

"But we never found the black box, Anne. As far as his flaps on takeoff go, you're *it*."

"No!" There was an alarm that should have sounded if Cable had tried to take off with his flaps up. "If he raised his flaps on takeoff, why wouldn't he hear the cockpit alarm?" she asked.

Ruble got up and walked to the window. "Another blown fuse. What do *you* think about PacLant maintenance?"

"No comment."

"I'm not taping you, and I won't attribute your answer."

"OK. Our maintenance is awful."

"So are your answers, frankly. *Did he raise his flaps on the runway?*"

"Have you talked to Danny?"

"Of course. We will again, when he's better. He's pretty much out of it now."

"Mr. Ruble, there was an Arizona Air Freight DC-10 behind us! I heard them on the radio! And they had just as good a look at Cable as I did!"

"You were closer."

"But have you talked to *them*?"

He looked at her steadily. " 'Flaps down, running lights on, normal, straight takeoff roll, until I lost sight of him in the rain.' That's what *their* copilot says."

She felt a surge of relief. "Well, then?"

"Sure!" he said. "Only he's a pilot, just like you. Hell, I was too. He's one of *us*. One of our great, silent brotherhood of the sky, which sees no evil, hears no evil, says no evil—"

"Would he *lie* about it?" she mumbled.

"Will *you*? For good old Danny? On the witness stand?"

"I'll be on the *stand*?"

"Look, we flew in thirteen investigators on our go team. I spent two weeks kicking the tin on that site, sixteen hours a day. We had experts from the FAA, NASA, photographers, surveyors. We had five pathologists, and twenty dental forensic experts, and a psychologist to analyze the flight crew's mental state! We had reps from PacLant and Boeing and Pratt and Whitney Engines! Fifty civil defense workers walked the crash path seven times, looking for that stupid box! So you *will* be on the stand!"

"I thought you'd *found* the cause. Design failure! The horizontal stabilizer! Aren't we suing Boeing?"

"Yes, you are. But I'm not satisfied. That's why you're here, six months after the fact. Stabilizers just don't fall off airplanes, I don't care where we found it. And his flight path is exactly consistent with a no-flap takeoff! We ran it on our computer."

"You don't *know* what happened, so you're gunning for the pilot. NTSB always does!"

"*Do* we, now?"

"Especially when he can't defend himself!"

"I think that's a cop-out, Anne. And I think you're hiding something."

She heard a landing L-1011 whistle by. Ruble grabbed a pencil, tore a piece of paper from a sketch pad, and slashed swiftly. Within two minutes he was finished. He shoved the sheet at her.

A faultlessly drawn 747, hurtling down the runway, seen from the copilot's seat of another, at night. The flaps were down, ten degrees, extending below the trailing edge of the wing, making a deep, dark slit.

"Down?" he demanded. "You saw that plane, I didn't!"

She didn't answer. He snatched back the sketch, slashed again, shoved it at her. The slit between the trailing edge of the wing and the flaps had disappeared: the flaps were up.

"Or *up*, goddamn it? Down or up?"

She swallowed. "Mr. Ruble, don't bully me. I was in another airplane: I don't know."

"Don't *know*, or just won't say? To save his reputation? Or . . . How's this? *Because you didn't try to stop him?*"

Her throat was too tight to answer. He waited, finally shook his head and waved toward the door, dismissing her.

The receptionist was gone from her desk in the outer office. Sitting on a chair was Gary Fremont.

She had not flown with him since Christmas, had not even seen him for months. He wore slacks and a sport shirt she had bought him in Hawaii, and loafers they had shopped for in Hong Kong.

"I left you a note in Flight Ops," he murmured. "You didn't even read it."

"No."

"I wish you had. I've left Yvonne."

"And she blames me, of course."

He smiled. "Who else?"

"Do you?"

"Anne!" he shook his head. "Come on! I love you. I've been calling. I want you back!"

She touched his cheek. "Gary, it wouldn't work."

"I think it would."

"I'll never marry another pilot. Two people can't fly and bring up a child."

"So hang up your wings!" he said. "*I* can't. Not yet."

"Hang up *my* wings? Thanks a lot!" She glanced at Ruble's office. "OK, I stuck with my report. You're next?"

"I guess."

She felt the tears coming. "Oh, Gary . . ."

Awkwardly, he took her into his arms. "Baby, what's wrong, what is it?"

"Two hundred people died, goddamn it!" she sobbed. "And he's really not sure why! And suppose he puts me on the stand? What do I do then?"

"You asking a lawyer or a lover, Anne?"

"I'm asking my best friend."

Clumsily, he patted her cheek. "Your best friend already told you, Anne, you didn't see a thing."

As he waited for Captain Fremont in his office, Mike Ruble sat at his desk, doodling the girl's face on his sketch pad. He wondered if she'd truly missed the flaps, which—in his mind—were the root cause of the crash, or if her recollections had grown cloudy, or if she was lying, and *knew*.

He himself had perfect recall. His memories, like his dreams, were in full color. He could paint from them as easily as if he had his subjects before him: The rusting aircraft hanging above his desk he had painted ten years after he had seen it.

If he could bear it, he could sketch Kitty, laughing with another stewardess, the first time he had ever seen her, lying poolside at the Miramar Hotel.

Or Anne Woodhouse: *"Mr. Ruble, don't bully me. I just don't know."*

He glanced at his sketch pad. He discovered that he had been blocking in her face again: square, honest, the eyes as vulnerable as Kitty's. And frightened, at the end.

Young enough to be their daughter.

He softened her cheek. His pencil broke. He flung it across the room.

His receptionist ushered in Captain Fremont. They shook hands. To Ruble, Fremont's eyes seemed guarded.

A waste of time, he decided: he'd heard Fremont was a part-time lawyer: he'd get nothing out of him.

CHAPTER 8

Anne Woodhouse sat on coarse gold sand, hugging her knees in the shade of Old Man's, the tattered grass shack in the center of San Onofre State Beach.

A hundred yards away, her father dozed in a beach chair in front of his shabby motor home. Warming in the sand beside him was a can of Coors. On a paint-flecked long board rising behind him was his sign: CHAIRMAN OF THE BOARD: Surfboard Repairs and Alterations.

A forest of the other seniors' battered long boards, jammed in the sand in the ancient way until the surf would rise, grew along the line of motor homes beside his.

The campers and trailers of veterans of the fifties and the sixties were backed to the creosoted logs that separated the parking lot from the sand. Their owners sat and stared out at the surf, as most of them had been doing all their lives.

The beach was almost within sight of the San Onofre nuclear power station, with its two nippled breasts desecrating the coast, and she often wondered if the plant's outfalls, which actually warmed the surf, were safe for Laurie.

But the tiny strand had always had consistent swells for long boarders and children. Her father had brought her here when she was six, gentled her onto the midget board he had made her—bright yellow with red polka-dots—and begun to teach her all he knew of the rhythms of the surf.

Now his granddaughter Laurie sat astride an identical board just inside the surf line, scanning the long, rolling greenbacks. They were fast becoming boomers, rising a half-mile out. When they curled and tumbled and crashed on the beach, Anne could feel them pounding through the sand.

She shivered in the shade. She had deliberately been staying out of the glare. From a lifetime of beach days from here to Cape Town, South Africa, she was already fighting crow's feet and laugh lines. This morning she had already used her allotment of sunlight astride her board, waiting for the long San Onofre swells.

She got up, shook her towel, and plodded through the hot sand to her father's motor home. She let her shadow wake him. When his eyes jerked open, she touched a spot on his head. His hair was gray, and thinning fast. "Did you ever hear of skin cancer?"

"What will be, will be." He flexed his shoulders, still firm from paddling boards, and yawned. He had an athlete's narrow, speculative eyes, dark green like her own.

On her tenth birthday he had quit United Airlines and bought the yellow World War II open-cockpit Stearman biplane for $9,000. He began to tow advertising banners and to skywrite.

When business was slack, which it mostly was, he would jam a leather helmet on her head. She would strap herself into the front seat and fiddle with a pair of goggles that were forever falling off. Then, while she craned into the whipping slipstream, he would fly her through the cloud castles over the Malibu peaks.

They would chase their shadow across fields of snow-white stratus. He would flutter down in a falling leaf, straighten and land on a cloud, or loop and slow roll and split S. Sometimes he would shake his stick, signaling her to take control. Though she could hardly reach the rudder pedals, she would fly the plane herself.

His last skywriting job was a message over Malibu Beach, for a lovesick movie actor: "Will you marry me, Suzie Q?"

The actor's check bounced, her father was cited by the sheriff's department for flat-hatting over Zuma Beach, and the finance company flew the plane away.

He started a glider school at Cherry Blossom, a dirt airstrip with a country store clinging to the rim of the Mojave. Anne soloed in a sailplane at fourteen. For two years, while her mother pounded out romances in their mobile home, she and her father soared like eagles, teasing the thermals and mountain waves of the Sierra's eastern slopes. They sold groceries, too, to rock hounds, but not enough. The school failed.

He went on a drunk in Vegas, discovered a navy nurse he had known in Yokosuka, and never returned to her mother and her.

He existed now on a tiny pension from the naval reserve, Social Security, surfboard repair, a few hours a week sanding foam cores for his "Kamikaze Surfboards" at his San Clemente surfing shop, and what flight instructing he could find.

"So, how's your love life, sweetie pie?" he asked, closing his eyes.

"Lousy."

"Maybe you should get Cal sprung from the funny farm."

"Sure, I'll do that." She had never told her father what Cal had done to her, out of fear of what he might try to do to Cal some day when he'd been drinking.

He opened his eyes. "He called me at the Surf Shop a couple of days ago."

"What?"

He had liked Cal and had helped her to teach him to surf. Cal had listened to his war stories like a son.

"Challenged me to a dogfight over Fresno in a perfect German accent. How's he do that?"

"He can do that," she explained, "because he doesn't give a damn, and he's got an ear for languages, and he's brilliant, and he's nuts. Where did he say he was calling from?"

"San Francisco. The VA."

OK, but she still didn't like it. "What else did he want?"

He shrugged. "We shot the breeze. He saw you in *People* magazine. He asked if I saw Laurie much."

"What did you tell him?"

"I said I don't. And *that's* the truth."

"You poor guy! Look, we've been down here half the summer."

He saw them both more than he deserved. He had a low threshold of boredom. She and Laurie stepped over it, usually, in the first hour they were here.

"You haven't been down here *enough*." He glowered at his beer. "Warm! How about your bring me out a cold one?"

For what she was going to have to tell him, she needed a beer herself. She entered the little motor home and found it unusually clean. She opened the refrigerator. Sure enough, it was stocked with food.

So a woman was living in it, obviously; otherwise it would be its usual shambles, and the refrigerator empty except for beer. In his rare attacks of celibacy, her father ate exclusively at the Taco Bell in San Clemente. Sometimes he seemed to live on Coors alone. She grabbed two beers and popped them.

She went outside and handed him the beer. He reached out impulsively, pulled her close, and hugged her. "You're a good kid, Annie Woodhouse."

"Thanks." She sat on the sand beside his chair and sipped her Coors. The beaded can felt good on her lips. She waited for the fire in her belly, welcomed the warmth when it came.

She looked out at the surf. Laurie was kneeling on her little board—if she grew much faster he'd have to build her something longer—and had her eye on a set, far to sea.

"Cal *is* harmless, isn't he?" her father murmured. She felt his hand on the crown of her head, turning it gently so that she was looking into his face. "He never hurt you, physically? Am I right?"

If Cal had taken to phoning him about Laurie, she had better tell the truth. "Wrong."

She told him for the first time about the scene in the TWA briefing room, and that it was Cal who had broken her wrist and jaw.

"I thought you did that skiing," he said.

"No."

The can crumpled slowly in his hand, spilling beer onto the sand. "Why didn't you tell me that back then?"

"Come on, Dad! What could you have done?"

"For openers, kill the son of a bitch."

"That's why."

"Are you safe from him now?"

"I guess, unless that article set him off." She searched the surf. Laurie was turning toward shore on a rising wave. Now she paddled faster, rose suddenly on her board, knees bent and tiny body crouched, and was in the curl.

Her father gazed seaward, at his granddaughter. "She's as good as you were on a board, already." He toyed with his beer. "Does he pay her support?"

"No problem," she mumbled.

"Meaning no."

She sighed. "Oh, what's the difference? How could he, in the VA, anyway?"

"I'm sorry I can't help."

From the pale cast of his upper lip, she knew that the two beers were not the first of the day, and that she must be very careful. He walked a razor's edge, when he drank, between good-fellowship and venom, and he often turned his inner guilts on her.

"I shouldn't *need* help, Dad," she said. "I make fifty grand a year."

He raised his eyebrows. "I'd have thought more."

"PacLant," she said bitterly, "isn't United."

"Yeah, United." He scowled at his crumpled beer can. "You think I should have hung in there?"

"You didn't ask me twenty years ago. Why are you asking now?"

"Well, if I'd stayed on like Danny Cable, I'd be retiring in September. On what, a hundred grand a year? Hey, with a hundred thousand bucks a year, I could have kept the house in Malibu!"

"*And* Mom," she murmured.

And me, she almost added. *But you never did lose me, and I guess you never will.*

"Well I don't *like* your mother very much, that's not a plus for me."

"She never was a plus, for you! But she wrote her buns off, and kept me fed, and got me a year of college, too!"

"She wrote her *husband* off, you mean! From the time she sold that first book, I was cooked."

"That isn't how *we* remember it."

"Then you remember wrong, sweetie-pie. Anyway, I was burned out with the airlines. I *had* to quit."

"Sure, the surf was up." She finished her beer. "The stewardesses were getting older, and I guess you just got bored!"

"You got it," he said coldly. "Right on, kid."

"And," she said finally, "*you* were lucky: look at Danny now."

"I have. Have you? He's back in Hoag Memorial again."

"Oh, no!" He'd weathered the crash with a broken hip and a crushed sternum, the only survivor on the flight deck. "Why?"

"Heart. They say he damaged it. Me, I think he broke it."

"Can he remember yet?"

"Most things, sure. He asked about *you*."

"But Christmas Eve?"

"Nothing. *Nada.* Zip." He shrugged. "I quit too soon, he quit too late. The way it goes, I guess."

"Well, you used to tell me: 'Flying is not inherently dangerous, but it is mercilessly unforgiving of human error.' "

"No 'human error' Christmas Eve. Not Danny."

"Not true." She had come for absolution: there might be no better time: "He pulled his flaps up, Dad. I saw him."

He stared at her. "What?"

"On the runway. Taking off."

"Bullshit!"

"I saw it, Dad, I *saw* it!"

He hurled his beer can toward a public garbage can some twenty feet from his motor home. It bounced off the swinging top and lay in the sand.

He had had too many beers to advise her. With her father, she was always picking the wrong time to talk, and the wrong place. "It's too hot to argue in the sun," she said. "Let's skip it."

But she had shaken him, and he wouldn't quit. "You saw his flaps up, and didn't *warn* him?"

"Almost, but—"

"But *what*? You let him prong a 747 in, just to be *polite*?"

"It was too late by the time I realized it. But the NTSB had me in yesterday. A guy named Ruble. He suspects."

"What did you tell him?"

"Nothing. So far."

"So *far*? What the hell do you mean?"

"They need help. I seem to be the key."

He sat back and closed his eyes. "Let me tell you about Danny. I got us lost off Chinhŭng-ni one night. He was on my wing. I was trying to fake it, scared to death, and Danny slid up and took the lead—"

"You've told me that one, Dad, about two hundred timcs." Danny Cable had saved them both, apparently, by finding their aircraft carrier off Korea, but she wanted no war stories, now.

"Ok, then," he growled. "If it weren't for Danny Cable, you wouldn't even *be*! So, Anne, you better warn him, right away."

"Me? No!"

"Yes."

"Oh, God . . ."

"But don't tell him what you saw."

"I know."

"Because if you do, you'll kill him, sure as hell!"

She spotted Laurie surfing in. The child rode out her wave, sank gracefully into his churn, whipped her board sideways, grabbed it, and emerged dripping from the surf. On the next wave, a slender redhead came ashore, hoisted her board under an arm, and trailed her up the beach.

She was perhaps thirty, with a freckled pug nose and gray eyes. She had lovely round hips and hardly any waist at all.

The girl tilted her head and began to pound water from an ear. "Hi! You're the jet pilot!"

"*Co*pilot," Anne said briefly. She threw a towel around Laurie and hugged her close. "You looked great, Doodle. You do us proud."

"This is Diane," her father announced. "I'm teaching her to fly, once I teach her how to cook."

Diane smiled down at Laurie. "This ninja turtle busted me off a wave, the little creep."

"I'm sorry," grinned Laurie. "I didn't see you."

"Oh, yes you did." Kneading the child's neck, she looked at Anne with interest. "I want to fly, like you."

"You can teach a woman to do almost anything," her father belched. "I've always said that."

"Yeah," snorted Diane. "Did you sweep your RV?" She glanced at the squashed beer cans by the GI can. "Stupid question, sorry."

She went inside, and began to sweep. Anne and Laurie gathered up their towels and boards. Her father went with them to her car.

"Hey," he said, as Laurie climbed in and Anne fumbled

with her keys. "Diane really likes Laurie, I do believe." He had an artless smile, quite ruinous to women, like McCann's. "Your next flight, can she bring her down surfing, while you're gone?"

Anne thought it over. "If she and Laurie want, OK."

"And, sweetie-pie, what do you think of that lovely ass?"

"I hate it, you old lecher." She kissed his stubbled cheek. "But then, we're used to that."

CHAPTER 9

Cal McCann grinned across the table at his psychiatrist, trying to make her smile. They sat overlooking the ocean, in the cafeteria of the San Francisco Veterans Administration Hospital.

The buildings were perched on the cliffs seaward of the Golden Gate Bridge. Mornings, the view was magnificent, with the breakers thundering below, but every summer afternoon, at 4 P.M., the fog glided in from the Farallons, setting the span's foghorn—as captive as he—to bellowing like a hungry water buffalo.

The furious sound, repeated interminably, probed his gut and drummed angry chords in the back of his head. By five each day the horn had him raging inside.

Tonight, to calm his own nerves, he was charming his psychiatrist.

Her name was Gail Flodden, and her name was prettier than she. He had spotted her eating alone and joined her, deliberately sitting opposite her in a slash of brassy daylight from a western pane, so the dying sun would paint a halo on his hair.

She was a rabbity woman, with earnest brown eyes behind glasses and nervous, active hands.

"We shouldn't be seeing each other like this," he grinned, "but the place is getting to me again. I thought you ought to know."

"I know, all right. I saw you acting out your hostility on that old man."

McCann had fallen into the food line behind a mustard-gassed, ninety-year-old veteran of World War I, who could not make up his mind whether he wanted roast pork, chicken, stew, or fish.

McCann had solved his dilemma—after a five-second delay—by grabbing the ladle from the server and slapping each selection on the doughboy's plate, one on top of the other, until the ancient tottered off.

Under the gaze of his psychiatrist, McCann kept the smile on his face. "So what's the problem?"

"You are a violent man," she said simply.

"Boorish I'll concede, but violent? Aren't you being judgmental?" *Judgmental* was a great group therapy word.

"I'm not sure we can keep you here, McCann."

"Then make me well: I'll go."

"You *are* well. You're dogging it here to stay out of the Orange County jail. You're here on the *slimmest* sufferance—"

"Look, I just helped him pick his dinner, I didn't push him off the cliff!"

"Are you likely to do that?" she asked quickly.

"Do I fantasize *murder*?" *Fantasize* was another word they used in group. "I'm learning. Give me time."

She changed the subject. "You didn't go to group therapy Wednesday."

"I'm the only ex-officer in your frigging sewing circle. They'd frag me if they had grenades. Why do I have to bare my soul to *them*?"

"I want you in GT, for the others. You liven things up. You're perceptive. And you went through their common experience."

"No I didn't."

"You did, barring combat."

In Nam, he had ached for combat, but Division had yanked him from the 101st and put him in Intelligence in Saigon because he spoke French.

"Barring combat," he said bitterly. "You got it."

She studied him. "Where were you Wednesday?"

"I had a pass."

"From whom?"

Her brown eyes remained unwavering. They made him uncomfortable.

"The chaplain," he said.

"The *chaplain*? It's so preposterous I almost believe you. Where'd you go?"

"Presidio. The National Cemetery. I don't want to talk about it."

She relaxed a little. "A buddy?" she asked softly.

He feigned reticence: "I don't want to talk about it. OK?"

"Well, *I* give out your passes," she said. "Not the chaplain."

"Good. I need another one. For Tuesday."

"What for?" she asked.

"I want to go to the Emporium's toy department. I need a panda bear."

"You're worse off than I thought."

He smiled. "Not for me. Next Friday's my daughter's birthday—"

"You pulled this same thing on Christmas, McCann, and you didn't get back for two days!"

"I will this time, Gail, believe me. I saw this ad, there's a panda there she needs. Jesus, I haven't seen her in so *long . . .*"

"You're not *allowed* to see her."

"I'm allowed to send her a goddamn panda!"

She arranged her tray and stood up. "Next Tuesday, a pass. Two hours, max, should do it."

"*Three* hours, instead? Or I'll just be AWOL."

She nodded.

He sat back and smiled. "You don't *look* like a doctor, Doctor. You're too young."

She blushed. "You're such a bullshitter, McCann!"

He watched her moving toward the trash disposal. Nice ass, nice moves. Not that bad, despite her buck teeth and twitchy nose.

Three hours meant, really, five or six. He could fly to Newport Beach and back, no strain.

CHAPTER 10

Anne Woodhouse, in uniform for another run to Shannon, stopped at Hoag Memorial Hospital on her way to the airport. Danny Cable had a private room on the third floor, overlooking the ocean at the end of Newport Bay.

She had brought him a basket of fruit from the gift shop downstairs. She paused at the door. She could hear his TV inside. She knocked and when she got no answer, eased in quietly. The room was full of dying flowers. A dejected yellow balloon floated above the foot of his bed.

Danny was snoring lightly. He was pale, with a six-month-old scar from the crash that ran from his temple to his lower jaw. He was sleeping with his mouth open: he had lost his teeth on impact, and the false ones gleamed too perfectly. His nose had been crumpled. He looked like an ancient boxer. Even his proud white hair had wilted.

She decided not to wake him, put the basket of fruit on his bureau, and began to sneak out.

"And where are *you* going?"

"Hi, Danny!" Anne kissed him. "You hanging in?"

"Yeah." He fingered her gold braid. "Coming or going, or just trying to make me sad?"

"Shannon. Post time in three hours. And my daddy sends his love."

"I don't want his, he's ugly, I want yours," he smiled weakly. His voice was hoarse. An electric motor whined as he raised the head of his bed, and she flounced up his pillows. He said: "I haven't seen you since that flight to Japan." He took her hand. "The girl with the gentle hands. You landed at Narita, right?"

"I was awful on that approach, Danny. I hope I'm better now."

He moved restlessly. "Look, tell me why I remember a normal landing at Narita, and *not* the only flight that counts?"

"Don't worry about it, Danny."

"I remember fighting to keep up the airspeed," he said vaguely. "Full power, and sinking . . . I remember that goddamn hill . . ."

"Don't try to remember, Danny. It's over."

" 'Retro . . . ' " he struggled. "It's called 'retro . . . ' Christ, now I've forgotten what it's *called*!"

" 'Retrograde amnesia,' Danny. Lots of people get it."

"Right." He reached for the control box on his bedside table and turned off his TV. "So, how are things in the great wild blue?"

"Hectic, awful, Crew Scheduling's out of control." She took a deep breath. It was time to tell him; there was no way out. "Danny, a guy named Ruble called me to the NTSB Monday. To ask about Christmas Eve—"

"Were *you* on my airplane? I didn't know."

Her heart dropped. "I taxied out behind you, from the ramp."

"Sure! I recall your daddy told me that, once. The NTSB called you in?"

"Some joker named Ruble," she told him again. "He's an awful man, and he's got this idea . . ."

He seemed a million miles away. "Ruble . . . Ruble? I think he talked to me, a long time ago."

"I'm sure he did."

"So what's he say *happened*, this guy?"

She took a deep breath. "He thinks your flaps were up."

"On *takeoff*?" Cable tried to sit up. His face was white. "Why would I take off with my flaps up, Anne?"

"You didn't," she lied. "Danny, lie down."

He lay back. His eyes were distant. "What *did* you see, Anne?"

"Nothing," she said. "I told him that."

"Thank you."

"But I'm sure he'll be in to see you, so I wanted you to know."

"He thinks I killed those people?" asked Cable. "And I don't even *know*?"

"Well, *I* know, Danny." She had a sudden compelling conviction that it wasn't Danny's fault. "If the flaps came up on that airplane, you didn't ask them to."

He reached out and squeezed her hand. "I hope not. Because all night long I wake up on that hillside. And lying there and bleeding . . ."

"Yes?"

"I hear a baby cry."

Anne Woodhouse sat with Ian in the red-brick Abbey Theatre near the River Liffey in downtown Dublin. It was first act intermission of Synge's *Playboy of the Western World*.

She wore a black silk cocktail dress that clung to her body. It was a strapless sheath. With its short tight skirt, it showed off her legs. She had bought it on sale on her credit card at Robinson's in Newport Beach. This was its maiden voyage, and she reveled in the feel of fabric along her thighs when she walked down the aisle with Ian.

On her neck she wore a plain golden choker, and on her ears gold button earrings. She wore black sandals, with three-inch heels, because he was so tall.

She felt, for the first time in years, that she was glorious: movie-star, Academy Award glorious, and that others felt it too.

Now, to give herself breathing room, she leafed through the program, trying to concentrate on the printed page.

The first act had gone well, and she loved the pulsing rhythm of the liquid Irish brogues. She wanted to remember the cast, and describe the play to Laurie.

But now Ian's deep blue eyes were on her, and they shook her focus. She turned and looked into his face.

"Yes?"

"I missed you, Anne."

Surprised, she stumbled: "Well, thank you, Ian, that's nice."

But the eyes did not waver. She put her hand on his arm. "You're staring, Ian. Stop it!"

"Why should I not? You're the loveliest thing in the theatre. On or off the stage."

She felt her cheeks grow hot. "Stop it!" she grinned.

"I'll not." The aisles were beginning to fill again. He jerked his chin at the advancing crowd. "You're a treat for us here. Yeats said: 'The wrong of unshapely things is a wrong too great to be told.' He knew Dublin: Look at all the *Irish* cows."

He took her hand and pressed it to his lips.

"Ian!" Anne whispered shakily, "you know about me and Gary Fremont, don't you?"

"Sure and who doesn't? The episode of the angry actress? But that's all finished, long ago."

"Well, I'm just getting over *him*. I think we'd better cool it, just a bit."

"Anne," he sighed, with his eyes still on hers, "I'm Irish, in love for the first time in my life—"

"Ian!"

"—and the proudest man in Dublin! Now why would I be coolin' that, my dear?"

Anne lay on a New Zealand lambskin in front of a peatburning stove in his sitting room. She was propped against an easy chair. By mutual agreement, she'd missed the last shuttle flight back to Shannon, and would have to spend the night.

The flat was well lived in, a one-bedroom apartment with a small kitchen, lined with books, on the first floor of a brick structure on Merrion Street.

Bright brass nameplates glittered under the streetlamp outside, and most of the digs were occupied by young doctors and lawyers; only a few, he said, held married couples, and there was not a child in the place. Laurie would be bored here, but he had a country place.

Now why, she wondered, did that touch her mind?

He poured scotch neat, from an ancient cut crystal decanter that he had drawn from a polished oak tantalus trimmed in brass.

She would have preferred coffee, to jar her into wakefulness, but didn't like to ask in case he had none. He kneeled beside her, poking the flames. His eyes, in the snapping firelight, were an even deeper blue.

"It's been a lovely evening," he said softly. "I *am* quite gone on you, you know. I love you, Anne. I do."

"Ian . . ." She swallowed a yawn. Gently, he took the glass from her hand and put it on the lamp table. Then he arose, and drew her into his bedroom. On his bedside table lay the *People* magazine.

"Oh, Ian," she murmured miserably, "I can't . . ."

"I know," he grinned, "you dozed off in Act II." He swung open his closet. "Well, Ireland's 'the Land of Time Enough.' I'll be in L.A. Wednesday, fighting for my budget. I've waited thirty-six years for you, so what's another week?"

"You're sweet," she said. "I'm a zombie."

"My pajama tops should strike you at your ankles: take your pick. We'll catch the early Shannon shuttle, never fear."

"If I do wake up . . . ," she yawned. "If I get cold . . ."

"Then look for me on the sheepskin, by the fire."

She stood on tiptoe, kissed him, hung up her dress, and crashed.

The next morning, she felt nineteen again. She had not slept so well in years.

CHAPTER
11

In her small, government-green office on the second floor of the San Francisco Veterans Administration Hospital, Dr. Gail Flodden left her desk and wandered to the window.

She could no longer delude herself. Cal McCann had evaporated. He was AWOL, thoroughly gone . . .

The foghorn groaned on the Golden Gate Bridge: McCann was always complaining of the sound. White fog choked the city. He was out in it somewhere, and she had no reason to believe that he'd return.

He had logged out this morning, at 9:05, on the three-hour pass she had signed for him to shop for his daughter's "birthday present" at the Emporium. Now it was 1:55 P.M.

So much for trusting the smiling eyes.

If he got into trouble, she was dead.

Last year the hospital chief of staff and the head of psychiatric services had both resisted his admission. He had been in and out of VA hospitals for years, and there was his suspended sentence from the Orange County court . . .

But McCann's lawyer, a dapper black ex-marine who specialized in handling veterans' affairs, had come on strongly, sitting here in her office: "Doctor, the guy loved his wife and lost her. He loves his daughter. He's lost her. He loved his job. He lost *it*. He's a veteran in trouble, he needs treatment, and he'll gladly commit himself."

"He's violent," she protested. "We can't handle violence here. He beat up his wife and broke her jaw."

"But she's in southern California! Five hundred miles away. This is a perfect answer. What's the VA for?"

"What can we do for him here?"

"Is there something they can do for him in the Orange County jail?" he asked. "The DA's willing to give him a break. Now, why the hell won't *you*?"

She had folded, of course, like an idiot, and convinced her superiors, and now McCann was gone, and they'd have to tell the Orange County judge.

Gone *where*? South?

She punched up his ex-wife's number on her computer. She had talked to her before. This time a child answered. She glanced at McCann's file on her computer screen.

"Is this Laurie?"

"Yes."

"Is your mother home?"

"She's on a flight to Ireland."

Thank God for that.

"Well, happy birthday, Laurie."

The child giggled. "Thank you, but it's not until October."

The lying bastard! She wondered if the child would ever get her panda.

She heard a car horn beep in the background. "I'm sorry,"

said Laurie. "I have to go surfing. Who is this?"

"A friend of your mother's. I'll call again next week."

She hung up. If the wife was out of danger, there was no use stirring things up. She looked at her clock.

Almost 2 P.M.

She'd wait until dinner, and if McCann wasn't back, she'd call the chief of staff.

Cal McCann stood hip-deep in the surge at San Onofre State Beach, upwind and up-current from the grass shack known as Old Man's. His ex-father-in-law's motor home was a quarter-mile down the beach.

McCann wore a graying, false moustache. He was searching the line of surfers for his daughter's blond ponytail or her yellow, polka-dotted surfboard.

If things went well, he would know in a few minutes whether he must try to kill her mother again to get her.

His rented surfboard was shackled to his ankle, nudging his thigh. He kept a hand on it and let the churn of the last wave swing it toward the surf line.

Months before, for two hundred dollars, a lithographer in the Haight-Ashbury had altered the ID card he'd kept when he was fired from PacLant. Now it pictured him wearing a moustache, and carried the name of a PacLant captain flying out of Denver.

With the card on his sport shirt, he had deadheaded free in the cockpit of an American shuttle to John Wayne Airport in Orange County. He rented an Avis car. He found the tennis club pool closed for cleaning: no junior classes today. He drove the five blocks to his ex-wife's condo.

He suspected that the gate guard had his description, so he parked across the street to make a battlefield estimate of the situation.

All at once he saw his former father-in-law's pickup truck nosing onto the street. A redheaded lady was driving. Beside her was Laurie.

Following them along the freeway had been easy. At San Onofre, from far down the parking lot, he watched them eat, sitting on the sand outside Harry's motor home.

Then the old man began to wax a surfboard. The redhead disappeared into his motor home.

And Laurie grabbed the yellow board, with the red polka dots, and paddled out into the surf.

At last, thank God, alone.

McCann rented a board, bought swimming trunks, and changed in his car. He crossed the sand and waded into the surge.

Now he spotted his daughter far beyond the set. He launched himself into a wave.

He had not surfed for five years. He was a skydiver, not really a surfer, but he was a natural athlete, and kept himself in shape in the VA gym.

In a steady, powerful rhythm, he headed out to the line of surfers sitting on their boards. Laurie was paddling idly near the end of the string, looking seaward, sizing up the surf.

She suddenly spotted the wave she wanted. She flopped on her belly, stroking mightily as the face of the wave soared above her. She turned the board in an instant, and caught the surge of it.

In a graceful, fluid motion, she rose and slanted down its slope. A teenager skimmed too closely to her wave. She cut in front of him, forcing him to climb to the top of the wave and to let it pass.

Good, nobody was going to steal Laurie's wave: she needed no help there. She rode it in, challenging and teasing it, until the last moment, then kicked out, swung her board to seaward, and started out again.

He yanked off his moustache and stuck it into his waistband. She regained the surf line and pirouetted her board to wait for the next wave. He called softly: "Pumpkin?"

She whirled, staring at him across thirty feet of rising, mirrored blue.

"Princess Laurie?" he called again.

"Daddy?" she muttered. "Daddy?"

He stayed where he was. "No: Sir Cal the Valorous. Back from the Forest of Glob."

She spun her board and skimmed across the space between them. Alongside, she peered into his face. "Where were you? Where have you been?"

"Hunting the fierce bunnydactyl. Tracking the saber-toothed frog."

She began to tremble. "Mom said you were in Honduras, or something!"

"Mom" had been "mommy" when he left . . .

"And 'Mom' must be right?"

"Where *do* you live?"

"In a foggy castle with a moat and a drawbridge made of gold."

"Stop it!"

He made his eyes grow wide in fright. "Imprisoned by a giant that roars all night!"

She rolled off her board and splashed onto his, sat lightly facing him until he gathered her into his arms. He hugged her.

"Are you ever coming home?" she begged. "Are you *ever* coming back?"

"I can't. The Witch of the Sky cast a spell."

She looked at him strangely. "Don't call her that, that's silly. So *are* you coming home?"

"Do you want me to?"

They rose together on the face of a wave, and dropped. Her little board, shackled to her ankle, bumped his.

"*Do* you, Pumpkin?"

She began to cry. "I thought you were mad at me."

"Not *you*."

She had shed six years in seconds, she seemed a baby again. "Did you hurt Mommy?"

He felt a stab of alarm. *The bitch!* "Did she say I did?"

"No."

"Then why did you ask?"

She shrugged. "Grandpa . . ."

"Grandpa *what*?"

"Grandpa asked me once," she said miserably.

He smiled and tilted up her chin. "Would Sir Cal hurt a lady?"

She managed a smile. "No."

"Even the Witch of the Sky?"

"No." She shook her head and looked suddenly younger still.

"Why not, Princess Laurie? Why would he not?"

"Because he feeds the hungry," she said, smiling faintly, "protects the weak . . ."

"Go on?"

She grinned, covered her nose, and giggled: "And gives his Pumpkin's nose a tweak!"

He tugged her hand away and pulled her nose. "Now how'd you like to ride Honda-wheelie to a castle built just for you?"

"Do you *still* have Honda-wheelie?"

"He roars and snorts and paws the ground. He's been waiting for you, Pumpkin."

"*What* castle? The giant's?"

"No, a real one."

He had once flown coke from Puerta Vallerta to Catalina Island. On the Sea of Cortez, nestled in a cove with Baja across the water, was a lovely, red-tiled estate he coveted. It stuck in his mind still.

Well, he still had a couple of hundred grand. It wouldn't get them *that*, but in Mexico, it ought to get them something. The important thing was to pry his daughter loose.

So he described the estate anyway, giving it an alabaster roof and an Olympic-sized pool.

"I'll buy it for you, Princess," he promised, "or something just as good."

She seemed dubious. "I can't. I'm on the club swimming team."

"I know. You won the freestyle. And somebody gave you a flower!"

"How'd you *know*?"

"A wizard told me."

"If we went to that castle, how would Mommy get her flights?"

Mommy, he told her silently, will be dusted, capped, quite thoroughly fragged. Don't worry about Mommy . . .

"Just you and me, Pumpkin. Sir Cal and the Princess, on our steed of gold."

She shook her head decisively. "She'd never let me go."

"Would you *want* to go?" He had to know.

She seemed scared, and didn't answer. Desperately, she glanced shoreward. "Here comes Diane."

"Who's Diane?"

"A friend of Grandpa's," she murmured. "She's cool. She came to get me, all the way to Newport."

"And if *I* came to get you, would you come to the Sea of Cortez?"

Her face twisted, as if she were about to cry again. "Daddy, I told you, Mom couldn't come! And she sure wouldn't let me go!"

The redhead, board held high, launched herself a quarter of a mile away. He craned, looking for Harry. If the old bastard found him out here, it could be very bad. He didn't see him.

But the redhead was approaching fast. She had a fabulous body: no time for that. "I have to go, Pumpkin." He lowered his voice an octave. "Tell no one I was here!"

"Why not?" She began to cry.

"Because it's a secret. From everyone!" He held up his palm toward her, waiting.

She remembered, slapped it doubtfully, and slowly crossed her heart. "It's a sacred secret," she intoned. "I'll never, never tell."

"And if you do, you'll turn into what?"

"A snail," she remembered. "A yukky, schlocky, crawly snail."

"And?"

"Get squished in the driveway and die!" She wrinkled her nose. "Daddy, come on! I'm almost ten!"

"A snail's a snail," he beamed. He held up his hand. She slapped it again and together they chanted: "Forever and ever, Amen!"

He hugged her briefly and watched her clamber onto her board and shoot away. He caught the next wave, almost lost it, but managed to kick out at the end without loss of face.

He trudged through the sand to his car. Laurie might or might not keep his secret: perhaps their private world was gone.

That, he'd worry about later. Now he had to get to John

Wayne Airport, and quick, or his scrawny shrink would kick him straight into the Orange County jail.

Dr. Gail Flodden toyed with the telephone on her desk. The foghorn on the bridge was bellowing hoarsely: "Fool . . . Fool . . . Fool . . ."

Almost seven o'clock, and she still hadn't had it in her to blow the whistle on McCann. She simply could wait no longer.

She picked up the phone. There was a quick rap on the door. Before she could answer, he walked in.

He carried a panda three feet tall. He looked as if he had spent the day on a park bench. His eyes were bloodshot and his cheeks stubbled. His khaki slacks were crumpled and there was a vomit stain on his corduroy jacket.

Even across the room, he smelled of booze.

"You got the panda," she said coldly.

"Yes."

"I talked to your daughter."

That seemed to shock him. "No, goddamn it!"

"Oh, yes. When's her birthday?"

"October, I lied."

"*You* lied?" she cried. "Cal McCann lied? Now that, I find hard to believe. Why'd you bother with the panda?"

"To con you with," he shrugged.

"Where *were* you?"

He roughed up the panda's head. "I got us a jug and took a cab to the cemetery again."

"That's sick."

"*I'm* sick, aren't I? Or why am I here?"

"You aren't." She tore a memo from her printer. "A

recommendation to discharge you."

"To where?"

"Back to custody, I guess," she said.

"Thanks. So much for the red, white, and blue."

"Well, where *were* you? I'm responsible!"

"At the cemetery, like I said."

"And you ended up drunk?"

He nodded. "In some broad's apartment by the Broadway Tunnel. Doing coke, a little booze. Right, Mao?"

The panda nodded, brown eyes twinkling.

McCann continued: "Long hair and glasses, Queen of Haight-Ashbury, circa '68 . . ." He regarded the panda. "Hey, how'd we meet *her*, Mao?"

The panda shrugged.

"If you're blacking out," she said heatedly, "then you've got another problem. If you're doing coke and screwing users you've got a third one: you'll probably end up with AIDS."

"Judgmental, judgmental! Now, look, you're all steamed up!" The foghorn blasted. He went to her window, cranked it open, and bellowed back. He turned with his little-boy smile. "And hey, I *didn't* screw her. I passed out."

Unaccountably, she felt a start of joy. She was being unprofessional, first angry and disturbed, now elated.

He was her patient, still, and she was supposed to help him, cooly and objectively, not torture him. She crumpled her memo, took aim, and ringed her basket.

"Well, maybe you didn't screw her, but you sure could have screwed me." Their eyes met. His were gleaming with mirth. He could see right through her, the bastard: it was supposed to be the other way around. "I mean, with the pass, and all," she finished weakly. "So we won't try that again."

Cal McCann picked up the panda. He looked into its face. "Nice lady?" he asked it.

"Velly nice," nodded the panda. "She get more better lookin' alla time."

"Get your bear butt out of here, Mao," she said. "You're just as bad as he."

Walking down the corridor, McCann squeezed the panda. Not a bad day: he'd seen Laurie, the shrink was ready as a plum gone ripe, and he was still safe in the hands of Uncle Sam.

He would never get Laurie while her mother lived, but at least he *knew* that now, and the Witch of the Sky would be checking out soon.

Because next time, he would not fail.

CHAPTER
12

Stanley Block Junior's corporate suite perched on the ninth floor of the PacLant Building, only a few blocks from the runways of Los Angeles International Airport. He stood at the window waiting for his security chief, Monty Starbuck.

Georgia O'Keeffe paintings—desert skulls and sunflowers—hung from the oaken paneling. A Remington bronze—*The End of the Trail*—sat on his massive desk, next to a model of an old DC-4.

In a walnut gun case hung a Winchester rifle and crossed Colt .45's, supposed to have belonged to Billy the Kid. A series of leather-bound Whitney studbooks lined his bookcases.

His office occupied the entire southwest corner of the floor. When Santa Ana winds off the desert whisked the smog to sea, he could spot the brick-red Spanish tiles of his home on the Palos Verdes cliffs, peering through a telescope he had mounted by the sweeping southern window for just this reason.

But now he was at the western window, fidgeting as he gazed through binoculars, down at a long line of taxiing aircraft.

A PacLant 737 was bobbing and curtsying toward the active runway in the conga line. It had been inching toward the takeoff spot for a full ten minutes.

Pilot pay was block-to-block. It started at push-back at the terminal building and continued until the plane was parked at its destination. A PacLant captain earned $75 an hour, taxiing or aloft.

To see one of his planes, fully manned and earthbound, gobbling flight-crew pay and gulping jet-A fuel at a buck-twenty-five a gallon, drove him frantic. Block could not escape a conviction that the unknown captain, who undoubtedly hated him, was simultaneously and deliberately carrying too much throttle and braking against it, so that his jet blast was leaving a trail of silver dollars rolling on the asphalt.

He heard the door open, and the whine of Monty Starbuck's wheelchair.

Starbuck was a white-haired, tanned ex-Treasury agent whose career as a T-man had ended when a wild-swinging boom in a yacht race shattered his spinal cord. He was a handsome man with deceptively gentle eyes and a quick and easy smile.

When the PacLant boardroom split had put every executive's loyalty to the test, he had sided with Stanley Junior, sensing that the son was going to win.

He was the only employee in PacLant who dared to call him "Junior" to his face. Junior valued him and feared him, too, for God knew what he had in his head, or in his files.

"Monty, will you look at that idiot down there, burning fuel?"

"What idiot is that?" asked Monty, taking the glasses and rolling closer to the window, where he could see over the ledge. He put the glasses to his eyes. "Flight 314?"

"I don't know who the captain is, but—"

"We'll see." Starbuck handed him back the glasses, reached into a case which hung from his armrest, and whipped out his lap-top computer. His fingers danced over the keys.

"Flight 314 to Salt Lake City." He tapped for a moment. "Captain Leonard Speakes. He's forty-seven. He has eleven thousand hours flight time . . . Dum de dum-dum . . . Argued against the strike in '84 but went out anyway . . . Reported a near-miss with United in '88, beating them to the punch and saving our asses . . . Oops, in 1989 he grounded a 737 in Hong Kong for three hours for repair of an oil leak . . . a *minor* oil leak."

"Three *hours*? You see what I mean? They got no more company loyalty than an RTD bus driver! And he taxis like a teenage girl trying to back a stick shift up the driveway! Have the chief pilot talk to him when he comes back." Block scowled down at the taxiway for a moment, then, with an effort, turned away from the window. "Well, I didn't call you here for that."

Block picked up a letter from his basket. "I got this from a flight engineer: 'Dear Mr. Block,' he says, 'I have certain confidential information that threatens this company's suit against Boeing.' Goes on: 'I got a feeling it would be a mistake to talk to anybody but you.' " He looked up. " 'J. D. Showalter.' S-h-o-w-a-l-t-e-r."

Starbuck typed in the name. The laptop squealed and groaned. He squinted at his screen.

" 'Showalter, John D.,' or 'Chinook.' Well, he struck in '84. Eight thousand hours. Unmarried. No loans from the credit union; no indication of financial problems. Two requests for accelerated promotion to first officer."

"On what grounds?" asked Block.

"He claims seniority over the scabs."

"Well, he shouldn't have struck," said Block.

"He's been rotting in an F/E seat for all these years: he must be just about next in line." Starbuck closed his computer and slipped it back into its slot on the arm of his wheelchair.

"He's due here now."

"Shall I stick around?"

Block knew that in a shoulder holster under Starbuck's coat rode a 9-millimeter Browning.

"Hell yes. These union assholes, you never know."

Starbuck's eyes twinkled. Block suspected that after McCann's visit, his security chief had never thought highly of his courage.

Angrily, he pressed his intercom. "Is Showalter out there? Send him in."

Block studied the little flight engineer.

"She started to call Cable on the *air*?"

"I think so. Lot of noise in our own cockpit, and I was busy. But *something* about his flaps. The captain stopped her."

"That crash was six months ago!" said Starbuck from his chair. "Why didn't you report it then?"

"Why didn't *she*?"

"Why are you here now?" demanded Block.

"Last week the NTSB hauled me down there. And every question this guy Ruble *asks* me is about Danny Cable's flaps!"

"So what did you tell him?"

"Well, I knew about our lawsuit against Boeing, so I didn't say a thing."

Block's eyes began to ache. The lawsuit . . .

A skin section of the horizontal stabilizer had been found almost a quarter of a mile short of the crash site. It could have been blown there by the force of the explosion, or it could have ripped loose and caused the crash. He was suing Boeing for a structural defect, just in case, and the last thing he wanted was to discover that his pilot had tried to take off with his flaps up.

Shutting up Showalter would be easy: his hand was out for a copilot's seat right now. The captain might be easy, too, if he thought he'd made a bad call. But what about the nervous goddamn woman in the right-hand seat?

He licked his lips. "What *did* she say about the flaps?"

"It's hard to say, right now," murmured Showalter. He was a dour, wizened man, but he was smiling now. "Cockpit noise, and . . . Well, it's a long way from the F/E's seat to the copilot's." His eyes met Block's. "A *long* long way."

The grandfather's clock in the corner ticked in the silence. Block cleared his throat.

"Maybe not," said Block. "It all depends."

"On the flaps, he means," explained Starbuck.

Showalter stood up. "What flaps?" he asked, and left.

After the flight engineer left, he and Starbuck sat silently for a long moment.

"Who was their captain?" asked Block.

"Fremont. If he kept her off the air, his ass is out a mile," said Starbuck. "He's a lawyer himself, but he's losing a very expensive divorce case now, and he needs his job. *I* can handle him, no sweat."

Block got up, crossed to his coffee table, picked up *People* magazine, and tossed it on his security chief's lap. "You see this?"

"Sure. A week ago."

"She's McCann's ex-wife!"

"Yep!" Starbuck nodded. "She sure is."

"Tell me something, Monty. How did she get past *you*?"

"Changed her name."

Not much of an answer, thought Block, but he let it go. He walked to the window and looked out. Flight 314 to Salt Lake City, thank God, had finally reached the runway.

He watched it accelerate, gather itself like a show horse nearing a fence, and leap into the coffee-colored sky. From this instant on, it was generating cash. He returned to his desk and closed the magazine.

"I was going to get rid of her. Now what'll I do?"

Starbuck heaved the laptop out of its case and opened it again. He tapped a few keys.

"Good evaluation sheets: she's bucking for that left-hand seat. She has an annual proficiency check coming up Monday. If she got a down, we'd *have* to fire her."

"Jesus, Monty, are you recommending I fire her? *Now?*"

"No, I'm recommending a leveraged buy-out: she sees it our way, she stays."

"Tit for tat," said Block.

Starbuck chuckled. He studied his screen. "Let's see. Divorced, got a little girl. Told Howie Ball she hated

PacLant, once. MasterCard has a garnishee on her wages. Hey! She was screwing that captain, the same one, Fremont! And it got broken off, just after that crash, too. That's interesting."

"You know all about her, *now*," sulked Junior. He had a throbbing headache. "Where do you get all that crap?"

"Well, let's see. Orange County DA, it says." He shrugged. "Superior Court Clerk, the DMV, the Orange County School District. I don't do this *myself*, Mr. Block: I hire the stupid: they're fun to watch."

"I'll have her up for a little talk," decided Block. "If I know she's solid, she stays. Otherwise, she gets a down on Monday."

"Shall I sit in?"

"*She* isn't going to assault me. No."

Starbuck snapped closed his laptop computer, dropped it into its case, and started for the door. He spun his wheelchair around.

"Just remember three things, Boss?"

"What?"

"She wants four stripes, she's got a kid to bring up, and she seems to be flat-ass broke."

Anne glanced at the office that McCann had invaded. Early OK Corral, she decided of the decor, more a cattle baron's than an airline executive's; just right for McCann's heroics with Block's gun. She followed Stanley Block to a leather couch that faced a hide-covered coffee table tooled with cattle brands.

She had decided to wear a black business suit and skirt instead of a uniform. She had picked modest jewelry: tiny jade earrings she had found with Gary in Bangkok, and a scrimshaw brooch he'd bought her on Tonga. She looked, she thought, like a lawyer on "L.A. Law."

He gestured for her to be seated and stepped to a coffee maker on a worm-eaten bar overlooking LAX.

"Black?"

"Yes, sir."

" 'Sir'?" he repeated dryly. "My relations with your family are improving: Your husband called me a bastard, the only time we met."

"*Ex*-husband."

He came back, placed her coffee on the table and joined her on the couch. He had the *People* issue in his hand and opened it to her picture.

"Now, I *liked* this story," he said. "Don't get me wrong."

"Good. Since Howie Ball talked me into letting them do it."

"Yes. Did we pay you for your time?"

"Yes."

He sighed. "There's just one thing: when we hired you fresh out of flight training, you might have mentioned that you were married to Cal McCann. Out of gratitude to a prospective employer?"

"If you'd had a slot for 'former spouse,' I would have filled it in. I'm *not* responsible for McCann! Or anything he did."

"Do you *know* what he did, Anne?"

She waved her hand at the office. "He broke in here and tried to cram a wage offer down your throat!"

"Was I right to fire him?"

"Of course. I'm sorry he's not in jail."

He stood up and walked to a telescope by the window. He looked toward Palos Verdes and the beaches stretching south.

"Do you know what *else* he did, Anne? Come here."

She joined him. He swung the telescope to the Palos Verdes cliffs, focused it, and pulled her close. She stiffened, disliking his touch.

"Take a look," he murmured.

She squinted through the scope. A mansion filled the field of view: red-tiled roofs, outbuildings, a pool. "Yes?"

"It's mine."

His hand was still around her waist. She stepped back. "Out of my price range, Mr. Block. Why show it to *me*?"

"Because Cal McCann broke in there once. McCann and a person unknown."

She stared at him. "He *didn't*!"

He was watching her intently. "Tried to kill our panther. And led my wife's mare into our living room—"

"When?"

"The last day of the strike," he said. "Sweet horse, gentle horse. Her name was Morningstar."

"Why would he do that?"

"He's a dangerous man, Anne Woodhouse. He cut the poor thing's throat."

"What?"

A jet screamed past on the taxiway below. Across the room she heard his grandfather's clock chime once.

"In front of our fireplace. My wife thinks she still smells the blood."

"Oh, God!" Her mouth was dry. She wanted to be home, with Laurie in her arms. "How do you know *he* did it?"

"Well, we proved it to the union," he shrugged. "My cook saw them. Identified his picture. That's why ALPA threw him out. An airline pilot! Christ!"

"Why didn't we hear about it?" she asked numbly.

"Because I promised them not to go public. I think that's what broke the strike."

"Why are you telling me all this, now?" she demanded.

He gazed at her for a moment. "You need a drink?"

"A glass of water," she said distractedly. "Or a tonic, I don't care."

He poured her seltzer over ice. "How did you *feel* about that strike?"

"Sympathetic."

"To me?"

"To ALPA."

"But you crossed their picket line, anyway."

"I crossed because he'd left me with no support."

"I see." He tinkled ice from a dispenser into a glass with the PacLant panther etched into it. He poured himself a careful shot of Black Label scotch. Swirling the liquor thoughtfully, he said: "And you're loyal to the company now, would you say?"

"Did I sound *disloyal* in that article?"

"No, but you told Howie Ball you hated us."

Thank you, Howie Ball . . .

"I hate the hours, I like the food, I need the pay. Loyalty? You didn't hire me as a personal secretary, you hired me to fly."

"Sit down, Anne, I want to talk." She sat on the couch and he stood by his desk. From it he picked up a model of an old Douglas DC-4.

"My daddy used to fly these," he said. "And so did Danny Cable, I guess." He ran the plane down the desk, lifted it, dove it toward the desk again and put it down. "You saw Cable crash last Christmas."

"Yes, sir."

"Anne, do you have a problem with his flaps?"

She chilled. The word was out. From whom? It didn't really matter.

"Arizona Air Freight says they were down," she said briskly. "So do I."

"Good. No discussion of his flaps in the cockpit?"

Chinook! Her mouth felt dry. "I can't recall."

"I hope there wasn't, Anne. Because we could go under on this crash. Insurance or not. We *have* to win our suit."

Junior had built a fortune on poor-mouthing: she discounted every word. "Well, then, I wish us luck."

He sipped his drink. "Legal's position is that Danny Cable was blameless."

"I agree. If those flaps came up, it wasn't Danny!"

"They *didn't* come up, and don't forget it! Boeing has deep pockets, Anne. Deeper than ours." He smiled. "So, there *was* no 'discussion' in the cockpit. Right?"

"I can't say that if I'm sworn," she warned. "I'm not going to jail for PacLant."

He walked around his desk and sat in his monstrous leather chair. He stared at her for a moment, put on glasses, and took a pile of papers from his basket.

"In no way," he said, "did I suggest that you perjure yourself. Thank you, for coming up."

"No problem, sir." She started for the door.

"Woodhouse?"

"Yes?" She turned.

"Legal has *another* position, too. Regarding you and Captain Fremont."

"A position on *us*? What?"

"If there *was* a discussion about those flaps, they advise me to discharge you both. *Before* the hearing and the Boeing suit. To cover ourselves."

"For God's sake, *why*?"

"For not calling our other aircraft! Or the tower!"

She went numb, and couldn't answer.

"They're very tough, our lawyer-types," he continued. " 'Negligence,' I think they said." He searched through the pile. " '*Criminal* negligence!' Yeah, Woodhouse, it's in here somewhere." He looked up, shaking his head. "So if there really *was* such a discussion . . . I just don't know, my dear. I guess it's up to you."

part two

IDIOT
LIGHTS

CHAPTER
13

At 11:30 P.M., in a Millbrae greasy spoon called Violet's Grill, Mike Ruble sat with a PacLant maintenance mechanic named Carl Rhinelander. They were only ten minutes via the Bayshore Highway from San Francisco International Airport, where Rhinelander was due for the graveyard shift at midnight.

Rhinelander had wispy red hair, a comfortable belly, and the globular nose of a peasant in van Gogh's *Potato Eaters*. He had sad eyes. He had complained freely of PacLant maintenance when Ruble questioned him after the Christmas crash. He was the only person Ruble trusted in all of PacLant Maintenance.

Now he found him almost furtive. They sat in a booth near the rear while a waitress in a dirty fuchsia apron slopped them coffee.

Rhinelander wore white overalls with the orange PacLant logo and the leaping panther on his chest. Under the logo a well-worn patch read: HYDRAULICS SYSTEMS: CREW #3.

Over the logo was pinned a yellowed, cracked PacLant ID badge. In the photo, Rhinelander seemed ten years younger.

Ruble could hear foghorns from the East Bay bleating like lambs through the steamy windows. He had flown up alone in an FAA Beechcraft, and landed on instruments here.

Even in the muggy cafe, he shivered from the damp. He wore only a light windbreaker, more suitable for LAX than San Francisco.

"Is this about the Christmas crash?" asked Rhinelander. "I thought it was all wrapped up."

"What makes you think that, Carl?" asked Ruble.

"Well, we're suing Boeing for design failure," Rhinelander said. "I heard it in the hangar."

"The horizontal stabilizer panel? I'm not happy with that theory."

"You got another one?" asked Rhinelander.

The golden rule of the NTSB investigator was "thou shalt not speculate." But Ruble decided to meet Rhinelander's openness with his own. "Yes. His flaps may have come up."

Rhinelander's face closed. "No! I *signed* for that hydraulic system!"

"OK, OK!" So much for his flight north in the fog. "Sorry, Carl, just a theory."

"If his flaps came up," insisted Rhinelander, "it was pilot error."

"Could be," said Ruble.

"Look, I told you all I know about that plane. And Braden damn near got me fired for telling you!"

Braden was Rhinelander's foreman. His turnaround time on hangar checks was the best at PacLant. Long ago he had launched a vendetta against Rhinelander for insisting on the letter of the law. Now he seemed to have the mechanic cowed.

"Braden?" said Ruble. "Now, there's a guy that PacLant *ought* to can."

"They'll fire me first, for whistle-blowing. He never changes. I found hairline cracks in a landing-gear oleo strut last week, but he signed for it anyway: 'Count the wings, sign her off, and get her out of the barn.' Pencil-whipping!"

"Oleo cracks? That's awful! And it's out there flying now?" demanded Ruble. "What's its tail number?"

Rhinelander winced, and Ruble backed off: "Never mind, I'll call our local inspector. He'll check every oleo you got, and nobody'll ever know."

"I hope not. Every morning I pray to Lord Jesus the union keeps my job for me."

Ruble stirred his coffee. "You born again, Carl?"

"Born again," Rhinelander said. "At the Evans Avenue Evangelical Church. This Easter, like my Christ. I was a drinker, Mr. Ruble, and I haven't had so much as a single beer since then. Are you a Christian, sir?"

"Jewish," said Ruble.

" '*The Lord loveth the gates of Zion,*' " murmured Rhinelander. "Anyway, don't let your wife fly PacLant."

"She was on PSA 1771 in '87," Ruble said bitterly. " 'Catch Our Smile.' "

Awkwardly, Rhinelander reached across and patted his forearm. "Then she's safe in the arms of the Lord, Mr. Ruble. That's comfort for you, I'm sure." He glanced at the door and tensed. "Look, I got a clock to punch. Thanks for the coffee. God bless."

He slid from the table abruptly and was gone. Puzzled, Ruble picked up the check and moved to the register.

Braden was seating himself on a counter stool. He was a stubby black with curling white hair and steel-gray eyes. He wore an orange PacLant windbreaker over his white overalls.

"Kaffeeklatsch over, Ruble?" he smiled. "You and Rhino? Was that about his goddamn main mount olco, or we got another crash?"

"Jesus, you had an *oleo* problem?" asked Ruble. "I'll get our inspector on it."

The hangar bay was enormous, as large as a soccer field, and brightly lighted. Carl Rhinelander punched in at a time clock near the entrance.

A lone 747 loomed like a cornered monster in the rear. High in the fuselage, someone working late from the swing shift was pounding a panel with a mallet, and the echos made the building seem even larger than it was.

He passed an empty security desk: to save money, PacLant had dispensed with hangar security guards years ago. He boarded the plane and trudged sullenly down the length of the 747's empty cabin, stepping from light to dark to light again, one pool of brightness to another.

Last night, disregarding the impatience of his foreman, he had properly hung a series of caged work lamps from the overhead baggage racks.

His hanging lights, which after all took hardly a quarter hour to string out, were almost his only remaining protest against Braden's nonchalance.

In the cockpit, he knelt painfully to remove a deck panel. Under the pedestal between the pilot's and the copilot's seat he traced a linkage with a beam from his flashlight, to make sure that it was not worn.

"Hey, man!" A metallic voice echoed along the length of the cabin. It was Paco Lopez, his apprentice. "Rhino!"

Rhinelander hated his nickname, which Braden had dreamed up. "Yo! I'm here in the cockpit."

Paco was a slim, cheerful youth from East L.A., frightened by gang warfare into a vocational school and a steady job as an apprentice machinist. He had moved to San Francisco with his mother when PacLant had expanded the SFO maintenance facility last year.

"Jesus, Boss," said Paco, "Braden's in the hangar already. And he's pissed. We were supposed to be out of this mother by now. What you doin' *there*?"

"Flap linkage check," said Rhino.

"No! Wrap it up, or he'll have our ass!" Winding the electrical light cable around his forearm, Paco said: "I saw you at Violet's, having coffee with that dude. Who's he?"

"Safety inspector, NTSB."

"You got guts, to talk to those guys," Paco muttered. "Or you're stupid, one. Braden's saying he'll get you off graveyard, you don't quit making waves!"

Rhinelander sighed. When he had found God this spring, he had thought that nothing could harm him, but the hands of the Lord were slow in warming. His wife had lost her job last month, and was still looking. If he lost his graveyard pay, they were in trouble.

There was a time when he would have challenged Braden openly on the hangar floor, and trusted to the union for protection. Now he was too scared, and spilling his guts to Ruble at the NTSB hardly eased his conscience.

The wicked in his pride doth persecute the poor . . .

He continued with his check.

"He don't even *want* that check," complained Paco, "unless there's a squawk."

"If he wants *my* signature, he gets the check!"

Paco sighed. "Here we go again . . ." He rumpled Rhinelander's hair affectionately.

Rhinelander swiped his hand away. It was hard to teach Paco the old ethics, when their foreman and their company scoffed at them. "*Remember* that, and do this every time."

"Nobody *does*, Rhino."

"You're supposed to. If you're *supposed* to, you *got* to." Lips pursed intently, Rhinelander felt for wear and leakage. "You got a license to protect!"

"I got a paycheck to protect!" said Paco. "I only seen one other guy do this, out by the terminal, a million years ago."

"By the *terminal*?" said Rhinelander, insulted. He was responsible for hydraulics, and he didn't need a backup. Angrily, he lined up the floor panel and slapped it into place. "Who?"

"I don't know," said Paco.

"When?" Rhinelander turned each dzus fastener slowly until it seated. He was finished.

"Christmas Eve."

"The night of the crash? Seven-seventy-one? Flight Fourteen?"

"Hell, I don't know."

"The plane that crashed?" demanded Rhinelander.

"I guess." They heard a bang as someone connected a tow bar to the nosewheel two stories below. The plane lurched. "Man, he wants this turkey *out* of here! Let's go!"

Punching out at 8 A.M., Rhinelander found Braden waiting at the timeclock. The foreman looked at him impassively. "You and Paco blowin' each other up there?"

"Checking linkages, hydraulic lines. Like the manual says."

" 'If it ain't broke, don't fix it.' "

"We're getting a bad reputation. Paco says he saw a guy from another shift rechecking my flaps Christmas Eve!"

"Let 'em. *We* ain't got time."

"We got to *make* time. 'Seest thou a man diligent in his business? He shall stand before kings.' "

"*You'll* be standing in line at Unemployment, you don't get off your ass," said Braden. He thought for a moment, filled out a change-of-shift slip, and said: "You don't like our reputation, Rhino? Good! Now you're on day shift, on the ramp. Start at 1 P.M. tomorrow."

"You can't do that!" Day shift would lose him his extra swing-shift pay, two dollars an hour, eighty bucks a week.

"Yeah, I can. You're hurting my turnaround time."

Rhinelander had suddenly had enough. *For which of those works do ye stone me?* God helped him who helped himself: there were no more cheeks to turn. "I'll file a grievance!"

"With who? That NTSB clown?"

"My shop steward!"

"Sing your troubles to Jesus, Rhino, the chaplain's gone ashore."

Blazing with anger, Rhinelander punched out on the clock and started toward the hangar door.

Braden's voice echoed after him: "And file the grievance on your own time, Rhino, not on ours!"

Rhinelander was in the parking lot, unlocking his battered old Bronco, when he saw the 747 leaving the hangar, immense and gleaming under the floodlights like a huge white whale.

Dwarfing its tractor tow, docile and good-humored, it rolled in dignity toward the line. In a few hours, it would howl down the runway and bank toward the sun, out of

Braden's careless hands and safe in the arms of Jesus.

At least its hydraulics would work.

Even when he had been a drinking man, he had followed the old rules, though the rules had been changing for years now, in the hangar, and the game was a new one: Braden's.

But as for me and my house, we will serve the Lord. There were still some who cared: himself and Ruble and the pilots themselves, and the nameless mechanic Paco had seen on Christmas Eve.

He wondered who he was. He climbed into his car, put his key in the ignition, and found himself staring at the plane as the tow truck trundled it to the terminal.

He wondered if anyone on day shift would double-check his work. The thought angered him. His signature was on the sheet.

And Christmas Eve? What if Paco's eager mechanic had stripped a fitting?

He visualized hydraulic fluid, red as blood, squirting from a connector as the plane gathered speed and the flaps eased up in the slipstream. For an instant he was impelled to call Ruble. Then he remembered his company's suit against Boeing. He was already tagged a whistle-blower: how far did he have to go?

From his glove compartment he drew a worn, plastic-covered Bible and thumbed it.

John 5:30: "I can of mine own self do nothing," said Jesus.

Well, if Lord Jesus could do nothing, how could he?

If an overconscientious technician on another shift had butchered his job, let the Safety Board worry, or Braden: his own conscience was clear. There was no way, he decided, he would ever get into that.

CHAPTER
14

Sitting outside on the rattling cable car to Fisherman's Wharf in the brisk morning air, Anne put her arm around her daughter and braced them both for the dizzy drop to North Beach. During the ride from downtown they had slid their way forward on the wooden seat, place by place as other passengers left, until they reached the car's front window.

It was a glittering San Francisco day, livid with reds and greens and brittle shards of sunlight. But the closer she got to her proficiency check, the more nervous she became.

Yesterday, she had driven their rental car across the Golden Gate Bridge to Marin, to lunch on the deck of *Sam's Landing*. In some mysterious way, the ride had backfired.

Crawling back to the city in the afternoon fog, Laurie had heard the horn on old Fort Point thundering below.

"Mom? If it's the Golden Gate Bridge, why don't they paint it gold?"

"Orange paint is cheaper than gold, I guess."

"Does Daddy live near here?"

Mercifully, brake lights came on ahead, to give Anne time to think. A lucky shot? A phone call, overheard?

"Why did you think that?"

"I just *did*, is all."

"Come on, Doodle! 'Just did'? There's got to be a reason!"

"No, there doesn't!" Laurie said hotly. "So does he live up here, or not?" She was gazing straight ahead. "My daddy?"

Anne took a deep breath. "Yes."

"Near here? By the bridge?"

"In the VA Hospital. They call it Fort Miley. I don't know where it is."

"Is he sick?"

"Not really, no."

"Then why's he in a hospital?"

"He's got problems."

"From Viet Nam? Like the grunts in *Platoon*?"

Not really, but it seemed the simplest answer. "You might say that."

"Why don't we go and see him?"

She almost drove out of her lane. "There isn't time: you're flying home tonight. And he hasn't tried to see *us* in years! So probably," she added weakly, "he wouldn't want to see us anyway."

Laurie took a breath, as if to speak, and then sat back quietly. She had been quiet all last evening, but during the night had awakened with a nightmare, screaming about a crawling snail.

Now, peering ahead from the cable car down at the wide blue bay, she seemed restless and moody. She turned from the window and swiped at her hair.

"Can we eat lunch at Mama Maxwell's? A Candy Dandy Sundae?"

Yesterday's lunch in Marin had cost a fortune. "We just ate breakfast, Laurie!"

"We're talking major starvation. Up here, it's like my body only *runs* on Candy Dandy sundaes."

"OK." After she put Laurie on her flight to L.A., she could economize tonight on a Big Mac, all alone.

The brakeman clanged his bell, there was a squeal from the cable under the tracks, and the car lurched over the brink.

Laurie hadn't mentioned her father again, but how in *hell* had she known he was in San Francisco?

Mama Maxwell's open-air cafe clung to a terrace in Ghirardelli Square, a brick complex with sweeping windows and blue canopies. Once the building had been a chocolate factory, and it still smelled of cocoa beans.

From under a yellow umbrella, Anne and Laurie watched rubberneckers passing in the bright sunshine on the street below. The three-masted bark *Balclutha* nuzzled the quay across the street. They had trudged through it yesterday, as they always did.

Laurie was toying with her Candy Dandy, an immense concoction of ice cream and chocolate.

"So," Anne asked idly, "you went surfing with Diane. Did my father go out too?"

Laurie glanced at her quickly and swung her eyes to the street. A black horse plodded by, drawing a surrey full of tow-headed German tourists. The driver wore a derby and seemed half-asleep. "Hey, Mom, *rad*! Can we go on that?"

"No. *Did* he surf? Your grandfather?"

The child dug her spoon into her Candy Dandy and churned the ice cream. "No. He drank too much beer, waxing up."

"And Diane let you go out alone?"

"*You* do."

"When I'm there, watching. Was *she* watching?"

"I guess." Laurie squirmed and stared after the departing carriage. "Some day, I want to live up here. And drive a buggy, just like that."

"Good." Something was seriously wrong. "Doodle?"

"What?"

"Did something happen? Surfing?"

Now Laurie's spoon was in full motion, and five dollars worth of ice cream was becoming a sea of mud. Laurie studied it intensely, as if in another world. Her lips pursed. *"Pwa, pwa, pwa . . ."* she whispered. *"Pwa . . ."*

"What?"

Laurie looked up quickly. "What *what*?"

Anne shivered. "You were mumbling. Like a child."

"I *am* a child."

"I mean a *baby*. Weird. What happened surfing, Laurie?"

"Nothing. The surf was *zip*."

"*Something*," insisted Anne. "What *was* it, Doodle?"

"Nothing happened!" flared Laurie. Her eyes were filling with tears. "I told you! So just get off my case!"

In the tiny IAM office at the San Francisco terminal, Carl Rhinelander was trying to file a grievance with George Tippet, the IAM shop steward.

His Lord seemed to have forsaken him. His cut in pay was devastating: eighty dollars a week. He would have to refinance his car payments. Months before, when his wife had lost her job, he had fallen behind in his rent. And the union—at least in the person of Tippet—wasn't helping him a bit.

Tippet was a bushy-haired young man with a walrus moustache, wearing loose khaki work pants, with his ID badge stuck into one of his wide red suspenders. Rhinelander had trained him in the hangar, found him a sloppy worker, and never trusted him. He had heard lately that Tippet wanted a strike.

"We can't get you back on graveyard," Tippet said. "Management's cutting down night checks."

"What do I pay dues for?"

"Forget it, Carl. You're a whistle-blower. You want to live like a hero—"

"I'm just trying to save my ticket. I taught *you* that. When I sign off an airplane—"

"Live like a hero, die like a hero. There's nothing we can do."

Rhinelander spun around and started for the door.

"Carl?" the shop steward said abruptly.

He turned. "Yeah?"

The man was studying him. "You had the balls to beat the bottle. You got the balls to go to Stanley Block with this?"

"I couldn't get in. And they'd fire me if I did. Like that crazy copilot."

"You trained half the guys in the hangar. He knows if he fires you, we'd strike."

"I want *graveyard*, I don't want a strike. *'If any will not work, neither let them eat'!* Just file the grievance, George, OK? I want my two bucks an hour back."

"No grievance," insisted Tippet. "Waste of time. Go down and see him, Carl."

Leaving the office, Rhinelander paused at a terminal phone, thinking. Perhaps the idea was not really Tippet's, but the Lord's. See Block? Why not, if it was the only way? After all, on PacLant, he flew free.

He made a reservation on the early morning flight, and went back to work on the ramp.

Anne Woodhouse sat blindfolded in the copilot's seat of an idle Boeing 747. It was parked in late afternoon sunlight at PacLant Departure Gate Number 22, San Francisco International.

Covering her eyes was a pair of the orange sleep shades that PacLant gave first-class and business-class passengers, along with their stereo earphones, on takeoff.

She was in her shirt-sleeve uniform, wearing her gold first-officer stripes on starched white epaulets; her tunic hung in the coat locker at the entrance to the flight deck.

She was sharpening her reflexes, for in twelve hours—at 4 A.M.—she would have her proficiency check in the 747 simulator a half-mile across the ramp in the PacLant training building.

"OK," she said. "Final Descent Checklist again. You challenge, I'll point and reply."

There was silence from the captain's seat. She lifted the eyeshades and peeked.

Laurie, dressed to travel, sat in the left-hand seat, wearing Anne's uniform cap, which came down around her ears. She was still moody, and had apparently lost interest in the drill: there were 48 dials, 135 warning lights, and 76 switches, of which Laurie knew nothing and cared less, spread before and above them. She was staring at a TWA plane howling past the pilot's window.

They had been here almost an hour chanting challenges and responses.

"OK, Laurie. Last landing."

Her daughter, lips pursed, scowled at the plastic checklist in her hand: "Final Descent Checklist: No Smoking signs?"

Anne dropped the blinders back over her eyes. Her hand flew to the no-smoking sign switch. "On."

"Flight and nav instruments?" chanted Laurie.

Anne's fingers, as if they had eyes of their own, flicked across them, one by one. "Cross-checked. No flags."

"Mom, I have to go to the biffy."

Last resort of the travel-weary child, and end of drill. Anne pushed up her blinders again. Laurie's plane was leaving in an hour: Anne would put her in care of a stewardess, and her grandmother would pick her up at the Los Angeles arrival terminal. It was time to quit. "First door to your left."

Anne picked up the cabin phone and flicked on the PA. Her voice echoed through the plane:

"Welcome to Los Angeles International Airport. The final landing was made by Laurie Woodhouse, age nine. Please remain seated while we taxi to the terminal, else our flight attendants will be forced to use their whips, clubs, and lashes."

She shut down the cockpit and led Laurie into the business-class lounge behind the flight deck, then down the spiral staircase to the main cabin.

She was shocked to find that they were not alone. A tubby mechanic peered around the bulkhead of the forward galley. He was kneeling and looked like a red-headed bear disturbed in his cave. He had comical pink cheeks and a full fat nose.

He heaved himself to his feet, stretching his back painfully. He was not pleased.

"You had *her* up on the flight deck?"

"What's the problem, for God's sake?"

"Do not use the name of the Lord Our Savior in vain." As she stared at him in disbelief, he said: "It's against FAA Regulations to have nonemployees on an unloaded aircraft without permission. *That's* the problem."

No, the problem is, she thought, *I'm a woman. Or else you know I crossed the line in '84.*

"Are you in Security?" she asked. "I mean, really!"

"Rules are rules."

She rested her hand on Laurie's head. "She's not a terrorist. And I was with her all the time."

If the mechs struck during their coming negotiations, she might be picketing with him in a month. And in the meantime, with Block threatening to fire her, she wanted no trouble with Security, Flight Ops, the chief pilot, or anyone else.

She squinted at his ID badge: "Rhinelander, Carl?" she murmured. She recognized his name and was not past buttering him up. "You're the A and P who won't sign off the turkeys?"

"Well, yeah," he blushed. "And you're our lady copilot, I see."

"I'm proud to meet you, Carl." She shook his hand. "And this is my daughter, Laurie."

"Hi," said Laurie, flashing him a smile even better than her mother's. "Why do you have the floor all apart?"

He grinned. He had nice teeth. "So your Mom will get where she's going, if it please the Lord."

Anne felt Laurie's grip tighten. "You mean if you didn't, she *wouldn't*?"

"Or if it didn't please *Him*, that's correct."

Anne glared at him. Laurie was capable of connecting life as an orphan with sloppy maintenance, and she didn't need an evangelical sermon, not tonight.

"But it always turns out just fine, Carl," she said evenly. "Am I right?"

"Oh, sure, oh sure, just fine."

"Thanks. We have to run, she has a plane to catch."

CHAPTER
15

Anne followed Lenny Hagler, chief flight instructor, through a door marked 747 Flight Simulator. PacLant's infamous monster sat in the center of the immense room, murmuring electronic threats.

It was a sterile white structure two stories high, supported like an enormous spider on six spindly cylinders. Awkward gray pipes, ventilating tubes, and oddly angled joists and levers clustered around its base.

On its side was painted a full-faced portrait of Sylvester the PacLant Panther, eyes half-closed, blood dripping from his teeth, feasting on a canary wearing a PacLant pilot's cap. Under the picture someone had written, in an angry scrawl, *"Sylvester's Den: Abandon Hope, All Ye Who Enter Here."*

Anne had grabbed a few hours sleep in the crew lounge. She carried her flight bag. It was 4 A.M. and raining on the deserted ramp outside: the PacLant 747 simulator worked a full twenty-four-hour-day.

The captain on the check ride—whoever he was—had not yet reported. He would be getting his annual check ride too. She hoped he was more confident than she.

She followed Hagler to Sylvester's ladder. They were trailed by a black flight engineer she had never met before. Somewhere in the building a radio blared scratchy rock.

Hagler was a bald man with yellowing teeth and a flat Oklahoma accent. In his hand was a clipboard with a pad of pilot-evaluation forms.

It was dawning on her that he himself was going to be the check pilot. But why would the chief flight instructor schedule himself at 4 A.M.?

She had flown the simulator last year and had barely passed her check. It was old, cranky, overly sensitive, and notoriously difficult to fly. It had the feel of a boogie board in the surf: slippery and unpredictable. It often "crashed." When it did, it tilted crazily on its foundation, and its technicians had to work for hours untangling ancient joints and muscles.

To crash Sylvester meant a down check, and maybe your job.

Hagler waved her up the gray steel stairway to the flight deck. Numbly, she counted the steps to the cockpit as she climbed. She had never noticed before, but there were thirteen.

The flight deck was a 747's, complete with the flight engineer's station and check pilot's jump seat behind the pilot's.

Beyond its windshields now lay a computer simulation of San Francisco International Airport, at night.

Dry-mouthed, she strapped herself into the copilot's seat. The flight engineer took his station at his panel behind her, facing the right bulkhead. Hagler settled into the jump seat behind the captain's place and turned on the computer panel. With it he could safely tickle Sylvester into any emergency known to the sky, some quite unsurvivable.

"Where's the captain?" he demanded. "Who is he, anyway?" He picked up the cockpit phone and called his secretary. "Who's scheduled for four?" Footsteps sounded on the ladder. "Never mind," said Hagler, and replaced the phone.

Gary Fremont, in civilian clothes, slipped into the seat beside her.

Gary? Oh, no, not now!

"Fremont," Hagler growled, "it costs a thousand bucks an hour to run this thing!"

"Blame our midnight express from L.A., Chief, not me."

Hagler put the computer keyboard on his lap, jabbed a key, and said: "Let's go."

Anne leaned across the pedestal to set Fremont's altimeter. "*Damn* it!" she whispered. "What are you *doing* here?"

"Not now," he said. "Turn One!" he ordered the flight engineer.

The rumble of the number one engine, perfectly counterfeited, filled the cockpit. "Rotation! Oil pressure, fifteen percent," said the flight engineer.

Gary reached below the throttles and jammed up the start lever. "Fuel flow, light up!" Automatically, Anne's eyes swung to the exhaust-gas temperature gage: a hot start in a real plane could cook an engine to a block of molten junk before they ever got out of the chocks. Sure enough, the temperature was rising.

"EGT coming up!" she piped.

"Hot start!" Gary called. "Securing Number One!"

He jammed the start lever back down and the rumble died

away. In the sudden silence he swung around in his seat. "Is this *it* for today, Chief," he asked, "or you going to let me fly?"

Hagler shrugged, punched a key, and said: "There's your engine back, Captain. Let's get this mother off the ground."

All through his two-hour captain's check—a vicious one, in which Hagler seemed vengefully bound to crash them, if he could—Gary sat in Sylvester's swaying cockpit, calm and solid as a Buddha, ending the flight with a two-engine approach to a full-stop landing at Los Angeles International.

Hagler looked up from his clipboard. "Five-minute pee call, then Woodhouse. You can hang out in the office, Captain; I'll critique you both when she's through."

"Wait a minute! Who's flying left-hand seat for *her*?"

"Me," said Hagler.

She stared at Hagler, appalled. "Why?"

"Because that's the way I want it."

"Bull*shit*, Chief!" snapped Gary. " '*Annual Proficiency Checks will be flown by full crews in the following order: captain (two hours), first officer (two hours), flight engineer (four hours, concurrently with captain and first officer). No changes in personnel will be permitted after the check begins.*' "

"*I* wrote that training manual, Fremont. I'm entering a change."

"I'm staying right here," Gary said. "I'm legal counsel to the master executive council. A check pilot in the left-hand seat sets a precedent ALPA doesn't like. And Junior doesn't need the hassle now."

Hagler seemed to think it over. "OK, *stay*, who gives a damn?" He stamped from the flight deck behind the engineer and plodded down the stairs.

Anne stared at Gary. Face shadowed, he was rubbing his eyeballs.

"You won't answer my notes in your mailbox," he muttered. "You never return a call . . ."

"You *idiot*!" she said, throat tight. "You got *yourself* scheduled for this!"

"Yeah, I pulled a switch."

"Why?" She studied her hands. They were shaking. "Look at that! How can you help me, anyway? What's *wrong* with me?"

"Your problem won't be shakiness: your problem's Stanley Block."

"What?"

"Why's Hagler working at 4 A.M.? To sandbag you, for Junior."

"Why?"

"They want the leverage to shut you up. They're afraid you'll blow the whistle in the hearing on those flaps."

She felt like crying. "What can I *do*, Gary?"

"*We!* Right now, we try to get you an up."

"And then?"

His eyes drilled into hers. "You do just as I say."

She somehow finished her air work: steep, heart-grabbing turns and stalls that no one could dare in a real 747, and then—to her surprise—she made a perfect approach to La Guardia and another to Heathrow outside London, on both of which Hagler failed an outboard engine.

Hagler gave her a three-engined missed approach at O'Hare in Chicago, and conjured up a near midair with a Marine Corps transport climbing out of El Toro, California. He punched in wind shear, thunderstorms, icing, and another loss of hydraulics over San Diego.

He triggered full electrical failure over Dallas and a loss of cabin pressure coming in to Adak in the Aleutians.

By the end of the first hour she was damp with sweat. By her final approach, descending with gear and flaps down through catastrophic turbulence over San Francisco Bay, she was exhausted.

Inside Sylvester's world, it was 7:00 P.M. local. In real time, *stomach* time, it was almost breakfast. She was nauseous from hunger, and queasy from the creaking, groaning motion of the flight deck. Her eyeballs stung and she was afraid to take her hands from the controls to rub them.

She glimpsed the lights of the San Mateo-Hayward Bridge drifting far below, under scudding clouds. She found them blurred. Hagler was simulating one of the night-time fogs that socked in SFO so frequently: ceiling 150 feet, visibility zilch.

All at once a red light began to flash on her glare shield. The flight engineer called: "We have a fire in Number Two!"

Automatically she yanked the number two throttle closed, then the number two fuel shut off valve. The plane swerved left. Delicately, she cranked in rudder trim, and added power to Number One.

"Pull the fire handles on Number Two and fire the bottle!" she ordered the flight engineer. She heard him pull the fire handle, shutting off everything to the engine and flooding it with foam.

She called San Francisco approach control, declared an emergency, and advised them that she was making a three-engine approach.

She came out of her turn lined up perfectly, she was sure,

with the invisible runway. Inside, she was suddenly singing. She had handled every glitch and failure perfectly. The fire was out.

Gary was smiling broadly. His arms were folded across his chest, but she saw one thumb go up.

After all the worry, a piece of cake! All she had to do, when they broke through, was land the plane.

On the instrument panel, a cheerful blue light began to blink as she crossed the San Francisco outer marker. She was tight on a glide path that would lead her to the end of the invisible runway in the fog.

She checked her gear and flaps again. Sylvester seemed steady as a rock.

At two hundred feet, as she was locking on to the localizer, another red light began to flash. Simultaneously, the flight engineer yelled: "*Now* there's a fire in Number *One!*"

"Pull fire handle Number One! Fire the bottle!" she yelled again. She cut the number one engine, killing the last of her thrust on the left wing. The wingtip dropped and the plane skewed heavily to port. She braced herself and stood on the right rudder pedal, fighting to hold course.

"Altitudes!" she gasped.

Gary began to chant the altimeter readings, softly: 170 feet, 160, 150. Now she was committed: no altitude left to trade for speed: no way to take a go-around if she missed. For an instant she tore her eyes from the panel and glanced through the dark windshield.

Through the fog, she saw the happy, golden glow of runway lights. Then Hagler's voice crackled over the speaker, lazy and amused: "PacLant Heavy Two-three-two! There's a vehicle on the runway! Go around!"

"Goddamn it!" barked Gary. "He can't *do* that!"

But Hagler had trapped her. Five miles beyond the runway lay the notch in the coastal range where Cable had crashed. There was no way she could climb out.

A mighty rage welled up inside her. She'd give Hagler a crash to remember.

"Go-around thrust!" she grunted, and the hell with the murderous yaw. She felt Gary backing her hand as she jammed her two good engines to the fire wall. "Flaps: twenty! Gear up!"

"Flaps: twenty! Gear up!" echoed Gary, hopelessly. "Look, Anne, no way!" He struggled out of his shoulder straps. "I'm not going to let him—"

"Gary! Wait!" Anne called, fighting the enormous torque—two engines, full power on her right wing, nothing but drag on her left. Her right thigh was throbbing with fatigue, and she had already rolled in full rudder trim.

The plane swerved dangerously, still descending. But dropping more slowly? Leveling off? One hundred feet, ninety-five, ninety . . .

She glanced ahead. The runway lights were clear now, and sure enough, a pair of headlights was crossing, heedless of her plight.

Cautiously, she eased up the nose. Ninety feet, then ninety-five . . . *Climbing*, on the knife-edge of a stall.

"Anne," grunted Gary, "now he's disabled your flaps!"

She heard the whine of flaps retracting. "Pull the breaker!" she yelled at the flight engineer. He lunged for the flap circuit breaker, just too late.

The stick shaker began to wobble, alerting her to a stall and very nearly breaking her grip upon the yoke. The stall-warning klaxon blasted in her ear. The cockpit tilted violently as the altimeter unwound. The hazy lights of San Francisco began to rotate beyond the glass.

She heard the howl of a rising slipstream. The flight deck lurched left, then right. Every instrument on her panel went berserk. In a cacophony of whistles, alarms, and a roaring crash from the speakers behind her, Sylvester stopped.

A cylinder creaked. Something bleeped. She smelled overworked electrical wiring, and sweat.

A tinny, stewardess voice on tape from somewhere said: "Thank you for flying PacLant. Have a nice day."

Anne found herself sitting at a thirty-degree angle in dead silence. She dug for the dark glasses in her flight bag. Hagler must not see her tears. She struggled from her seat and faced him on the canted flight deck.

"That wasn't fair!" she cried. "I never had a prayer!"

He shrugged. "You crashed, Woodhouse. Sorry. It's a down."

Gary twisted in his seat. "I don't think so."

"No, Captain Fremont? Why is that?"

" 'First Officer's Annual Proficiency Check,' " quoted Gary: " 'Basic air work, one three-engine approach, and one three-engine missed approach to 100 feet.' And that's all."

"That's right, and she *crashed* on the missed approach." Hagler began to write on his clipboard.

Gary slipped from his seat and slammed his hand on Hagler's forearm, stopping the pencil dead. "No. *One* missed approach. She already *had* her 'up' from O'Hare, when you pulled that horseshit here!"

Hagler looked up from his clipboard. "O'Hare was just her warm-up. I don't remember *what* I gave her there."

"And that was two hours ago, so the cockpit voice recorder's erased?"

"Right!" said Hagler. He disengaged his arm and continued to write. "I heard you're a lawyer, Captain, take it to court. It's just your word against mine."

"But there are two of us," Gary reminded him.

"Well, you're not exactly strangers to each other, are you?"

"Have I got an up?" asked the flight engineer suddenly.

"Yeah," said Hagler, "you're OK."

"Give me my sheet."

Hagler signed it and handed it to him. He glanced at it, folded it carefully, and put it in his pocket. "Thanks, Chief. Only, now it's three to one, 'cause I'm with them."

Gary Fremont shook his head. "No, *four* to one, Hagler, you son of a bitch."

"How so?"

Gary reached into his sport jacket pocket and pulled out a pocket dictating recorder. "If you can't trust PacLant's cockpit voice recorder, you bring your own."

She collapsed in a window seat on PacLant's morning shuttle to L.A. Gary Fremont slung her flight bag into the overhead locker and sat down.

"I can't believe you did it," she murmured. "I can't believe it worked."

"I *didn't* do it, Anne, *we* did."

"I never want to fly again, just sleep," she yawned. "That bastard! I was just a sitting duck to him."

"Well, Junior wants to can you, and he'll find another way."

"So Gary, what'll I do under oath?"

"Who knows what you saw but *you*? Tell Junior you'll testify 'flaps down,' oath or not! That's all he wants, Anne. *Do* it!"

"I want it too," she said. "I think Danny Cable's God

Almighty. And Gary, I think his flaps came up all by themselves!"

"That's bullshit! He blew it. But I stopped you from warning him, and—"

"I was too late, anyway," she said quickly. "It wasn't *your* fault."

"Well, I want his flaps *down* in that hearing, sure as hell."

"And Chinook?"

"It's our word against his, in a noisy cockpit. What does an F/E know?"

She closed her eyes. She didn't want to think about it. "Anyway, for now, you saved my tail, my friend."

" 'Friend?' " he repeated. "Jeff Henlein's your 'friend.' Poor old Captain Plover, he's your 'friend.' Your Chicano security guard—Eduardo? He's your 'friend.' For Christ's sake, Anne, I'd rather be your enemy than a '*friend*.' "

"I'll die before I'll let you be my enemy, Gary."

"Good. Lover, again?"

She touched his hand. "No, Gary."

He stared straight ahead. "I know. You're bidding Shannon nowadays?"

"Yes."

"What's there?"

"Rain and fog."

"*Who's* there?"

"Well . . . nobody, at first. Then, our station manager, maybe, I don't know."

"Costello?"

"Corello." She gazed out the window. They were taxiing toward the runway—Cable's runway—and in her mind it was Christmas, once again.

She fought off the memory. "Gary, I'm whacked. Can we—"

"Does he tell you to return my notes? Corello?"

"Don't be silly!"

"And *not* return phone calls? To your dumb machine: 'We're busy now. But if you'll leave your name and number, after the beep—' "

"I'm sorry. I'll change the message."

"Don't bother. Anne, this *is* after the beep!" He took a deep breath. "Anne, I miss you. I never should have let you get away."

She squeezed his hand. "Oh, Gary . . ."

"I miss the hotel in Papeete," he said, "and the big stone fireplace in Aukland. I miss watching you wake up. You ponder, and puzzle, and frown, and think, and nibble your lips, as if you're trying to solve the Rubik's Cube."

"I don't sleep very well any more."

"Does *he* watch you wake up now? Corello?"

She could not bear his eyes on hers, and looked out the window.

"Not yet."

A taxiing Northwest aircraft dipped and nodded to the center line, squared off, and gathered speed. She could plainly see his wing flaps as he sped past. Ten degrees down, steady and unbudging, as the plane roared off.

"Anne?" Gently, Gary took her chin and turned her face to his. "*Did* I let you get away? Or were you going anyway? I want to know."

"Your wife *drove* me away, she was right, we were wrong. And now it's just too late."

Ignoring the seat-belt sign, he unbuckled and stood up.

"Where are you going?"

"To see if they'll let me ride jump seat until we let down."

"Why?" she asked.

"Because I still love you, damn it, and there's nothing I can do!"

"Gary, sit down!"

But he was gone.

Reading his Bible somewhere over Paso Robles, Carl Rhinelander, master machinist, fell off the wagon. The businessman next to him ordered a Bloody Mary from the liquor cart and Rhinelander absentmindedly ordered a beer. Aghast, he stared at it on his tray.

Look not thou upon the wine when it is red . . .

Ashamed to return it, he drank half, and when the cart returned, found himself buying a shot of bourbon.

Now he had a boilermaker, which he tossed down in a ruddy haze, loving the bitterness, hating himself, and already begging forgiveness from his Lord.

He wore a shiny polyester suit of navy blue he'd bought last year at C & R, to wear to church, and his light green Christmas tie. His old brown shoes were polished to an air force sheen. He wore white socks.

In his wallet he carried his Airframe and Engine Certificate, which he intended to slap onto Junior's desk, to emphasize his years of service.

He heard the rattle of the cart again, behind him. Uncertainly, he returned his Bible, which he had been studying since take off, to his breast pocket.

Look not behind thee . . .

"Another, sir?" the stewardess asked his seat mate.

The lips of a strange woman drip as a honeycomb, and her mouth is smoother than oil . . .

Rhinelander stumbled past her and lurched toward the toilet to escape. Passing down the aisle, he saw the pretty copilot. "Morning, ma'am." His tongue felt thick. "Where's your little girl?"

She looked tired and he was sure that she'd been crying. "I put her on our 6 P.M. last night."

Perhaps Jesus would forgive him if he brought her to the fold. Perhaps he'd had the booze for just that reason. He took a deep breath and slipped into the empty seat beside her.

The time has come for Thee to reap; for the harvest of the earth is ripe.

He had been born again too recently to have brought any sheep to the Lord, but they were there in the pastures: you saw them gathered in on TV every Sunday.

"I shouldn't have said that to your little girl last night," he began. "About our maintenance: 'So your mom will get where she's going.' I hope I didn't scare her, ma'am."

"Everybody knows about PacLant maintenance," she shrugged. "She sees the newspapers, Carl."

"Just the same . . . But the other part, about the Lord . . . Are you a Christian, ma'am?"

"I guess. I'm not Jewish, if that's what you mean."

"Not exactly." He smiled. He felt wonderful: this was the Glory they'd promised him, and the joy. "You look sad."

He took out the Bible and thumbed through the pages, remembering how, so recently, its passages had been tangled and dark, and he could never find anything in it, Old Testament or New. Now he knew it like his hand. "Listen to Nehemieh 8:9: *'This day is holy unto the Lord your God; mourn not, nor weep.'* " He sat back and smiled at her. "A day 'Holy unto the Lord.' " He found Thessalonians 5:8: *" 'Let us be sober; putting on the breastplate of faith and love, and for a helmet—an helmet, it says, excuse me—'for an helmet the hope of salvation.' "*

She was staring at him as if he were crazy. If only people would *believe*, it was all there in the Book. He grabbed her arm. " *'For an helmet the hope of salvation!'* " he repeated. "Christians wear that helmet, *that's* what Christians wear! Wouldn't that ease your burden, ma'am? Whatever it might be?"

"I guess." She was looking into his eyes. He felt twenty years younger. "Carl? You're a hydraulic expert?"

"Yes," he said proudly. He was instantly ashamed. *Let not the wise man glory in his wisdom.*

"I have a question: technical, not spiritual. About the 747."

He was hurt. He'd found her passages to comfort her, read her chapter and verse, and she wanted to talk shop! *"Everything* is spiritual."

"Whatever. But I was watching a Northwest 747 take off back there. In that Christmas crash, was there any way Cable's flaps could have come up on takeoff?"

"Only if he *pulled* them up. You know that. Look, I signed that plane off, less than an hour before it went in!"

"Then why didn't the cockpit alarm go off?"

Her question made him nervous, for he—theoretically— was the last to have checked the alarm.

Her eyes were on him, green as the emerald earrings his wife had bought at K Mart, before she lost her job. A first officer, he marveled, think of that! Some day, maybe captain?

He didn't want her to think he'd pencil-whipped the cockpit alarm through check.

"Well, I wasn't the *last* mech to fool with those flaps."

He found himself blurting out Paco's story. By the time he was through, his mouth was dry and his head was throbbing. He longed for another boilermaker, but the plane was already descending into the San Fernando smog, and the stewardesses had trundled the drinks cart out of sight.

The girl's face was white, as if she were airsick.

"What's wrong, ma'am?"

"We *switched* planes in Flight Ops that night," she murmured. "At the very last minute. Or *that* plane would have been mine! I wonder . . ."

"What?" he asked.

"Nothing." A handsome man with a blue-stubbled jaw was leaving the cockpit and heading aft. "We're landing, Carl," she said, "and Captain Fremont's sitting in that seat."

Rhinelander arose. He felt like an idiot: he had spilled her the very thing he had promised to keep to himself. *A prudent man concealeth knowledge: but the heart of fools proclaimeth foolishness.* He put the Bible in his pocket and lurched back to his seat.

Anne searched Gary's face. It was closed and grim.

"Sabotage? That's crazy, Anne! By one of our own mechs?"

"Maybe a flight engineer, in mechanic's overalls? Chinook! He'd known the hydraulic system, wouldn't he?"

"Maybe, but *why*?"

"Me."

He stared. "You?"

"I scabbed. I jumped over him and a hundred other F/Es, smack into the right-hand seat! He hates my guts! They all do! You know that!"

"So Chinook tries to *kill* you? And me? And himself? And a planeload of people?"

"Not *kill* me, no. Panic me! I'm the one reading the checklist. We start to roll. The flaps start up, the cockpit alarm stays off, Chinook catches it, I don't, you abort, he's a hero, and I'm through for life!"

"Well, you wouldn't have panicked."

"Thanks. But I damn near *did*, when I saw those flaps, and I wasn't even in the plane!"

He faced her sadly, shaking his head. "You're saying he just sat there, after we switched planes, and let Danny kill two hundred people? Come on, Anne, lighten up!"

He searched her eyes with genuine concern. My God, she thought, I'm getting paranoid.

"OK, I'm sorry. It *is* insane. You're right."

CHAPTER 16

Across his desk, over a just-completed model of a nineteenth-century clipper ship, Monty Starbuck regarded the tall Irishman.

For an instant, Starbuck hated him. He was loose and rangy, as Starbuck had been once. He reflected that if Corello wanted to, after their conference, he could jog, or bicycle, or make love on a sandy beach, or sail a boat to Avalon.

His wheelchair seemed to grow smaller, gripping his butt too tightly. He toyed with a pencil on his desk. "Come on, Ian! Why would the IRA pick on PacLant?"

The man's eyes, uncomfortably direct and very blue, rested on his. "And why not? We've just been lucky, so far."

Starbuck wished he had not allowed him to come to L.A. But the FAA had forced his hand: on test runs in the past six months, its agents had sneaked two pistols and a six-inch

Buck hunting knife through the PacLant gate at Shannon.

"We increased your budget last quarter, Ian. What other airline has German shepherds on patrol?"

"I asked for bomb sniffers. What I got was untrained dogs, rented from a breeder, to impress the ticket lines. And a Brit for a station security chief that I didn't even want."

Starbuck had, in accordance with PacLant's global policy, hired the Englishman to keep an eye on the Irishman. In Japan's Narita Airport, he had a Korean watching a Japanese manager, and in London's Heathrow, he had an Irishman watching a Limey. It seemed to work very well.

He rolled his wheelchair to the personal computer by his desk. He banged a few keys and loaded his foreign-manager personnel file onto the screen.

CORELLO, IAN MARCUS . . .

He scrolled past Corello's resumé, employment record, and work history. Due for salary review. Unmarried . . .

Cambridge '75. Light drinker. Member Dublin Rowing Club. Sometimes dates PacLant stewardesses. . . .

The most recent item was apparently entered by the new Shannon security chief, a Londoner who seemed to have his own agenda and a ready knife:

Unauthorized private use of company vehicle: Station Manager was observed by security guard departing ramp area in company van. Passengers were a uniformed female first officer and a stewardess, both entitled to scheduled shuttle bus at no cost to the company.

Female first officer . . . Anne Woodhouse was turning up everywhere he looked. He closed out the file and turned away from his computer.

"I'll try to get you a supplementary thirty thousand for additional security personnel. You flying back tonight?"

Corello put his papers back into his briefcase. "No. A few days' holiday, since I'm here. Disneyland, Knott's Berry Farm. A child's involved: you know the drill."

Disneyland? Starbuck had a stroke of intuition. "With Anne Woodhouse? And her daughter?"

Corello smiled. "Yes. This company *is* a bloody fishbowl, isn't it?" He got up, stretching his shoulders. "Thank you for your time, then, Mr. Starbuck."

"You've asked for a salary review while you're here?" asked Starbuck suddenly.

"Yes. I'm on my way to Personnel."

"Good luck." They shook hands. "She's a pretty girl," said Starbuck, "Anne Woodhouse."

"Rather more than that, I think. I've fallen quite in love."

Starbuck's Chelsea ship's clock, from the sloop that had crippled him, chimed from his wall. Six bells: 3 P.M.

"Then you can do her a favor, Ian."

"And what would that be, now?"

"She's muddying up the investigation about that Christmas crash. She may have to testify before the NTSB. There's a feeling that she lacks . . . Well, company *loyalty*."

"What you're saying is that she won't testify our way."

"You got it, Ian. Mr. Block wants to fire her."

"For refusing to lie?"

"For screwing up a lawsuit against Boeing."

"And you think a word from me might change her mind?" Starbuck shrugged. "How close *are* you? It couldn't hurt."

"Or hurt my salary negotiations with Personnel?"

Starbuck suspected that Corello wasn't buying it, but decided to go the course. "*I* didn't say that, *you* did. But you're right."

"How right, Mr. Starbuck? Two thousand quid a year?"

"Why not?"

The Irishman smiled. "If pig shit were music, Starbuck, you'd all be a bloody brass band!"

He pushed through the door and left.

Anne lay with Laurie by the condo pool. New Boys on the Block blasted from Laurie's boombox. Laurie had been sulking ever since San Francisco. Anne still did not know why.

"What is it?" she begged. "What's bugging you, Doodle? Do you want me to bid local flights?"

Laurie tossed her hair. "No."

"What *do* you want?"

"Nothing." She kicked at the water. "Yes. Something. Daddy's picture."

Anne tensed. As calmly as she could, she asked her why.

"Why not? Kimiko's got *her* dad's picture on her bureau, and *she* sees him every night!"

"I don't think . . ."

"You don't think we have one?" The golden eyes swung to her scornfully, and Anne sensed that she'd found the only remaining picture of McCann, hidden in a file in the den.

"There is one, of course. If you want it on your bureau, you can have it."

Anne went back to the condo and dug McCann's photo from under a pile of her mother's old galleys, deep in a file cabinet. "My God," her mother muttered, "I forgot that thing was there."

"Well, Laurie knows it, she must have been in your files. She wants it in her room."

"Why, now? All of a sudden?"

"Because he's her *daddy*, Mom."

They stared at the photo. Cal, strapped into his parachute gear, wearing helmet, bandoliers, and more artillery than she believed a man could carry, was climbing aboard a C-130 air force troop carrier in the brilliant Georgia sun. One thumb up, eyes laughing, he beamed back at her triumphantly, with the innocent little-boy grin.

She marched with the picture to Laurie's bedroom, dusted the glass, polished the silver frame with a sock, and plunked it on Laurie's cluttered dresser, dead center in the mess. *That's one for you, you bastard*, she told him, *but this is as close as you come.*

CHAPTER 17

Stanley Block, Junior, stared across his desk at Monty Starbuck. "So what *do* we do about Miss PacLant, the Pride of the Great Silver Fleet?"

"I struck out with her Irish boyfriend, but I'm giving it some thought." The beeper on his wheelchair began to chirp. He spun to Block's desk, punched a phone number, and said: "Starbuck, here. I'm in Mr. Block's office. You beeping me?"

He listened for a moment and said: "Give me his full name and social security number. And you better pat him down."

He waited, hand over phone. "First-floor security," he reported to Block. "Some mech's demanding to see you, from Maintenance, SFO." He pulled his laptop onto his knees and picked up the phone again. " 'R' and then 'H'?" He tapped the keys, studied his screen. "OK, Bucko, put him on . . . Rhinelander? I'm sorry, Mr. Rhinelander, I know

he'd like to see you, but he's in Washington all week long."
Slowly, he hung up.

"Who the hell was that?" demanded Block.

"That whistle-blower mech from San Francisco."

"I've heard of him. He wanted to see *me*?"

"They threw him off the graveyard shift."

"Who does he think he is, trying to get in here? Another McCann? It's time we canned that son of a bitch! Call Personnel!"

"Wait," warned Starbuck. "He signed off on that Christmas plane. Don't turn him loose quite yet."

"I don't care," growled Block. "I'm tired of this crap!"

"Now, come on, Stanley," Starbuck murmured, "he trained half the slobs on the hangar floor! What if they walk? Suppose the *union* sent him down here just for this!"

Reluctantly, Block agreed. Starbuck rolled to the southern window and gazed toward Palos Verdes. His home was only three blocks inland of Junior's own: their wives played tennis daily. He half rose in his wheelchair, trying to see through the eyepiece of Block's telescope.

Block joined him: "Let me drop that tripod for you, Monty. You think Madge has a lover?"

"Leave it up, I don't want to know." He seemed to fall into deep thought. "Junior, does *your* wife go to Horace Vezzano?"

"Don't they all?" Vezzano was the current pet of Palos Verdes housewives. His hypnotic biofeedback sessions were said to be effective for everything from frigidity to migraine. "Yeah, Dotty goes, for her PMS. Why?"

"So does Madge," said Starbuck.

"So?" asked Block.

"Just a passing thought," said Starbuck, "about that damn-fool girl."

● ● ●

At Los Angeles International Airport, Mike Ruble sat at a window table in the PacLant terminal restaurant. He watched Carl Rhinelander wrestle with his conscience.

Dressed in a shiny blue suit, the mechanic seemed ill at ease and angry. An overnight bag lay across his knees: a cup of coffee steamed before him. They had less than five minutes before the mechanic's plane left for San Francisco.

"FAA needs that list, Carl," urged Ruble. He had dropped everything to get here, and now he sensed that Rhinelander was having second thoughts. "I'll see that it gets to the right guy. And they'll never know where it came from."

"They'll know where it came from, all right. They know I'm here, I tried to see Block. Somebody said he's in Washington. I don't believe him."

He dug suddenly into his bag and pulled out a brown manila envelope. He slid it across the table. "Every plane we've pencil-whipped out of that place in the last three years. Plus omitted check procedures, plus the dates."

"Thanks," said Ruble, doodling on the envelope with his pencil.

"The Bible says: '*Let me see thy vengeance on them; for unto thee I have revealed my cause:* Jeremiah 11:20.' Will you be working on these, yourself?"

Ruble glanced out the window. A Lockheed-1011 was descending from the haze, flaps down, gear groping for the runway.

"No. I'll pass it on to the FAA inspector. A plane has to crash to bring me in. Besides, I'm still working the Christmas thing."

"The Christmas thing," mused Rhinelander. "Mr. Ruble, suppose somebody fooled with those flap hydraulics *after* I looked at them?"

"*Fooled* with them?"

"Rechecking them, maybe. My apprentice on graveyard told me the other day . . ."

His voice trailed away.

Ruble glanced at the envelope. Under his doodling pencil, Rhinelander's face had appeared on the flap, quite magically.

Narrow the eyes, furrow the forehead, change the mouth . . . There! He had caught perplexity, thought, the elusive recollection. He removed the list and skidded the envelope across the desk.

"Hey," beamed Rhinelander, "look at that!"

"Keep it, Carl." There was something in the air, a question unresolved. "Your apprentice told you *what*?"

Rhinelander shrugged. "He said that on Christmas Eve he saw one of the line mechs checking flap linkages after I signed off a plane."

Ruble tensed. "Who *was* the line mech? What's his name?"

"I don't know."

"Why would he check the flaps again, after a thousand-hour check?"

"Maybe he didn't trust us guys on Braden's shift."

"Your apprentice saw this? What's his name?" He whipped a notebook from his pocket, but Rhinelander shook his head.

"No! I don't want him in it."

"I can *get* his name, Carl. You know that."

"Paco," conceded Rhinelander. "Paco Lopez. But his mother's a wetback with false papers. He won't want to get involved."

"Will he *talk* to me?"

"You're federal government. I don't think so."

Ruble's heart began to pound. He took a deep breath and tried to relax: his doctor wanted him to retire, and he would, too, when the Christmas crash was solved. It was consuming him, as if it had some relation to Kitty's death, years ago.

But that was insane: Kitty had been the innocent victim of a mass murderer on PSA 1771, a random casualty of an on-the-job feud between a psychotic ticket agent and his supervisor.

While PacLant's Christmas crash was pilot error, or maintenance failure, or something structural . . .

Still, flaps didn't just *creep* up on takeoff, or they'd all be dead.

"Carl, I've got to see this guy."

"I don't have him any more. I'm out on the ramp all alone."

"You have to set it up for me!" said Ruble.

"No. I was kicked off graveyard for talking to you. You can't have Paco, too."

The PA system squawked: *PacLant International announces the departure of Flight One-one-eight for San Francisco* . . .

Rhinelander stood up. Carefully, he put the empty envelope into his overnight bag, smiling at the sketch. "Got to go, Mr. Ruble. Thanks for this."

Ruble tried a parting shot: "I want to talk to Paco, Carl! Suppose I intercede with Immigration to keep them off his mother's back?"

Rhinelander sighed. "OK, Mr. Ruble. I'll see what I can do."

CHAPTER 18

Bored with his visitor, Cal McCann sat on a green plastic bench on the cliff outside the VA cafeteria. He watched the fog slide in like a great roll of cotton, from the Farallon Islands far to sea.

Next to him his old top sergeant, J. B. Stolak, sat staring out at the water. He had made the trip up the coast on McCann's Honda, and brought him some crack. McCann passed him back the glass pipe.

Dullsville, USA. The smell of the cafeteria drifted over the lawn. A radio blasted golden oldies from some ward behind the trees. The old geezer from World War I shuffled along the cliffside path, a doughboy fore-and-aft cap, as always, on his head.

"Gassed," he pointed out to Stolak, "making the world safe for democracy."

"You *look* gassed."

"*Him*, asshole. Not me."

Stolak studied the old man languidly, eyelids half-masted. "Jesus, he's gotta be . . . What?"

"Ninety, ninety-five? He lives down the corridor. Half the time he's still in France, and he coughs all the goddamn night."

"At least, *he* got a parade when he came home."

If Stolak started the embittered veteran act, he'd have to strangle him where he sat.

In a moment, McCann knew, the foghorn would start. The Top had never heard it: it would make his pony-tail stand up. The boredom fled. He chuckled, and the chuckle got away from him and turned into a long, high giggle.

"What?" drawled Stolak, inhaling. "What's crackin' *you* up? *Crack's* crackin' you up."

Stoned, decided McCann. The Top was stoned, and so, thank God, was he. Felt good, saw things clearly, had answers he had never had before.

Like, if they really wanted, when the fogbanks reached the cliff, they could step onto them and plough their way to the Farallons, Hawaii, Nam. They had the time: time was God: there was no other.

They gave you a slice of the god named time, and then you died. Like Charlie-Charlie.

"Hey, Charlie-Charlie!" McCann murmured, dredging up the memory to crowd Stolak. "Remember Charlie-Charlie, Top?" Charlie-Charlie had been a teenage VC scout who would not break. "Wham! Gone!" he sighed. "Prime of life."

"What brought *that* up? Crack?"

"Just thinking. And what was your excuse? 'I didn't know there was one in the chamber, Lieutenant.' "

"Well, I didn't," shrugged the Top. "I took the clip out! You saw that!"

"You're a real pro, you know?" he said sarcastically. "Regular army. Jesus!"

"Hey, even Joe Montana fumbles, sometimes!" grinned the Top. "You weren't all that great at Fort Benning."

"But I saved our asses with Charlie-Charlie," McCann reminded him. He had convinced G2 that the prisoner had grabbed the weapon and committed suicide.

"No. Your gold bar saved our asses, McCann. Not you."

"Umm . . ." McCann regarded the fog bank speculatively. He'd lost his chain of thought, over Charlie-Charlie. Fog . . .

Hell, he could drive the *bike* to Saigon, across the billowing clouds. Better yet, to Mexico, with Laurie riding postilion. Why fly, when you could ride, and leave the driving to us?

"My bike OK?" he asked Stolak. "You clean the points?"

"Points?"

"I told you to do the points," he flared. "And grease the chain. Before you started north."

"Yeah, I forgot."

The foghorn suddenly blasted, setting the bench to quivering and driving needles of sound into his nerves. Stolak jumped and almost dropped the pipe. "Jesus!"

"Welcome to the voice of San Francisco, Top."

"That thing go off all the time?"

"No. You won't hear it again," McCann said slyly.

The horn bellowed immediately. The Top jumped once more, and McCann chortled.

"Hey, that ribbon in your ponytail turned green!"

"Funny, funny, funny. How do you stand it here?"

"I go AWOL quite a bit. I won't be here long."

"Good." The Top took a last suck on the pipe, knocked out the ash, and ground it into the path with his foot. "Get your butt back south, Lieutenant, and set us up some drops off Catalina. I'm not makin' it on abalones, very good."

The horn roared again. As always, the noise of it tied knots in McCann's stomach. And he was coming down too quickly from the crack.

He waited until the horn stopped, and said: "You got access to a sewing machine down there? Heavy-duty?"

"Sewing machine? What for?"

"Canvas webbing."

"Canvas—".

"Well, do you or don't you?" *Jesus, ask a simple question . . .*

"Maybe. I sell a little meth to a guy with a sail loft. Why?"

"I'm going to want to use it, when I come."

"No problem, Lieutenant." Stolak yawned, got up, stretched his arms, and tucked away the pipe. "Long ride back. Goin' to stay in San Luis Obispo tonight."

His freedom angered McCann. What right did Stolak have with *his* bike, to take the open road, when he was chained to this?

The hell with him. "OK, go! Don't forget the points, OK?"

"Sure, sure, you gonna walk me to the lot?"

"No." If he walked to the bike, he'd probably take off for southern California with him, and now was not the time. Tomorrow, maybe, and alone.

Churning inside, he watched Stolak move into the mist. The foghorn thundered. Restlessly, he got up and wandered to the cliffside path. The fog was suddenly upon him; he could hardly see ten feet.

He heard the old man wheezing, and the slow, incessant tapping of his cane. Suddenly the geezer was upon him, rounding the path in the fog.

The tired old eyes peered up at him. "Buddy? *Tu es Américain?*"

The old fart had finally lost it! "*Non, non, mon petit,*" smiled Cal McCann. "*Je suis le Général Foch.*"

The wasted shoulders went back, the heels slammed together, the toothless chin went in. The cane rose to present arms—one, two—with the snap of a drill marine.

McCann returned the salute, then grasped the cane. He had a wild impulse to shove him over the rail.

To hear his strangled cry from the mist below, the thud of his body on the rocks, the sound of his cane, clattering down the crags? To sleep tonight without the old man's racking cough?

No. The heat would screw up all his plans. He let go the cane. "*Bon soir, mon vieux.* Stay loose."

The foghorn roared. It was almost time for dinner. He went in.

CHAPTER 19

Anne seated herself and watched Dr. Horace Vezzano, Ph.D., take his place behind his ebony desk. He was a fresh-faced young man with a confident grin and brown eyes that he was trying to charm her with.

She was tense, angry at being forced away from Laurie. Last night a nurse from PacLant Medical had phoned. Her chronic jet lag was on her record, and the company flight surgeon was insisting that she consult a specialist on sleep disorders in Palos Verdes. "You're scheduled for Shannon next week, so we made you an appointment tomorrow at nine."

Vezzano's office lay in a quiet corner of the Palos Verdes Village shopping mall, above a branch of Red Carpet Realty. The decor was restrained: furniture in greens and grays, a cream-colored couch along half the length of the room, and geraniums in the window boxes beneath leaded panes of glass.

Vezzano seemed a Mercedes freak. A three-pointed silver star hood ornament glittered on his desk set; another shone on a wall-poster on the door. A framed diploma from USC hung on the wall.

He smiled at her, shaking his head. "You used to take Halcion tablets?"

"They worked," she said peevishly. "And now I can't. They might show on a urine test. I've given up worrying about sleeping, Doctor. Jet lag comes with the job."

"How did you sleep last night?"

"Not worth a damn." How could she sleep, with the president of her company gunning for her, and the Christmas crash, and bills to pay, and always, in the background, Cal McCann?

"Do you sleep alone?"

"Yes. Is that a sleep disorder, or bad luck?" *Or an offer, you phoney bastard?* she added silently.

"Sometimes bad, sometimes good. Did you go to bed last night with something on your mind?"

"I always do. We won't go into that."

He looked doubtful: " 'Not going into that' may be your problem."

"Then the problem will remain," she said. "I don't really want analysis, Doctor. I'm here on the airline's orders. I'd rather have stayed on the pills."

He studied her, tapping a pencil on his desk. "Is there something you want to remember, and can't?"

"No."

"Or something you want to forget?"

She thought of the Christmas crash. *None of his business.* "No."

"I think there is. Have you thought of hypnosis? To get it out from under the rug, and sweep it all away?"

Despite herself, she was intrigued. "Can you *do* that?"

"Sometimes. I'm pretty good."

She thought it over. Without the pills, some day she'd be in trouble. She *had* to lick the jet lag, or quit flying.

"Ok." Anything was better than the awful, fretful nights. "Go ahead and zap me, Doctor: shoot."

He lowered Venetian blinds behind him and turned his desk set so that the hood ornament was facing her. "Just concentrate on the center of that Mercedes star, let your mind roam free, and we'll see what we can do. You've got a nice tan. You're a beach person? You surf?"

"Yes," she murmured.

"Me too. OK, now I want you to relax, relax, relax. Your body is heavy, and you're lying on the beach. The breakers are booming. They echo off the cliff behind you . . . You're deep in the sound of the surf . . ."

She tried to focus on the star, letting her mind go blank. She saw herself under the cliff, the Palos Verdes cliff. Far above her Block's Spanish mansion shone in the bright sunlight . . .

Block. His home could not be far from here.

Why was she in a classy Palos Verdes office at PacLant's expense, instead of—PacLant style—with some two-bit psychologist in a smoggy medical building near the airport?

She popped her eyes open. "Doctor, do you know Stanley Block?"

Vezzano's jaw tightened. "No."

"His wife?"

"Just concentrate on the star!"

"*Do* you?"

"I'm an ethical psychologist. You know that I can't answer that."

She stood up.

"You just did, Svengali. And you're not getting into my head!"

CHAPTER 20

She sat with Ian at a window table in the Theme Restaurant, atop the soaring, arched centerpiece of Los Angeles International Airport. He had wanted to meet Laurie and take them to Disneyland but Laurie—quite strangely—had begged to stay home and play tennis.

Anne picked a nacho from the appetizer plate.

"Starbuck said *what*?" she demanded.

"Starbuck said 'if it's love, you can do her a favor.' Well, it's love, that's sure. But I'd be doing you no favor, would I, if I told you to lie on the stand?"

"I don't know."

She stared out toward the runways. A quarter of a mile away, the PacLant terminal, with the evening flights filling, swarmed with traffic. She was beginning to think of the company as a Nazi state, devouring her whole life.

She had never heard of Starbuck before. "And this guy's in charge of *Security*?"

He nodded. "More than that, love. He's the corporate éminence grise. Junior made him a vice-president, last year."

"So he's sitting over at headquarters, playing with our lives? Did he set me up with that hypnotist, too?"

"Probably."

"My God! Was this outfit always like this?"

"Yes. Your lovely digs in Newport Beach are coming very dear. Is it really worth the candle?"

"Where else can I get to the left-hand seat of a 747!" she flared. "Why should I settle for less?"

"Steady, lass." He put his hand on hers. Her anger fled. "Less may be better, if it's wrecking your life."

"Ian, I need the goddamn job! So what else can I do?"

"Well, you've not seen my place on the Liffey. We'll talk of this there, next week."

His eyes were warm and full of calm. She let herself slide into their depths. "OK. Shall we order?" he asked softly.

She shrugged.

"Anne?"

"Yes?"

"How hungry are you, really?"

"Not hungry at all."

"Or tired?"

"Not tired either, Ian." She pressed his hand to her lips. "Let's go."

She awakened slowly in the Hyatt Airport Hotel near Los Angeles International, to the pulse of the pulse of the synthesizer from the piano bar below. *Boomp ... boomp ... boomp ...*

Ian slept beside her, his arm thrown back over his eyes. Though the bed was enormous, he was so tall that his toes reached its foot.

Traffic moved silently and eternally down Century Boule-

vard, bound for LAX. She watched the play of its light across
his features. She was impelled to trace his profile with her
finger, but he was in sleep so deep that she could not bear to
awaken him. He breathed slowly: she found herself holding
her own breath, waiting for his next.

Carefully, she turned away and lay face up, watching the
dance of light across the ceiling. She heard the faint howl
of a departing jet, discordant against the beat from below.

Boomp . . . boomp . . . boomp . . .

Midnight, or thereabouts, she estimated. Before two, anyway, or the piano bar would be closed already.

There was an illuminated clock on her bedside table.
Carefully, she eased it around. Almost midnight.

She had to get a painting estimate on the Mazda's door.
But when? Tomorrow she had to finish proofing her mother's book. The next day she had a flight to Shannon—Ian
would be on it. The day after that was Laurie's swim meet:
she was going to miss another chunk of her daughter's life.

The nighttime worries were gathering, planning their
attack.

*Gary: "Tell Junior you'll testify 'flaps-down,' oath or
not! That's all he wants, Anne. Do it!"*

*Ian: "I'd be doing you no favor, would I, if I told you
to lie on the stand?"*

Then Ian stirred, and she turned to him, and tomorrow
was aeons away.

Aeons . . . Ian . . . Aeons with Ian . . .

His eyes opened, pools of sapphire blue.

"Hello, there, you," he murmured softly.

"Hi . . ."

"And did you sleep, then?"

"Yes."

He drew her into his arms and shut off time again.

CHAPTER 21

Cal McCann sat in the VA cafeteria. Outside, below the cliff, the morning sun was burning fog off the Pacific, but the horn on old Fort Point was bellowing, as if to call it back. He was waiting for his shrink, and she was late.

Jabbing at a sausage, he watched the old doughboy hobble to the steam table and begin his morning deliberations. A line of other patients formed behind him.

Last night he had missed his chance to make a farewell gesture to his fellow sufferers: if he'd dumped the old bastard off the cliff, the chow line would bless him forever.

"Hello," the shrink said, behind him. Her voice was shaky and uncertain. As she put down her tray, her cup rattled in its saucer. "This is stupid, McCann, but I'm here."

Her hair was down, her eyes made up. For the first time he was seeing her without her glasses. *Nervous, but ready for plucking.*

"Good *morning*, Dr. Flodden, ma'am! Why do you rise so soon? To chase away the little stars, and far outshine the moon?"

"I rose so soon because you asked me. What was your problem?" She stirred her coffee and squinted at him nearsightedly. "You're too cheerful, McCann. Why's that?"

"Manic."

"Oh, great!"

"I'm 'feeling good about myself.' I've 'come to terms with my self-image.' I 'like myself as a person.' I'm 'acting out.' "

She smiled. She had a brilliant smile, today. "Oh, God, I've created a monster!"

"I've *swallowed* all that group can teach me, Gail, and now—"

"I know. But I told you once, no private therapy."

Now she was really blushing. Jesus, it was only 9 A.M., and already she was in estrus. He could probably have her on the table, if he wanted.

"You're the doctor," he said, resignedly.

She toyed with her cereal, smiling. "Once you said 'you don't look like a doctor, you're too young.' And I called *you* a bullshitter."

"You're *still* too young."

"You're still a bullshitter."

"Can I come up at ten and bullshit? After rounds? I want to talk about leaving here."

She seemed shocked. She moistened her lips. "Oh, hell, why not? Ten sharp."

At five minutes to ten he knocked on her door. There was no one inside. He eased it open and went in.

He was curious about his own psychiatric file. He tried her desk. It was locked.

He was trying the drawers in a file cabinet when he sensed her presence in the doorway.

"What the *hell* are you doing?" she whispered.

He turned. She had never looked better.

"Jesus, Gail, you're *beautiful*!"

She moved swiftly across the office, and tested the drawer. "OK. It's locked, it *stays* locked."

"Sure, fine." He smiled into her face. "You're prettier when you're pissed."

"Those files are confidential!"

"I wanted to see how I'm doing."

"You'd do fine if you'd go to group therapy."

"I'm doing fine anyway. I want a two-week pass."

Give me a two-week start on the Orange County sheriff, he promised silently, *and I'll never see you or Fort Miley again.*

"If it were up to me I'd give you a discharge, not a pass."

"And inform the Orange County Court about it, right?"

"Of course. It's a condition of your suspended sentence."

"Which I'd have to serve. No thanks."

"I thought so. Why do you want a two-week pass?"

"Family matter."

"Family? Look, your parents are dead, and if you get within a hundred yards of your ex-wife or your daughter, you go to jail. What family are we talking about?"

"My kid sister. She's in Seattle, teaching French."

"In Seattle . . ." She whirled and strode to the file cabinet, unlocked it, and drew out his file. "You're such a *liar*, McCann. Your sister, according to your preliminary interview, drowned when she was two. Did you think I wasn't listening, or what?"

His gut clenched. "It wasn't my fault," he blurted.

Her eyes widened. "*What* wasn't your fault?"

Get out of my head! And out of my way . . .

"Look, Gail . . ."

" 'Doctor' is better, I think, for now."

"Just give me the goddamn pass!"

She shook her head and sat down behind her desk. Her mood had changed. "How did she drown, Cal? Swimming?"

The foghorn blared. He could feel it reach into his gut, turn it inside out. "Bath."

She reached into her desk drawer and pulled out a pair of glasses. They magnified her eyes, which probed his own. "And who was giving her the bath, Cal?"

He shook his head. His mouth was dry and his hands were trembling with anger. "Nobody. Herself." He rested his hands on the desk, so that she wouldn't see them shaking. "Just give me the fucking pass, Gail. That's all you got to do."

"*Herself?* At two? No way. *Who* was giving her that bath, Cal? I really want to know."

"Get off it, Gail!"

The foghorn blared distantly. It became suddenly the braying of a Paris ambulance, outside his childhood home on Avenue Macmahon. The ornate, stuffy apartment was filled with calm professionals in white, and his baby sister's wet, rubbery body lay limp on the dining room table under a mask. His mother was out: shopping, she claimed, but more likely drinking in the bar at the Meurice; his father was God knew where.

The local gendarme, his hero until now, was staring at

him coldly while he repeated, again and again, that he had
left her only for a moment . . .

"Left her, *mon fils*? *Pourquois*?"

The shrink's voice was shrilling: "You *left* her, and she
drowned, Cal? Was that it, all the time?"

He rounded the desk, drew her to him, clamped his mouth
over hers, and shut her up. He could feel her struggling, then
growing soft, pressing her thighs to his. Her lips relaxed,
and he probed for her tongue. His hand slid down her back
to her buttocks: they were taut and warm.

He scooped her up in his arms, carried her to the door,
and locked it. "What kind of goddamn shrink are you, no
couch?"

She said nothing. He eased her to the floor in front of
her desk. He was unzipping her skirt when he heard the
foghorn blaring again, making the floor vibrate. He found
himself ripping off the dress.

Her eyes widened. "Take it easy! McCann! Let me go!"
Now she was fighting him in earnest. Her voice rose. "Let
me go, you son of a bitch!"

She opened her mouth to scream. He clapped his palm
over it, and clamped her nostrils between thumb and fore-
finger, cutting off her breath. Her eyeglasses fell and her
eyeballs bulged. Like a VC scout jabbed with a cattle prod,
she kicked and struggled to be free.

When finally she passed out, he raped her in giant,
convulsive thrusts: a waste, for she never knew. Then he
pressed his thumbs on her throat and counted to a hundred,
slowly, to make sure that she was dead.

Her telephone began to ring. He left it ringing and locked
her door behind him. He went to his ward. On a chair by
his bed sat the panda. He packed his suitcase. He unfolded
the Emporium shopping bag, emblazoned with bunnies,

chipmunks, and fawns, and jammed the panda in.

He walked through the grounds to the VA bus stop. He rode to the downtown airline terminal. On a VISA card, he bought a United ticket to Seattle under his own name, to mislead pursuit. In a stall in the men's room, he pasted on his false moustache.

At the Alaska Airline counter he bought another ticket, for cash, under a false name, to L.A. Buckled safely aboard a 737, he sat back.

Not good, not bad. She'd made him kill her, and now there'd be heat until he made his move, but what the hell? He was ready: moustache, colored contact lenses, passport, the whole schmear.

At least he'd never have to listen to the goddamn horn again.

CHAPTER 22

Mike Ruble sat with Carl Rhinelander at a table in a South San Francisco McDonald's, near the apprentice's home. Rhinelander had picked the place.

When Paco sauntered in, he wore a Giant's baseball cap. Ruble captured his image, head to toe: He was slender, dark, with laughing black eyes, a wispy moustache, and a gang tattoo in the web of his thumb.

"Miss you, man," Paco said to Rhinelander, mussing his hair. He regarded Ruble with suspicion, and when Ruble stuck out his hand, studied it for a moment before he shook it limply and slid into the booth. "You got Rhino slam-dunked onto day shift, man. What you gonna to do for me?"

"First, buy you breakfast," said Ruble. "Let's eat, and then we'll talk."

They sat over the remnants of Eggs McMuffin, staring at Ruble's sketch. It was his first attempt at forensic art, and had taken almost an hour. He filled in the shadows. Paco craned at the face. "Put a cap on him. Like mine, only 'PacLant.' "

"I get his cheeks right?"

"Too fat, maybe." Paco chewed his thumbnail, squinting at the sketch. "No, it's OK! Hey, we got Diego Rivera sittin' with us, Rhino," marveled Paco. "Look at that!"

" 'Neglect not the gift that is in thee.' Remember that, Paco, OK?"

Carefully, Ruble turned the sketch toward Rhinelander. "Anybody you know?"

Rhinelander inspected it. "No, sir. And I know everybody on every shift. Night *and* day."

"You think he screwed them flaps up, man?" Paco asked. "You think that's why it crashed?"

"I don't know," said Ruble. "Maybe."

Paco shook his head sadly. " 'If it ain't broke don't fix it,' Rhino, right? Maybe they should have left our flaps alone."

Ruble slipped his sketchbook back into his briefcase. "Maybe they should have, at that."

CHAPTER 23

Anne sat in morning sunlight at her dining room table, editing. Her mother's latest work lay in two neat piles before her: pages already finished to her right, barely one inch high: unread pages to her left, three full inches yet to go.

> *Martha squirmed sensuously on the warm Malibu*
> *sand at the memory of Howley Markham III and*
> *his trim body, his full and knowing lips . . .*

Anne felt chained between the piles of paper. Even her mother, who was leaving for a romance writers' convention in Houston this afternoon, was escaping the manuscript's woes.

Outside, on the porch, the wild canary she loved was trilling gloriously, free to fly away. She could hear golfers on the fairway below, discussing interest rates, free to quit if they wanted to. Laurie was with Kimiko, free to leave the TV and stroll to the club, or the ice-cream parlor at Eastbluff.

Anne, scheduled for a Shannon flight tomorrow night, shifted restlessly. Everything pulled at her to leave the table and flee her mother's prose.

The doorbell chimed. Gratefully, she went to answer it.

The man wore a madras sport shirt and chino pants. He had a scarred forehead and a twisted smile. He showed her a wallet with a gold badge in it.

"Anne McCann?"

" 'Woodhouse.' I dropped the 'McCann.' "

"You were smart. I'm Duane Prettyman, Fugitives and Warrants, Orange County Sheriff's Department. Do you have any reason to know why I'm here?"

"No," she said, frightened. An accident at Kimiko's, the club? "It's not about my child?"

"No, about McCann."

"Come in."

She led him to the front porch, far away from her mother, who was in her bedroom packing. They stood for a moment at the rail, looking over the golf course. "Pretty," he said. "Very nice."

"What happened?"

"Well, he killed his psychiatrist, up north. A woman. Then he took off."

She sat down heavily. "Oh, God!"

"Flodden," he nodded. "Doctor Gail Flodden."

"McCann *killed* her?"

"That's what they say, up there. And raped her, too, they think."

"Where is he?"

"Seattle, maybe. If he isn't . . ." He turned from the golf course and sat down on a patio chair. "Do *you* feel you'll be in danger, Anne?"

"Of course! He broke my jaw once."

"I know. And threatened you last Christmas. Has he threatened you since?"

"No."

"Is there something I might not know about him?"

She tried to think. "He cut a horse's throat once."

He looked surprised. "That's not in his file."

"He wasn't prosecuted. Why did he kill his doctor?" she asked.

"You tell me."

"I haven't seen him since the court order."

"You're lucky."

"But my mother *thought* she saw him, at Newport Beach Tennis Club, about a week ago."

"That doesn't check out, he was north. But whether or not she did . . ." He took a deep breath, seemed to brace himself, and began to speak.

He told her that he had just completed a two-hour crash course on Cal McCann. The SFPD had faxed him a duplicate of his personality profile, found in the shrink's office. He had read his arrest record, too.

"I'd rather tackle a Colombian goon," he said, "than a guy like him in a family fight. And I wish I could get you protection. I just can't."

"We *have* protection. You saw the guardhouse."

"Eduardo's no protection against McCann." He swept his hand at the steep drop to the canyon below. "That arroyo isn't protection, this guy's an athlete." He scratched Bonnie's head. "Your dog isn't protection: she's in love with me already."

"We have a burglar alarm."

"Fine. Newport Beach would respond in five minutes. Can you fight him off that long?"

Her throat grew tight. "What shall I *do* then?"

"You won't do it," he shrugged. "Nobody does."

"No, I want to know. What?"

"OK. Get out of here. Tonight."

CHAPTER 24

Cal McCann sat in the damp cabin of Stolak's abalone-diving boat, *Wet Dream*, sucking on a can of Bud. The afternoon sun, beaming through a porthole that had not been washed since he had lived on the boat, gleamed on the Top's shiny, knife-edge nose.

Once, after Anne had thrown him out, they had worked well together diving for abalone: McCann tending the air hose and kelp knife on deck, Stolak on the bottom, in a hookah face mask and wet suit, fighting the emerald cold.

Later still, when the ab beds failed, they had maintained their position: McCann on top, flying lightplanes up from Baja, dropping coke; Stolak below, gathering the fruit.

The dope drops had made them a fortune. Stolak's was probably long gone.

"So," asked Stolak, slurred and a little foggy, "what you got in mind? There's no more abs out there."

"Well, Top, how about I rent a little Cessna . . ."

"I like that."

"And find Rodriguez, down in Baja . . ."

"Good, good . . ."

"And then I make a run up the coast from Rosarito Beach?"

"Fantastic!"

Now was the sticky part. McCann studied his beaded beer can, pondering.

He had told Stolak nothing of the murder, but even down here, it might pop up on TV or in the *L.A. Times*.

Having fled, he was surely a prime suspect, perhaps the only one.

There was no way they could trace him here—the abalone boat was tied to a filthy dock near the Henry Ford Bridge, in Los Angeles Harbor, in untraveled water that only a barnacle could love—but convincing Stolak of that was another matter.

The boat rocked gently in the wake of a vessel passing close.

He got up quickly and peered out the porthole, thinking Coast Guard, LAPD, or California Fish and Game. But the craft was an innocent yawl, dirtying her skirts in the slums, heading for the Los Angeles Yacht Club. He sat down again.

"I had a little problem up there at the VA."

"You had a problem when they *put* you there, Lieutenant."

McCann nodded. "Not like this one. My shrink was trying to keep me there forever, and I guess I just went ape."

"You *hit* him?"

"No, *her*. A broad. I strangled her."

He crumpled the beer can, took careful aim, and tossed it out the starboard port hole, dead center. It clattered

on the deck outside. "I *dusted* her, Top." He studied his
fingernails. "Hey, did you clean the points on my bike?"

"*Fuck* your bike!" yelled Stolak. "You *killed* her?"

"Shh . . . *Calma, calma* . . . Yes. Totally capped. *Kaput.
Fini.*"

Stolak looked like a moray eel surprised in his hole,
gasping with righteous anger. "So you come down *here*
to get me busted too? Get off my boat!"

"Now, Top, that's no way. Think of all the nights at Tay
Ninh . . . Think of Charlie-Charlie."

Stolak's lips went white. "Charlie-Charlie was fifteen
years ago, McCann!"

"No statute of limitations on murder," McCann pointed
out. "And you're on an army pension."

"What's my pension got to do with it?"

"You kick me out in the cold," shrugged McCann, "they
pick me up, I'm no hero, I mention the horse that night
in Palos Verdes, and cop a plea? Or, like I say, Charlie-
Charlie? It gets to the media! A blot on the Screaming
Eagles? Can't have that. You don't know *what* the army'd
do."

"You're scaring the hell out of me," scoffed Stolak, but
McCann caught a note of uncertainty in his voice.

"Nothing to be scared of, if you let me stay aboard. In the
first place, they think I'm in Seattle. In the second place . . .
Hang on."

He dug through his gear, stepped into the cramped, stink-
ing head, and transformed himself: blue contact lenses,
the moustache, dental cotton cylinders between gums and
cheeks to fill his face, a whisk of rosy blush. He checked
himself in the cracked mirror.

He was fatter, older, and—with the ruddy cheekbones—
somehow Gallic. He slipped back into the main cabin.

Stolak was staring angrily ahead.

"Is this *me*, Top? Is this the McCann you've learned to love? Who *am* I?"

Stolak gave him the barest glance. "I don't know," he sulked.

"François Le Clerc, of Marseilles, your line tender. I used to handle Cousteau's gear. I'ave no English, sir. Je regrette, monsieur le flic, je ne parle pas l'anglais. C'est OK?"

Stolak appraised him more carefully. "You going to *stay* like that?"

"No matter what."

"Rent the plane for the run," Stolack decided. "I'll fuel the boat. But she can't outrun her own wake, now, so first we clean the barnacles off her bottom." He dragged a wet suit out of a foul-smelling locker. "Suit up!"

McCann had always hated scraping her hull: Stolak, in command, was Captain Bligh. "My makeup would run. I'll tend your line."

After all, he thought, he was scraping the bottom, already. But not for long.

CHAPTER
25

Anne sat with Laurie in the Mazda outside Kimiko's home, a block from the tennis club. She had packed her own clothes, and Laurie's, and it was all in the rear with her flight bag. Her mother had taken the airport shuttle bus to LAX, and would be safely on her way to Houston in two hours. Bonnie was at the boarding kennel. There was nothing else to do but to check into a motel.

And to tell Laurie . . .

"He *was* up there in San Francisco, Doodle, I told you that, and they were trying to make him well."

"In the castle, by the moat," Laurie said dully. "With the giant that roared all night."

"What?"

"Nothing," said Laurie.

"What 'giant'?"

"Never mind, Mom!"

"Well, now he's gone from the hospital, and we don't

know where he is. He's sick, and hates me, Laurie." She took Laurie's hand, but it was limp and passive. "And so, we have to hide until tomorrow."

"*We?* No! I'm staying here with Kimiko, right? For your Shannon flight?"

"No. You're *going* on the Shannon flight, with me."

"What about the swim meet Saturday?"

"I'm sorry." The time had come to tell her the rest, for McCann might make the TV news tonight. Anne took a deep, shuddering breath: "They think he killed somebody, Doodle: the lady doctor trying to help him."

Laurie's eyes grew wide. "No, he didn't!"

Anne drew her close. Her body was rigid. "I hope not, Doodle."

"He *didn't.* He wouldn't hurt a lady, even the Witch of—"

Anne stared at her. "What are you talking about? The Witch of *what?*"

"The Witch of the Sky," said Laurie dully. "When we played Prince Cal and the Pumpkin Princess." She began to cry.

"Laurie, baby . . ." Anne tried to pull her closer, but she resisted. "I'm the Witch of the Sky?"

"I don't know. I guess."

"Laurie, how can you *remember* that? From when you were a baby?"

"Because he came to see me," Laurie muttered. "Last week, while you were flying."

She had known it, somehow, had been certain, but now that she heard it, was weak with fear.

"Surfing?" she guessed. "When Diane took you to San Onofre. Right?"

"Yes."

"Where?"

"Out on the surf line."

"What did he want?"

"To take me to Mexico. I said you wouldn't let me, I was scared."

"Why didn't you *tell* me, Doodle?"

She licked her lips. "Because he made me promise not to. Or else . . ."

The bastard! "Or what, honey?"

"Baby talk. You wouldn't understand."

"Or *what*?" Anne repeated. "Just try me."

The child was shivering, and her lips seemed blue. Anne began to knead her shoulders.

"Or, I'd get run over, and die. Mommy, don't tell *anybody* he was there! I don't *want* him to go to jail." Laurie's face was white with fear. "If you tell, I'll never, never tell you anything again!"

"I'll *have* to tell," said Anne. "They're after him for *murder*, don't you see?"

They checked into a cheap motel near the airport. She phoned Ian and told him about McCann.

"I'll be there directly and we'll all go out to dinner."

"No, pick up a pizza and bring it here."

She felt safer in their room.

In *Wet Dream*'s cabin, Cal McCann finished his call to Crew Scheduling and replaced Stolak's phone on the chart table.

Through the planks of the hull, he could hear the crunch and grind of the Top scraping barnacles below. The air compressor, which he was supposed to be tending, wheezed and snorted on deck.

His plans were going beautifully. The bike was ready, he

had a five-hundred-dollar passport, done by San Francisco's best passport forger, and he spoke really good Spanish, besides.

The scraping on the hull had stopped. He jumped to the hatch. Stolak, beard dripping, was climbing up the boarding ladder, steaming mad.

"Jesus, McCann—"

"Hey!" McCann looked pained. "Not 'McCann.' 'François,' s'il vous plaît! *You're* the one that thinks the heat's too high!"

"What you doin' in the cabin? You let my air hose kink! *You* scrape!" He thrust out his scraper. "*I'll* tend the goddamn hose."

McCann smiled righteously. "I called Ensenada."

"Use the pay phone on the dock for dope!"

"Simmer down. I found Rodriguez. Thirty kilos, Top."

"Say *what*?" Stolak stood staring, frozen, the scraper out before him. "*Thirty keys?*"

"Is that worth all your aggravation and your pain?"

McCann read doubt on his face: Thirty kilos could cost almost a quarter-million.

"You still got that much dough?" asked Stolak.

"*I've* been living on Uncle Sam," said McCann, "while you been blowing yours. Besides, I found a partner in North Beach."

Stolak's eyes glinted. "Same split with me?"

"Eighty-twenty. I'm the bank."

"Seventy-thirty, or no boat."

He shrugged and slapped Stolak's hand. "Hey, what the hell, why not?"

"Thirty keys," murmured Stolak, shaking his head. "*Thirty!* Half a million bucks?"

"And I'll drop on Little Harbor Friday night."

Stolak, dripping, sat down on the blanketed bunk.

"How many passes you going to make?"

"One pass, one drop."

Stolak looked at him as if he were insane. "Packed in *what*? That's almost seventy pounds! You'll scatter those bags over half the cove. Suppose some yachtie sees me driving around to pick them up?"

"One pass, one bag on a cargo chute. We're talking Screaming Eagle, now."

Stolak thought it over. "You *got* a cargo chute?"

"I think so. In my mini-storage, somewhere with my tools." He stretched. "Now, do I *still* have to scrape this mother, or can we smoke a little dope?"

"Let the barnacles *fall* off, man," grinned Stolak. He smiled so seldom that Cal had forgotten how stained and crooked his teeth were.

You are a thoroughly unattractive man, old buddy: it will almost be a pleasure to put out your goddamn lights.

ALTITUDE ZERO

CHAPTER 26

Montgomery Starbuck, Vice-President (Security) of PacLant International, shifted uncomfortably in his wheelchair at his desk. He watched Captain Gary Fremont settle back in his leather chair. The captain seemed depressed.

"OK, Gary, how went the great charade?"

"Hagler loved it. He crashed her in the simulator, then I crashed him with a tape recorder. The *check* worked out just fine."

"And was she properly grateful?"

"Well, she said I'd saved her tail."

"So she's back in your sack and no problem?"

Fremont reddened. "She's not in my sack. But, flying home, I reminded her of how it had to be when she takes the witness stand."

"And? Come on, you're making me nervous."

"Making *you* nervous? Jesus, Monty," Fremont exploded, "I'm a member of the bar, an officer of the *court*, and you got me there at twenty thousand feet, suborning perjury?"

"Don't blame me, your butt's out too. You have to know how she'll testify, yourself. So, *how*?"

"Well, she loves old Cable, so she's grasping at straws. Somebody saw a mechanic in Cable's cockpit just before the flight. What's *her* reaction? Sabotage!"

"I don't give a rat's ass what she *thinks*!" said Starbuck. "What'll she *say* on the stand?"

Fremont rubbed his jaw. It was blue with five-o'clock shadow. "I don't know."

"Jesus," said Starbuck. "That goddamn woman! We even got her to a hypnotist!"

"Why?"

"You've heard of *People vs. Shirley*, you're a lawyer."

Fremont nodded slowly. "A California case? 'Testimony of a witness inadmissible after hypnosis'? So now she *can't* testify?" Relief shone in his eyes. "Who came up with *that*? PacLant Legal?"

"Modesty forbids me."

"Monty, you're fantastic!"

"Except," said Starbuck grimly, "it didn't work at all. She smelled it and walked out."

"Oh, shit," muttered Fremont. "That figured."

"Look, Fremont, I've got a meeting with Junior in ten minutes! I got to know how she'll testify! Do we drop that suit, or not?"

Fremont got up and walked to a Neiman painting of a cutter under full sail, charging on a starboard reach. For a moment he stared at it blindly. Then he turned. "How are you with Scheduling?"

"Well, I got you into that simulator, didn't I?"

"OK. Get Scheduling to fly me on her next hop. She'll probably bid for Shannon, and I'll try again."

• • •

Starbuck watched Ruble lay out his sketches. He rolled his wheelchair reluctantly to the conference table and inspected them.

The drawings lay in the lee of a three-foot-long scale-model racing sloop he had finished just last week. There were a half-dozen portraits, all wearing a PacLant maintenance cap: a bearded face, as described to Ruble by the apprentice mechanic; then the same man, unbearded, moustached; again, more heavily moustached, then with short hair; then with long.

They seemed professional and polished, almost too good for a forensic artist. They made Starbuck uncomfortable.

He didn't want the lawsuit against Boeing rocked by Ruble or anyone else. If they found a cockpit saboteur, Boeing was off the hook and he, as PacLant security chief, was on it.

Starbuck shook his head. "You want us to check these against three thousand PacLant mechanics? My God, Mr. Ruble! Do you know how long that'd take?"

"Well," said Ruble, "Rhinelander says he's not in your San Francisco shop. So who *was* he, Mr. Starbuck? The ghost of Christmas past?"

"The trouble is . . . Jesus! Sabotage? I don't believe it. Have you turned these over to the FBI?"

Ruble nodded. "They made up their mind six months ago: no sabotage. So they filed them carefully away."

"So *you're* going to play detective?"

"Yes, I am. Now, of course," Ruble suggested softly, "he might *not* have been a PacLant employee."

Starbuck stiffened. That theory threatened his turf. "Somebody off the street? No way!"

"How tight *are* you? With your badges and coded door

locks?" Ruble arose, moved to the window, looked down at the airport.

"We're very tight."

"That's what PSA said. Well, I lost my wife on their LAX-San Francisco flight in '87."

"I'm sorry, Mr. Ruble. A terrible thing, that goddamn maniac—"

"Well, some stupid bastard in Security let him get a .45 automatic on that plane. They found it in the wreckage."

"I remember," murmured Starbuck, "but—"

Ruble fumbled inside his sport shirt, and yanked a gold chain out. On it was the Star of David and a plain gold ring. "They also found a piece of my wife's hand, with my name in her wedding ring." His voice was shaking. "So, I have a problem with airline security, Mr. Starbuck, can you see that?"

"But, that was *PSA* Security, Mike. Not PacLant."

Ruble looked him in the eye. "You had three FAA security violations last year: one in Denver and two in Shannon."

Starbuck stiffened. "We paid our fines, Mr. Ruble. Who'd want to sabotage us, anyway?"

"Everybody in your San Francisco local hates your guts."

"Except on payday," Starbuck shrugged.

"You ever have any labor sabotage?"

"Once . . . Not sabotage, assault. On Stanley Block. Some idiot copilot named McCann broke into his office. And once in a while, graffiti on the hangar walls. No sabotage." He picked up the sketches, and squared them away. "I'll get on these right away, and then you'll *know* how tight a ship we run, just wait."

He watched Ruble go. The investigator, with his speculation on union sabotage, had given him an idea. If the Boeing suit failed, maybe they could pin the crash on the aviation machinists' union, just before the strike.

CHAPTER
27

Cal McCann parked his rental car outside his twelve-by-fourteen-foot mini-storage locker at the San Pedro U-Store lot. He unlocked the padlock, jerked up the hanging door, and stepped inside.

The storage was dank and dusty. He had not been in the place for years. His PacLant cap sat jauntily on a packing crate. His old PacLant uniforms hung under plastic covers on a clothes rack. His army uniforms hung beside them, with a dusty maroon beret of the Airborne stuffed under the epaulet of his service dress tunic.

He opened a padlocked field locker stenciled *McCann, Calvin M. 2ND LT USA*. From it he drew a .45 army issue automatic, wrapped in a towel. He removed its clip and field-stripped it. He oiled it, reassembled it, and cocked it. A photo of Anne—wearing her TWA stewardess uniform—lay on top of a pile of snapshots on a table. He propped it up, aimed at her picture, squeezed off a dry round, recocked, and did it again. It felt good.

He slammed the ammo clip back in the grip and stuck the weapon into his belt. From a battered bureau, he took out the three six-inch animal darts and the bottle of M-99 etorphine he had lifted from Block's tack house in '84.

He unscrewed the feathered base of each dart, checked the CO_2 cartridges for corrosion, and found none. He noticed that the inertia of impact would pierce the CO_2 cartridges and drive fluid from a reservoir through the dart's hollow point. He sprayed all three darts with lubricant, reinserted the CO_2 cartridges, and screwed on the bases again.

He stood the darts on their tails and unscrewed the points. The hollow needles were barbed to hang on to the animal's flesh. Behind each, in the shaft of the dart, was its reservoir.

He rummaged through the top bureau drawer and found a plastic syringe. He picked up the bottle of M-99 etorphine and read the label and its warnings: to large animals, in small doses, it was an instant immobilizing tranquilizer; to humans, in any dosage, instant death.

He found a pair of work gloves and drew them on. He filled the syringe from the bottle and topped the reservoir of each dart to the brim with the yellow fluid. Then he screwed the needles back. He was very careful: according to the label, a scratch on his finger could be fatal.

When he was through, he stood for a moment, puzzled. He reread the label.

From the body-weight chart, he decided that Stolak, the night of the raid on Junior's estate, had hit PacLant's panther with enough M-99 to bring down an elephant in musth.

Then why was Sylvester still alive? He'd seen him in PacLant TV spots. Had they got a vet there with an antidote in time to save it?

Or had the stuff been too old? He glanced at the bottle's expiration date: 1984. Marginal, and it was even older now. He'd have to run a test.

He filled the syringe again. He emptied a plastic crayon box that he'd got for Laurie just before the split, and never given her. He packed the darts and syringe inside.

He drew from his hip pocket a notebook, with a list of the other items he would need. He moved around the room, checking them one by one. When he was through he had filled a leather PacLant flight bag and half of a duffle bag.

He bundled everything up, trundled it to the rental Camaro, and dumped it all in the trunk next to Mao. He drove to the Luff Life sail loft in Marina del Rey.

Here he wrestled unsuccessfully for some time with a heavy-duty sewing machine, contributed by Stolak's coke-sniffing client, a laid-back, dough-faced sailmaker who—for two lines of coke—finally did most of the work himself, especially the surgery on Mao.

When he was through, McCann drove to the Wilmington branch of the L.A. Public Library. He removed the syringe from the crayon box.

Palming the syringe in his hand, he strolled to the periodical reading room.

The homeless clients of the library were gathered there, some reading newspapers, some merely staring blankly. A bag lady, complete with market basket, crooned to herself in a corner.

In the rear sat a grizzled seaman in a watch cap, nodding over a week-old *L.A. Times.*

McCann wandered over and rustled the racked newspapers behind him. The seaman did not stir. McCann drew a paper from the rack and scanned the room. Nobody had even noticed him.

He leaned over the man, laid the paper on the table next to him, and jabbed the palmed syringe into his jugular next to the Adam's apple. He squeezed it quickly and yanked it out.

The man made a half-grab at his throat, stiffened, shuddered, and slumped. McCann picked up the paper, returned it to the rack, and sauntered across the room.

He looked back from the door. The old man was sliding silently to the floor behind the table. In an instant he was hidden, except for one quivering foot. It drummed a jig against the table leg for a long, long time, then stopped.

McCann stepped whistling into the bright sunlight and drove to the marina. He parked in the shadow of the Henry Ford Bridge, next to his Honda Gold-Wing. He left Mao in the trunk of the car.

He could hear the air compressor running on *Wet Dream*'s deck: *pukka, pukka, pukka, pukka . . .*

Passing the bike, he touched its saddle. He had checked Stolak's work on the points, cleaned the carburetor, changed the oil. He had ridden it this morning, gliding along the freeways with the wind in his hair. The bike was ready as it could get.

"Do you still have Honda-wheelie?"

"He roars and snorts and paws the ground. He's been waiting for you, Pumpkin."

With the .45 heavy in his belt beneath his jacket, he walked down the ramp to the dock. An air hose led over *Wet Dream*'s rail: Stolak had apparently decided to finish cleaning her bottom, and was scraping away, below the surface. Good . . .

A shabby, deflated Avon life raft, stolen years before, was stowed on deck near the boarding ladder. Moving softly, so that Stolak would not hear his footsteps through the hull, he pulled the automatic from his belt and stuffed it into the Avon's rubbery guts.

Then he kinked the air hose and stepped on it, cutting off Stolak's air. In a moment the Top appeared at the surface sputtering and angry.

"You tryin' to kill me, you son of a bitch?"

"Top! What a thing to say!"

He drew Stolak below and cracked two beers. It was time to plan tomorrow's drop.

CHAPTER 28

The phone rang in the tiny motel room, and Anne told Ian to come up. She glanced at Laurie, sulking in her swimming suit on the bed, watching "Night Court." There was a brush fire in Santa Barbara, so Cal McCann, thank God, had not made the local news.

"Laurie, you *have* to meet him, so—"

"Not me," said Laurie, starting up. "I'm going down to check out the pool."

"Stay right where you are! What's *wrong* with you?"

There was a knock, and Anne opened the door. Ian loomed with the sunlight behind him, an enormous pizza box in his hand. She kissed him swiftly.

"Bumper to bumper all the way," he said, "and smog like barley broth. So much for your huddled masses, yearning to breathe free. I've checked out of the Hyatt, I've a bed just two doors down." He squinted into the room and the blue eyes shimmered. "And this is Laurie!"

Reluctantly, Laurie arose. "Hello." Their eyes met, hers hostile, with the gold flecks glinting light. "Mom, I'm really not hungry at all." She bolted out the door.

Anne turned to Ian. "Ian, I'm so sorry. She never acts like this!"

"And has she ever heard her father called a murderer before?"

"No . . ." she admitted.

"Then isn't this a temporary problem?"

"I hope so, God, I hope so," she said.

"That's an eight-hour flight tomorrow, Anne, and we're going to land the best of friends, you'll see."

She doubted it: "There's no room for you in her right now. Her father killed someone besides that woman, Ian."

"Who?"

"A prince she thought she knew."

CHAPTER
29

In his office, Mike Ruble was lost in a paperwork jungle. He had spent all Saturday afternoon rereading the records on the Christmas crash, and preparing an overview for the hearing examiners.

A half-dozen bound reports were stacked on his desk: data from the "go team" and those who came later: airframe specialists, stress engineers, mappers and surveyors, medics, coroners, dentists.

He had loose-leaf binders with reports from PacLant Maintenance and Boeing and Pratt and Whitney Engines.

He had a "background profile" from the flight psychologist who had tried to recreate Captain Danny Cable's mental state on Christmas Eve.

"Cable had been driven to the airport by his wife. She states that he was cheerful. However, he was anxious to see his grandson, who lives in Denver, before the child was put to bed."

So anxious that he drove two hundred passengers into a hillside? At fifty-eight, with twenty-five thousand hours in the air and thirty-five non-fatal Christmas Eves behind him?

Bull!

He shoved back his chair and rubbed his eyes, remembering. The Los Angeles terminal had been in Christmas colors the last time he saw Kitty.

They had been late, and the holiday rush was starting. He had floored the gas pedal all the way to the airport, taken short-cuts only pilots knew, so that she could see their granddaughter before Christmas.

"The white zone is for loading and unloading only."

And if only he'd parked to see her off, and taken her bag, and walked her to the gate as he always did, he'd have slowed her up and she would have missed the plane.

Parking in their carport at home, hand on the ignition key, he'd heard the first report: "A PSA airliner with thirty-nine passengers aboard crashed tonight near Harmony, California, after the pilot reported gunfire in the cabin . . ."

"She didn't get aboard!" he'd roared, to God and the rafters above. "She missed it, missed it, *missed* it, we were late!"

But God had remained unconvinced that night, and the next, and finally won the argument in the end.

"One must wonder," the NTSB psychologist had written, post-crash, of Danny Cable—at God only knew how much per word—"if Captain Cable, who had flown five hours already on December 24, was disturbed at the necessity of rechecking his weight and balance and refiling his flight plan after the equipment change . . ."

Absolute crap, but it reminded him that if PacLant Flight Ops had not switched planes, the pretty copilot would be dead.

And if he'd spent a couple of bucks to park and see Kitty off . . .

"Hey," she smiled at him now, *"I took a plane with a murderer! How could you stop that?"*

She was right, of course. Woodhouse was simply lucky; Kitty, a stewardess for thirty years, had used up her luck already.

He dumped the paperwork into his briefcase to take home.

CHAPTER
30

The LAX shuttle bus from flight-crew parking inched to the curb at the PacLant departure area. Anne, in uniform for her Shannon flight, tugged Laurie's Samsonite from the luggage rack, and then her own worn suitcase and battered leather flight bag.

It was 6 P.M: two hours before departure. Laurie had been silent since they left the motel.

The curbside was jammed. Anne's suitcase skimmed along the pavement, running smoothly on its wheels. She tried a smile on Laurie: "Gear down, three green lights, and touchdown: Shannon, here we come."

Laurie, squirming into the sagging red backpack she used for school books, said nothing. She had refused to call Kimiko to say good-bye, refused, in the motel, even to eat her lunch.

Ian was turning in his car to Hertz. In the terminal, they passed through the security gate and began the long walk to the Royal Panther Club, a PacLant frequent-traveler lounge where they would meet him.

All at once she saw Gary Fremont passing the ticket counters. He was hurrying toward the PacLant terminal, in uniform, carrying his suitcase. There were no other PacLant international flights but hers scheduled until the morning flight to Paris.

"Gary!" she called. "Are you scheduled *tonight*?"

He stopped and waited. "Yes. To Shannon."

"What?" she asked.

"And you?" he smiled.

"Shannon, of course."

He grinned down at Laurie. "An international traveler, Laurie? Off to see the world?"

Laurie had always liked him, but now she barely nodded: "Yes."

"Wait a minute," Anne protested. "Captain Plover's taking this hop!"

"No. You got a problem flying with me, Anne? My deodorant's in my bag."

She couldn't fathom it. "I'll see you down in Flight Ops, Gary. I'm tucking her into the Panther Club lounge, to wait for Ian Corello."

Carrying Mao and a camera bag, Cal McCann grinned at the pretty Chicana security guard at the metal detector.

He wore a sport shirt, a cashmere sport jacket, and brown slacks. On his lapel rode the ALPA emblem.

When he had left Stolak in the boat, he had been François Le Clerc. Parked on a dead-end street in San Pedro, he had metamorphosed again. Now he was Arthur O'Brien, a white-haired PacLant captain, grown old on the Path of the Panther.

His hair was snow white. His eyes, behind gray contact lenses and glasses, showed none of their golden flecks. He had added two more cotton dental pads between his teeth and gums, and put on twenty pounds.

He had selected O'Brien—apparently domiciled in Phoenix, Arizona—from a list of almost a thousand PacLant captains he had lifted when he was fired. For another two hundred dollars, he had had his old PacLant ID card further altered by the forger in San Francisco, and his picture, as O'Brien, substituted for his own. For three hundred dollars she had issued him an Arizona driver's license and for another five hundred dollars a US passport in O'Brien's name, good enough to get him on an international flight.

Today, he had snorted a line before he left the boat. He looked sixty but felt eighteen. He had no fears at all about his disguise. Anne, he would try to avoid.

Mao wore a red kerchief around his neck, with a birthday card pinned to it. On its chest were fastened the PacLant wings that stewardesses gave to children.

The prettiest of the security guards tickled the panda under his chin.

"Where's he going?"

"Ireland. For my niece."

"*He* gets to go to Ireland? I never been out of California!"

"Maybe next time." He patted her arm, sat Mao on the moving belt, and placed his camera bag behind him.

In it was a Nikon, a flash, and several lenses. The crayon box with the three darts was in it, too, packed in a lead-impregnated anti-X-ray film bag he had bought at the photo shop, along with a dozen 35-millimeter rolls of color film he had stuffed around the crayon box as cover in case they felt the bag.

But the key ring in his pocket set off the alarm at the gate, as he had planned, distracting the girls. He removed the key ring, handed it to the pretty one, strolled through, and picked up Mao and the overnight bag. Overkill: he doubted that the darts had even shown on her X-ray screen.

When he reached the departure lounge he stopped at one of the phone booths lining the wall. He pulled a phone number from his wallet and punched it in. He dropped in a quarter and a dime, and a woman answered in a heavy Spanish accent: "Block residence."

"Mr. Block, please?"

"*No es en casa.* Here is la senora."

"Hello?" A polished Texas drawl, easy and sexy.

"Mrs. Block, Howard Olsen from the comptroller's office. Mr. Block wanted some figures before the weekend. He left before I got them."

"He's not home yet." She sounded as if she'd had a belt or two. "And *how* you got this number I have simply no idea!"

Right off the phone in your den, he thought, *right from the horse's mouth.*

"Sorry, ma'am. So what time should I call back?"

"Dinner's at seven. Please, not after that."

"Have a nice evening," he said, and hung up.

He sat Mao in a chair near the counter and showed his ID card to the departure agent. His free ticket—under O'Brien's name—was waiting and confirmed. "Passport, Captain?"

He produced the phoney passport. She hardly glanced at it. "Aisle seat, sir?"

"Yes." He paid the extra fare for business class, on the top deck, behind the cockpit. "Look, I'm going down to meet the skipper. Can you give me this week's door code?"

"Three-three-eight, sir."

He strolled to an unmarked door, punched in the code, and headed for Flight Operations.

Anne sat Laurie in front of a TV in the Royal Panther Club, off the departure lounge.

"Wait here for Ian, and don't wander. He's changing his seat to economy class, so you can sit together."

"I don't want to sit with him! I don't even want to go!"

"Doodle! Please?" Anne kissed her gently on the forehead. "See you in Shannon, OK?"

Tight with anger at McCann, she left for Flight Ops. Emerald Isle? The Land of Oz?

As usual, he had spoiled it all.

CHAPTER 31

Mike Ruble sat alone at the dinette table in his Redondo Beach apartment, staring at the remnants of his microwaved chicken. Against his doctor's orders, he was sipping at a glass of Chablis.

He was still unsettled, and did not know why. He finished his wine, threw his dishes into the dishwasher, and poured another glass. He roamed into the living room, turned on the TV, then turned it off.

The Christmas crash obsessed him. Anne Woodhouse was on his mind, and, somehow, Starbuck, PacLant's security chief.

He did not trust the man at all, but something he had said teased his memory . . .

"Not sabotage, assault. Some idiot copilot named McCann."

McCann? He had seen the name in print, and recently, but could not remember where.

The late afternoon light was shafting into the room. He found himself at his drawing board, pencil in hand, sketching. A jungle clearing grew on his pad, besieged by ominous shapes. The eyes of a panther glowed in the darkness, and forms that might have been human hung from fences and from trees.

His heart was beating too fast: he tried to stop, and couldn't.

The sketch became surreal, like a Dali print: he was nowhere on earth, and everywhere; not on the oak-studded hillside where Kitty had died, nor the scene of the Christmas crash, but at every crash site he'd ever trod, reeking of jet fuel and death.

In the clearing grew a man, kneeling before the ruined pedestal of a Boeing 747. He was bearded, and wore a PacLant cap.

Ruble was suddenly certain that the figure was McCann's.

But who *was* McCann, and why did he have him worshipping at the twisted altar in the clearing?

"Jesus!" he breathed.

He flung his pencil across the room and rushed to his bedroom. On his bedside table sat a lamp, and a six-inch stack of magazines. Heart pumping, he dug through them. When he got to the issue with Anne Woodhouse, his hands began to shake.

He leafed through it, found her picture, turned a page.

"When she split with McCann, a Viet Nam vet and himself a former PacLant copilot, she resumed her maiden name, Anne Woodhouse."

McCann!

All right. Assume estrangement deep enough to motivate murder. But would an airline employee kill a planeload of people in order to murder one?

Absurd.

Still, David Burke, on PSA 1771, was an airline employee who had done exactly that.

He should have shown his sketches to Anne Woodhouse, not to Starbuck! He lunged for his briefcase and found her number in his file of the Christmas Crash.

"We're busy now, but if you'll leave your name and number . . ."

He left his home number and hung up. He called PacLant Security, but Starbuck had left for the day.

He felt his pulse. He was supposed to lie down and rest if it rose past ninety.

Ninety-eight.

He began to pace the room.

CHAPTER 32

Cal McCann strolled into Flight Ops and stared at the crew list behind the counter.

Flight 408: Captain G. S. Fremont . . .

Fremont? He felt a thrill of elation. He had phoned crew scheduling this morning, and expected an aging captain named Oscar Plover, whom he'd flown with years ago.

But Fremont?

Fremont was rumored to have screwed his favorite copilot in every airline hotel from L.A. to Bangkok. He had never met the man but had cheerfully tried to kill him on Christmas Eve with Anne.

The poor bastard should have dumped the Witch of the Sky, while he was still ahead.

He read the rest of the crew list: *F/O A. Woodhouse, F/E B. Katz, Purser J. Henlein . . .*

He recalled Henlein, faggy but funny, clowning to keep the cockpit awake, and he remembered one of the stewardesses well: Jackie Foley; a boozer, but not a bad lay.

Sorry, Jackie Foley, you were fun.

None of them would know him in disguise.

He scanned the room. There was only one four-striper in it: he must be Fremont. He was talking to a flight engineer—presumably Katz—at the NOTAM table, with a "Notices to Airmen" clipboard in his hand.

The flight engineer was young, but out of shape, a cockpit potato. Fremont was of medium build, medium size, well over forty, probably soft with flying, too. No problem there.

The flight engineer left for his preflight. McCann took a deep breath, strode to the table, and stuck out his hand.

"Captain Fremont? Art O'Brien, PacLant captain. We met in Denver, once."

Fremont seemed preoccupied. "Yeah? Denver?"

"Years ago. You're flying me to Ireland tonight."

"Glad to have you." Fremont waved toward the weather synopses hanging on the wall. "There's a low east of Iceland, but we'll try to find you Shannon in the goop."

Common airline courtesy demanded an invitation to the cockpit. But Fremont was turning away.

"Would you mind," McCann asked swiftly, "if I rode jumpseat?"

Fremont rubbed his chin.

"Well, I got our lady first officer tonight, and I think she'd prefer a sterile cockpit—"

"I'll keep my hands to myself. I'm fifty-eight."

Fremont barely smiled. "—a sterile cockpit, because she's new on the 747, a little weak. She asked me for the takeoff. I don't want any more pressure on her than she's got."

"How about after we're airborne, then?"

A phone behind the Flight Ops counter rang; faintly, McCann heard cargo rumbling past outside; a jet engine wound down on the line, leaving a void of silence. Fremont drummed his fingers, thinking.

"Maybe," he decided finally, "after we level off. Call me up and see."

McCann thanked him and climbed back up the stairs before Fremont could change his mind. Someone on the other side of the security lock was punching in the code. He waited in the darkness until the door opened. When he saw that it was a woman, he held it back politely.

On her sleeves she wore three stripes: *his* three stripes, if you thought about it. Around her clung the gentle scent of Norell perfume.

It was Anne. They performed a little dance on the stairs, right, left, right. She smiled in embarrassment.

He stepped aside to let her pass and watched her hurry down the stairs.

Sayonara, Annie, you're dead meat.

Anne stood with Gary Fremont at the counter and watched the computer's print head skidding across the paper, grinding out their flight plan.

"Anne," he murmured, "I'm glad I'm flying this hop. Because I'd like to get our stories straight. That hearing's in two weeks."

"*My* story *is* straight! If they swear me, I'll tell them what I saw! Look, did you know McCann is out?" she said. "He killed a woman?"

"I heard."

"And you still want me to sit up there for eight hours and discuss last Christmas Eve? Look, Laurie's all screwed up,

I'm going to get canned, I'm flat-assed broke, we can't go
on with life until they find McCann, and I'm not going to lie
and go to jail for you, or Cable, *or* the goddamn company,
so . . ."

"Shh . . ." he cautioned, glancing up the counter. He
seemed furtive. An awful suspicion began to grow. "Gary?"

"Um?"

"Look at me."

He turned his head but could not hold her gaze.

She went on: "You're a very senior captain. You can bid
any flight you want. You hate this run, you told me that
in Tahiti. You hate France, you hate Germany, you hate
Ireland. So why are you here at all?"

"I told you, I was on reserve, Plover's taking the Paris
flight, and—"

"Gary, did they *make* you bid this flight? Junior? Or that
Starbuck guy?"

"What do you mean, *make* me?"

"You're trying to con me, Gary. And that simulator ride
was a setup, too!"

"I'm trying to save both our careers, Anne."

"Not mine," she said dully. "Yours. Get out of my life,
now, Gary! And don't try to get back in."

His eyes went dead. "You know," he murmured, "I never
met McCann."

"So what?"

He smiled. "I've finally come to understand how you
drove the poor guy nuts."

"You rotten son of a *bitch*!" she whispered. She ripped
off the flight plan, slapped it into his palm, and wandered
to the weather map to hide her tears.

The weather east of Iceland seemed to be deteriorating:
it would be bumpy descending, and she knew that Laurie

was often airsick. She studied the map until she felt ready to board the plane.

In the cockpit, she found Gary unfolding the printout.

"Flipper departure," he said coldly. "Seal Beach to Las Vegas . . . Top of climb at twenty-nine thousand . . . Jet one-oh-seven to Dupree . . . Now we're in Canada . . . Direct to Riona . . . Flight level thirty-three."

She knew the route by heart: she had been droning along it for months. He was rigid in his seat. "Now, our way points, Woodhouse: Seal Beach: Thirty-three forty-seven point zero north, one-one-eight point zero-three west . . ."

She repeated the latitude and longitude as she punched the way point into the inertial navigation system.

Gary peered at the INS, nodded, circled the way point on his flight plan, and chanted: "Las Vegas: thirty-six oh-four point eight north . . ."

The INS would guide them through their twelve invisible way points in the sky, within yards in either direction, as they hurtled east over the Sierras, the Rockies, Manitoba, Labrador, and the North Atlantic. Old-time aerial navigators, peering through their bubble octants for the stars, would have marveled at the precision of the gyroscopes in the INS that did it all, the same gyros that surfaced a Trident submarine, after months below without star fixes or radios, within yards of a channel buoy.

"Fifty-four north, fifteen west," Gary finished. "And then"—he folded up the flight plan—"begin descent to Shannon." He handed her the plan and stretched. "Where's our flight engineer? Talking to his broker on the phone? I'll have his ass."

She looked into his empty eyes and did not answer. Katz opened the cockpit door and took his seat behind her. She could hear the business-class passengers climbing the staircase and settling themselves into their seats, and caught Jeff Henlein's voice aft of the door.

She called Henlein on the cabin phone and told him that Laurie was aboard. "She's downstairs in coach, and not too happy with life. She's with Ian. If you have time, cheer her up."

Jeff's voice echoed from the cockpit speaker. "Ian! Who's Ian, I wonder?"

"Just go down and make her laugh, please Jeff." She did not feel like joking.

"OK, sweetie, sir, ma'am. You guys want filet mignon or chicken Dijon?"

"Whatever costs the company the most," said Katz.

"Steak," said Fremont.

"Just coffee, Jeff," decided Anne, knowing she could not eat.

"And Captain," said Henlein, "there's another PacLant Sky King here who says he's riding jumpseat."

"Antsy bastard," muttered Gary, taking the phone. "*When* we get to cruising altitude! I told him!" He replaced the phone. "We're three minutes late already, First Officer. OK?"

"Gear lever and lights?" she began.

"Down and checked . . ." answered Gary.

"Brakes?"

"Parked . . ."

"Start levers?" she mumbled. She was crying inside, with anger and grief, and the night had just begun.

CHAPTER 33

When the workshop telephone rang in the Palos Verdes home of Monty Starbuck, a quarter-mile from his chief's mansion on the cliff, Starbuck was carefully brushing glue on a tiny wooden plank. It was to be fitted on the deck of his four-foot-long, radio-controlled model of the racing yacht *Koh-i-noor*.

A fresh scotch on the rocks sat on the workbench, in a glass etched with his last yacht's name. Dinner, he assumed, was cooking below. He was in a thank-God-it's-Friday mood: he intended, this weekend, to get the model decked and to start detailing the hull.

He resented the phone, but it might be Junior, asking him over for a drink. He picked it up.

"Starbuck here."

"Mr. Starbuck, it's Mike Ruble."

The stubby Jew with the sad-assed eyes! Calling him at *home*?

"Well, it's Friday evening, Mike, the sun's over the yardarm, I was just sitting down for a drink. But what can I do for you?"

"I have to know more about McCann."

He winced. Ruble had developed tunnel vision on the Christmas crash. Starbuck knew the symptoms. At Treasury, he had seen investigators obsessed with their current counterfeiting cases all the time. You humored them, but on Friday night?

"McCann?" he murmured. "Like I said, bad news. A radical."

"You said he assaulted Block in his office. You seem to have voluminous files. Is there anything else you know?"

Starbuck thought quickly. They had promised ALPA not to release the story of the panther and the horse, but what the hell: it was all over years ago.

"Sure. When he got fired, he busted onto Block's estate out here in Palos Verdes. He had an accomplice. First he tried to kill our panther, and then he led a prize mare into their living room—"

"My God!"

"—and cut her throat," concluded Starbuck. "That bad enough?"

There was a long silence. Then Ruble said: "You misled me, Mr. Starbuck. This man's insane!"

"Could very well be." Starbuck switched his phone to "speaker," picked up his deck plank, gauged it against its position on the deck, and laid it in place. He inspected the seam. Damn! Ruble had distracted him: the plank was laid askew.

"Do you know he's Woodhouse's ex-husband?" Ruble asked.

"Yep. It's in *People* magazine." He pried up the plank

and glared at it. "But why are we discussing him at this hour on a Friday evening?"

"Because I think *he* was the guy in the cockpit that apprentice saw! He was trying to kill his ex-wife!"

"And just happened to pick the wrong airplane, Mike? Come on!"

"The planes were switched by your Flight Ops," Ruble said. His voice sounded strained. "Switched at the last minute. Anne Woodhouse should have been *flying* that plane."

Starbuck carefully retrieved the plank that had dropped from his fingers. He tried to recover: "From killing a horse to killing his ex, plus a planeful of passengers? Now, that is quite a leap!"

"Believe me, it could happen."

He tempered his scorn. This was no time—on the eve of the hearing—to piss off an investigator from the NTSB.

"*Motive,* Mike! With this airline's divorce rate, if *every* copilot wanted to murder his ex-wife, we'd be asshole deep in bodies. You need *motive.*"

"Not if he's nuts."

Or jealous, thought Starbuck, fleetingly. Woodhouse and Fremont were lovers. The whole line knew it, and there was no reason to think that McCann, wherever he was, would not have heard.

No! Ridiculous! He rejected Ruble's inference that PacLant security was slack.

"It doesn't hold up," he said. "You need *opportunity*, too. How'd McCann get into that cockpit?"

"With his old ID?" said Ruble.

Starbuck winced.

"No way he could keep his ID card," he said, with more assurance than he felt.

"A forgery, then," said Ruble.

Starbuck preferred not to think of that. San Francisco, he knew from his years at Treasury, was full of forgers.

"OK, Mike," he said. "We'll check your sketches Monday with his picture. Have a good weekend, and thanks a lot."

He hung up and thought for a moment. Woodhouse was scheduled for Shannon tonight. He wheeled to a desk in the corner of his workshop. On it was a Compaq computer. He booted it up. Through its modem he punched up tonight's schedule, straight from Flight Ops.

Flight 408: Shannon: Departure 2000 hours: Fremont, Woodhouse, Katz . . .

Suppose McCann *was* the mystery mechanic, jealous, waiting? And tried again? *Tonight?*

He calculated swiftly the cost of delaying the plane to check for sabotage. Canceled tickets, missed connections, scheduling fines; ground crew, flight-crew overtime! A Chinese fire drill!

Ten thousand bucks, easily, and all charged to Security's budget! All on a half-baked hunch . . . He wished he hadn't answered the phone.

The ship's clock on his workshop wall chimed cheerfully: *ding-ding, ding-ding, ding-ding, ding-ding.*

Eight bells . . . 2000 hours . . . 8 P.M. sharp.

Flight 408 was pushing back from the chocks right now.

He picked up the phone, studied it, and put it back.

He got half a dozen bomb threats every month. You assumed a hoax and let the plane take off. Nothing had ever happened.

He glided back to his workbench and began to sandpaper the dried glue off his plank.

• • •

Mike Ruble stood at his easel, staring blankly at his latest oil. He was sagging with fatigue.

Starbuck was right: the gap between McCann and sabotage was too wide: his theory stank.

He studied his work. He was doing the painting from memory, a Portuguese inn near Estoril, where he and Kitty had spent a week.

A flagstone path led to the low, oaken lintel, and roses climbed the whitewashed walls. He had got the roses wrong: he remembered a deeper shade, almost a burgundy.

He was reaching for his brush when the awful pain began: first his shoulder, then his chest. His easel toppled, tossing paints and brushes to the floor. He dropped among them. The dying sun splashed reds and umbers on the ceiling and the walls.

He was suddenly crawling up the flagstone pathway toward a figure in the door.

"Kitty?" he called, astonished.

She smiled, and it all turned gold.

CHAPTER 34

As the aircraft hurled itself into the dusk, McCann sat back in his seat. He had assumed that he would be in the cockpit during takeoff: barred until cruising altitude, he had changes to make in his flight plan. He began to recalculate his estimated times of arrival and way points on his ancient E6B flight plotter.

Business class was only one-third full, so Mao sat comfortably beside him, on the aisle, strapped in like all the other passengers.

As they approached Daggett, in the midst of the darkened Mojave, the seat-belt sign went out. He stepped to the in-flight pay phone on the bulkhead and made another call to the red phone in Block's den, using a stolen credit-card number he had bought from the boyfriend of the San Francisco forger.

This time Block himself answered: "Hello?"

"Junior!"

The voice was icy: "Stanley Block, yes."

"Am I interrupting dinner?"

"As a matter of fact, you are. Who the hell *is* this, and how'd you get this number?"

"This is God," he said. "Bon appétit."

Then he hung up.

Henlein, preparing his beverage tray in the galley, peered at him in the shadowy light. "Have we flown together, Captain?"

"I think so," said McCann. "I used to fly this route."

Stanley Block sat toying with his salad, angry and disturbed. His daughter, who eschewed dinner for a regimen of Slim-Fast and diet Pepsis, was on the phone in her bedroom, as always, arranging her love life.

"So what if some idiot found out that number?" his wife said comfortably. "We'll change it tomorrow morning."

"You're damn right we will."

"Now, eat your dinner, Stan!"

Unmollified, he glared at her. "How'd he get it? I'll bet our ding-a-ling daughter gave it to some stud."

"I doubt if Marjorie knows that number herself!"

"Good. It's for Starbuck, or Flight Ops, if somebody clobbers a plane. Or the Board, if somebody's stealing the company. That's exactly why it's red."

She tinkled the bell for the maid. "Well, they know that number in your comptroller's office."

He put down his fork. "The hell they do!"

"They called with some figures you asked for. Just before you got home."

"I never asked them for any figures." He slammed down his napkin. "It's some nut!"

"Calm down!"

He picked up his fork. She didn't understand his fear, and he couldn't admit he was scared.

Three shifts of his personal body guards cost the corporation a quarter of a million dollars a year. Their home had a $20,000 alarm system, updated since Morningstar's death. She thought all of this would protect them. But what if she were wrong?

"IAM!" he said suddenly.

"What?"

"The machinists! They're going out, or hadn't you heard? Some IAM clown's got that number, sure as hell!"

His wife arose, took his hand, and tugged him into the den. She picked up the red phone and pulled its jack. She tossed the phone into his wastebasket.

"How's that, Stan?"

Too late, he thought, *whoever they are, they know I'm home*. But he let her lead him back to dinner, summoned a smile, and lifted his wineglass.

"Bon appétit."

CHAPTER
35

Anne put the plane on autopilot and sat back in the copilot's seat. The murk of the Los Angeles Basin was behind them, and the darkening wastes of the Mojave lay below. A lopsided silver moon was rising dead ahead.

She relaxed, gratefully. She had made a smooth, gentle takeoff, now all she had to do was stay awake. For the next eight hours she was severed from bills, McCann, her mother, even the hearing, for Gary had retreated into himself.

Laurie was with her, Ian was too; the plane was a womb.

She had already scratched two of their fixed way points— Seal Beach and Daggett—from the twelve on their flight plan. They were still climbing, and would cross the next— Las Vegas—at precisely the altitude she had punched into the computer.

Gary Fremont was silently brooding. Katz was reading *Forbes*, his lap-top computer still in its case. He was gloomy:

anticipating the IAM strike, he had sold PacLant short, and yesterday it had zoomed on rumors of a takeover attempt by the pilots' union.

He was twelve grand down already, he said, and dreading Monday morning.

The plane reached its T/C—top of climb—and dropped its nose, groping for their flight level. It overshot by fifty feet, hesitated, and eased down.

"PacLant Four-zero-eight Heavy," called Los Angeles Center, "you have traffic at one o'clock, twenty miles, opposite direction. Level three-four-zero."

She spotted red and green running lights next to the moon, and a flashing strobe.

"PacLant Four-zero-eight Heavy," she answered. "Roger. We have him in sight."

In thirty seconds the other plane had passed above. Las Vegas glittered ahead, in red and green and gold. The desert air was crystal. She could see Caesar's Palace, the Desert Inn, and all of the nameless casinos down the strip.

Beyond the city, Lake Mead and the Colorado were etched in silver.

She picked up her cabin phone, not wanting Laurie to miss Vegas. "This is your first officer. We're at cruising altitude of twenty-nine-thousand feet—five and a half miles high. Those of you on the left will see Lake Mead, shortly, and Boulder Dam, and the Colorado River in the moonlight. And the lights ahead, of course, are Vegas."

"Vegas," muttered Katz. "I'd be doing better there."

She ignored him and continued on the phone: "Sit back and have a pleasant flight. And thank you for flying PacLant, the Path of the Panther."

"Cruising altitude!" Katz reminded them. "That deadhead captain, remember?"

Gary picked up the cabin phone. "Henlein, let that old guy in."

Cal McCann finished his estimate of fuel on board and relaxed in his first-row window seat.

Climbing toward Vegas at 480 knots, burning a gallon—almost seven pounds—of fuel each second, he decided that they had probably wasted 22,000 pounds already, and they'd be down to 217,000 pounds—a hundred tons of fuel—by the time he turned back and descended into the L.A. Basin.

Henlein stepped from the galley. He chuckled when he noticed the ancient plotter. "My God, Captain! I haven't seen one of those in thirty years. Don't you trust the crew?"

McCann slipped it into his bag and dropped his voice. "On *our* airline, Jeff, I don't even trust the wings."

"Shh," whispered Henlein. "The jump seat's ready, if you want to go in."

McCann unbuckled Mao and picked him up.

"Him *too*?" Henlein looked dubious.

"Your copilot wanted to see him." He flicked the silver insignia on the panda's chest. "He's for my niece in Dublin, he has to earn his wings."

The purser led him to the cockpit door, rapped twice, inserted a key, opened it, and stepped aside.

All was quiet in the yellow glow of the panel. The captain, scrunched in the left-hand seat, seemed dejected; Anne in the right-hand seat looked fragile and unaware; the flight engineer behind her at his panel was reading *Forbes*.

He took a deep breath. He was there.

Anne watched the aircraft settle on its course to Milford. It was time to eat. She thought of the extra mouth to feed in the cockpit, and twisted around.

"Did you order dinner, Captain? He can bring it up with ours."

"Thanks."

His voice was muffled. He was silhouetted by the dim light from the flight engineer's panel. He seemed bulky and overweight. On the rear jump seat he was placing a stuffed panda with a redkerchief around its neck. Its eyes glittered vacantly as O'Brien straightened.

Weird . . .

"Your friend's already catcn?" she asked.

"Three bamboo shoots and an egg roll." The visitor slipped into the forward jump seat, scanning the instrument panel swiftly as he did. "We haven't flown together. I'm Art O'Brien."

He was all teeth and eyeballs in the somber light. She smiled politely. "Anne Woodhouse, Captain, glad to meet you."

"Woodhouse . . ." he reflected. "Hey, I knew Cal McCann!"

"Yes?" She flipped her VOR receiver to the Milford omni range. "Norra Intersection at forty-three," she said to Gary.

"Thank you, Anne."

"Nice guy, McCann," said O'Brien.

"Lovely. He's wanted for murder." She reached for her pencil and called back to the flight engineer: "How much did we burn on climb out, Barney?"

"*Murder?*" the stranger interjected. "You're kidding, of course?"

"No," she said stiffly. She sensed that he was standing again, and had moved behind Gary. He was scanning the instruments, but why, she had no idea. Katz hadn't answered her question about the climb. "Barney," she asked again, "how much did we burn?"

The plane heaved gently. She adjusted the autopilot sensitivity. From the corner of her eye, she saw Gary slap at his neck. Mosquitoes in the cockpit? Great! No sprays aboard . . .

All at once she heard Gary gagging. "Anne?" he croaked hoarsely. "Anne!"

She looked up from the autopilot. He was staring at her with bulging eyes, grimacing in agony.

"What's wrong?" she cried. "Oh, Gary!"

He tore at his safety belt, went rigid in his seat; she could feel his feet drumming on the rudder pedals, through her own. He began to shake violently. A heart attack!

"Put him on the deck!" she yelled to O'Brien. She yanked down her emergency oxygen mask and tried to stretch it toward the captain. It would not reach. "Give him your oxygen mask! Barney!" she yelled at Katz. "Get the steward up here!"

Katz did not answer, but O'Brien moved swiftly. He unsnapped the captain's belt, jerked him out of his seat and over the control pedestal as if he were an empty sack. He laid him on the deck.

They had just overflown the runway lights of McCarran International, outside Vegas. Swiftly, she decided to declare an emergency, ask for an ambulance, and land. She flicked off the autopilot and began a steep left turn. O'Brien was back beside her in an instant.

She handed him the cabin phone, "Call Station One! Get Henlein! He needs CPR, right now!"

"He's way past CPR," O'Brien murmured.

She glanced at Gary. Blood was oozing from his neck, next to his Adam's apple, and something was impaled there, glittering.

"What—"

"Way past CPR," repeated O'Brien, "And so's your scab F/E."

Hijacker!

She had lived hijackings a dozen times, in fantasy and training. Her reaction was quicker than fear. She grabbed for the transponder switch, but the stranger trapped her wrist.

"No way, Annie."

The voice had changed, and told her everything.

"Cal!" she screamed. "McCann?"

He pulled her close. In the light from the instruments, she saw a needle-nosed cylinder poised like a dart between his fingers. She flailed out and knocked his hand away. The dart struck the throttles and fell to the deck, rolling under her seat.

McCann swore, grabbed her jaw, yanked her head around, and pressed his lips to hers. She twisted loose, and her earphones fell off. For an awful instant, his tongue probed her ear: a signal for their foreplay, a million years ago. She arched her back, brought up her hands together, and caught him under the chin.

She flailed at his face with doubled fists. He only grinned. She barked her knuckles on the landing-light switches in the overhead panel, and all at once the sky ahead turned garish as the landing lights went on. He grabbed at her wrists, and trapped both in one hand.

He was crushing them, and she screamed in pain. Pressing them tighter, he kneeled between the seats, feeling with his other hand for whatever he had dropped. She kicked at his hand and heard him grunt.

"Shit," he murmured, and gave up his search. He rose and pressed her back into her seat. For a moment he grinned into her eyes. He released her seat belt, yanked at her blouse, popping its buttons, and hauled her to her feet. Braced on the pedestal between the seats, he jammed her body close to his. She bit his ear, his lips, brought up her knee into his groin.

He grunted and hurled her back into the copilot's seat. His free hand closed on her throat.

Air, she needed air . . .

"The wicked witch," he said, "is dead."

Her body arched, her knee hit the yoke, her hand pounded at the pedestal, again and again. The plane lurched into a wide, spiraling dive to the left: she had disengaged the autopilot.

Air . . . She must have air . . .

She was suddenly submerged, tumbling under a curl of ebony water, the grandfather of every motherless wave she'd surfed.

It was slamming her toward foaming reefs of white.

CHAPTER 36

Kurt van Osten, a skinny loner with a scraggly beard and a bent for computer games, seethed with anger at his console in the Los Angeles Control Center, a tan, monolithic building fifty miles from L.A. in the desert town of Palmdale.

His PacLant blip, the female one, had crossed his Norra fix at 29,000 feet on schedule, but now it was beginning an insane, sweeping turn northwest.

The darkened, windowless second floor was hushed and busy. Thirty-five scopes, each on a console with a keyboard beneath it, lay in four long rows. Before each scope sat a flight controller, wearing earphones and a boom mike, face green from the blips on the screen.

The air conditioning hummed softly. Otherwise, except for a quiet radio transmission now and then, the room was silent as an aquarium.

Van Osten was responsible for Sector Eight, starting

fifteen miles south of Las Vegas and extending to the southern border of Utah. The PacLant blip, labeled Flight 408, was screwing up the symmetry of his scope.

He had worked in the Palmdale Center since his graduation from the FAA Academy in Oklahoma City in 1981, when Reagan had fired PATCO strikers.

Until then, he had never commanded anything more powerful than a diaper-service truck, but now he regularly shepherded 150-ton airliners across the skies.

He had lightning reflexes. He regarded his job as an elaborate video game.

To win the game, you simply kept the crowded blips five miles apart horizontally, a thousand feet vertically.

If you lost, and the blips strayed closer, a computer in the basement of the center told your supervisor, who warned you.

If you lost again, you were sent to retraining. If you lost yet again, you were put to pasture in less crowded airways. If you lost even there, you'd be promoted, and allowed to play no more.

The Los Angeles Center handled two million aircraft a year, five thousand a day. There were 250 aircraft on its screens at this moment, seven of them on his own console.

Last year, on three occasions, aircraft controlled by the center had come within a mile—three seconds—of colliding. Such incidents were "deals."

Controllers in this room were among the best in the country, and paid accordingly. Nevertheless, because of the swarm of blips they handled, they had typically four times the near-misses of controllers on less crowded sectors.

Van Osten loved the game. Given enough Cokes and

sandwiches, he would have worked for free. But, to play it, incredibly, they paid him a thousand bucks a week.

Relieved every two hours for a break, he repaired to the "Break Room," where he played video games with his fellow controllers. Usually he won.

Outside the Center's quiet womb, in supermarkets or singles bars where people thronged and jostled, he won at video games, but nothing else.

Inside, among his blips, he never lost. He had never had a "deal."

Now he scowled at the errant target on his scope. Behind it crawled another blip, a United Parcel freighter five miles astern.

"Holy jumping Jesus Christ," he muttered, adjusting his mike. "PacLant Four-zero-eight! You are turning north!"

McCann, alarmed by the steepening turn, relaxed his grip and slipped into the captain's seat. His ex-wife sat slumped in her own. Dead, he decided, or unconscious: it made no difference, she was doomed with the rest.

He scanned the captain's panel. All seemed normal, but he eased the wings level, re-engaged the autopilot, and turned off the landing lights.

A midair collision could ruin his whole day, so he flicked the transponder to emergency to attract the Center's attention and clear the airways ahead of him.

He drew his flight plan from his pocket. Reading from it, he began to punch new way points into the INS. He knew that the cabin crew would shortly notice the turn, and then the passengers would too. He wanted to work, while he could, undisturbed.

The most westward way point on his flight plan was well to the seaward of Catalina Island.

He eased back the throttles, turned the central knob of the autopilot, began a standard-rate turn to the right, and a five hundred foot-per-minute descent. The radio came suddenly alive: "PacLant Four-zero-eight Heavy! Now you're turning *south*!"

He ignored the transmission.

"PacLant Four-zero-eight Heavy! Do you read me?"

The controller sounded strained. Good. He had always hated the disembodied voices that shuttled him about.

"PacLant Four-zero-eight Heavy! You are in a descent! You are a thousand feet below assigned altitude!"

The controller's voice was rising. McCann flicked on his automatic direction finder receiver. He dialed through the commercial stations until he found an AM country music station out of Los Angeles.

Johnny Cash: *"I woke up Sunday morning with no way to hold my head that didn't hurt . . ."*

He turned up the volume, then pressed his transmitter button to give them a blast of Johnny in their cocoon in Palmdale.

He rolled out of his turn on course to Los Angeles. He would not touch the controls again, but let the INS guide the plane through the way points that he had punched in, each one lower than the preceding.

The cabin phone began to chime. He picked up the handset. "Yeah?"

It was Henlein's voice, low and puzzled. "Captain, did we turn?"

"Yeah. This is O'Brien. Captain's busy. So's Woodhouse and Katz."

"Why'd he turn on the landing lights?"

"Electrical problem. A short."

A long silence. Then: "Anything *I* ought to know?"

"His alternators are cutting out. No sweat. I think he's going back to LAX."

"Will he make an announcement, sir?"

"Wait . . ." He paused for a moment. "OK, no announcement, not just yet. He says, serve 'em chow, but not up here, stay out of the cockpit, and smile."

Food should keep the flight attendants busy, and the passengers happy, too.

In Los Angeles Control Center, van Osten's supervisor glared at the PacLant blip. Every time they tried to call it, someone was blanking out the frequency with country music.

"Try raising her on Boulder City VOR. Then try Daggett!"

"Later, boss, there isn't time." For an awful moment van Osten thought the game was lost: The PacLant blip was showing 25,000, hurtling headlong into the UPS freighter, who was at 23,000: behind UPS, climbing through 21,000, was American 232 to Denver.

"I'm going to declare a 'no radio,' " the supervisor decided, "and clear out the whole L.A. Basin!"

An alarm on the console began to beep.

"Watch it!" screamed the supervisor.

Van Osten barked: "UPS, make an immediate right turn to zero-nine-zero. You have opposing traffic at your altitude! Climb to twenty-five!"

United Parcel came back: "One-two-one, roger."

The UPS blip sounded shaken, but van Osten was already working on the next one: "American Two-three-two—"

"Jesus, Van, there's *people* in that one," muttered the supervisor, as if he'd never thought of it. "Not just freight . . ."

Van Osten shot him a savage glance: American was a *blip*, just like all the rest. He pressed his mike. "American, immediate left to three-three-zero!"

Obediently, the little American star on his screen began to swing off course. The next one was TWA. Quick! Climb or dive? Right or left? Quick, quick, quick!

That one he dove. Then another TWA, right turn, then Delta for New York, but by this time UPS was inbound, miles off track, too close to Continental 406, for Denver.

His eyes began to ache. Blips or people, games or real, the damn-fool woman—or her captain—was trying to change the rules!

CHAPTER 37

In his workshop, as Monty Starbuck pressed his errant plank once more to the deck of his model, the phone rang again.

It was Frank Trout, Block's operations director, a new favorite of Junior's. Starbuck distrusted him and would have liked to pry his fingers from the corporate ladder.

Trout sounded shaken: "Monty, a security matter: we may have a hijacking. Flight 408, to Shannon."

He chilled, remembering Ruble's call. McCann? Impossible!

"Why a security matter? Is he squawking hijack?"

"No, emergency."

"Then it's not a security matter. Why call me?"

"Well, he won't answer Air Traffic Control, and he won't answer the *company* phone. He's a loose cannon up there, heading back to L.A."

Trout was obviously at Flight Ops: Starbuck could hear air controllers' transmissions in the background. "Now he's descending on the coastline, heading seaward!"

"Call Block!"

"Line's busy."

"That's his daughter, she's on it all the time. Use the red phone!"

"It doesn't answer." Trout cleared his throat. "Monty, *you* live out there. Could you run over there and tell him?"

Junior had a habit of killing the messenger. No way, sorry, Trout . . .

"I don't run so good," he pointed out. "Frank, the red phone's in his den. If he doesn't answer *it,* he isn't home."

"What'll we do?"

Not 'we,' Frankie-boy, your watch, not mine.

"Relax." He sat back in his wheelchair. "Maybe it's his landing gear, or a passenger having a baby. Throw in total radio failure, and there you are."

"There are half a dozen radios in that cockpit! Suppose you're wrong?"

"Then *you* got Block's red number, Frank. Keep punching."

Jeff Henlein was in trouble. The moment the plane had turned back, half the passengers in business class had noticed it. So Jeff handled his passengers in the PSA way: "Catch Our Smile." From his bag he produced a chef's hat to serve dinner, hoping to ease the strain.

But business class was a hard room to play. He got nothing but a few thin smiles, and more questions from a twitchy blonde up front.

Now, with the meal served, he called the cockpit again. Captain O'Brien answered. Henlein cleared his throat.

"Let me speak to the first officer, sir?"

"She's *busy,* Henlein."

"I know. But will she tell the passengers *why*?"

"Oh, hell! I'll do it myself!"

O'Brien's voice crackled from the cabin speakers, in a dry midwestern drawl: "This is Captain O'Brien. Captain Fremont would like to inform you that we have a minor electrical problem. We're returning to L.A. They'll fix us up and we'll resume our flight to Shannon. In the meantime, complimentary drinks for all. Thank you for flying the Path of the Panther, and thanks for your patience, too."

Henlein peered from the galley porthole. Already he could see the lights of the San Fernando Valley. Slowly, through the murk, appeared the tentacles of the Los Angeles freeway system.

Something was very wrong in their approach, and he wanted Laurie Woodhouse up here, where he could see her. He swung down the spiral staircase to first class.

Jackie Foley, the senior stewardess, was slamming dirty meal trays into the forward galley locker. "Hey, Hemline?"

" 'Henlein,' sweetie, OK? I'm gay, I'm not hilarious."

"What's the *real* god-poop? Why are they klutzing around over beautiful downtown Burbank?"

"I know no more than you do, gorgeous." He jammed his chef's cap on her head. "Where's Anne Woodhouse's kid?"

"Seat 28A." She ripped off the chef's hat and crammed it into the garbage. "Is it too late now to bid another flight?"

Anne had tumbled in the surf too long: now, lungs searing, she sounded for the smooth, golden sand below: better to drown on the bottom than to slam into the grinding, foaming rocks ahead.

She found a strand of kelp and clung to it. Her body flowed with the surge. When she sensed that the killer set had passed above, she relaxed her grip and began a long, strangled climb along a shard of golden sunlight . . .

She was all at once in the darkened cockpit of an airplane. From somewhere, she heard a flattened voice: "PacLant Four-zero-eight, this is Los Angeles Approach Control . . . Are you attempting an *approach*? PacLant! Do you read?"

Approach? To Shannon or L.A.?

The world went dark and slipped away again.

Jeff Henlein found Laurie Woodhouse sitting with Ian Corello, her face scrunched to the window. There was an empty seat between them. She turned from the window, blank-faced. "Hi, Jeff."

He hadn't seen her in a year. She'd be even prettier if she smiled more.

"Did you like your dinner, Laurie?"

"Not all that much."

"Sure, she must be starving again, by now," said Corello.

"I've got Dreyers ice cream in business class," Jeff told her. "Come up and try it?"

She flashed a smile. It was lovely. "That's cool."

As she released her belt, Henlein glanced out her window. Now they were over moonlit water, and low: six, seven thousand feet, he estimated.

Corello, standing up to let her out, looked at him strangely. "Something wrong?" he murmured.

Jeff shrugged. "Maybe."

"Then sure I'm coming too."

Leading them up the spiral staircase, Henlein felt a deceleration, then a gentle lift as the flaps groaned down. As they reached the top step, the landing gear ground into place with a brutal, final *thunk*.

Landing, then, for sure. But still no word to the cabin crew?

He had duties toward his passengers if anything was going wrong. He decided that he'd had enough secrecy from the cockpit: he'd make a real fast end to *that*.

Cal McCann crossed Los Angeles at ten thousand feet, descending seaward. Forty miles at sea, south of Los Angeles International Airport at six thousand feet, he flicked off the last of his VHF receivers, and the country music as well.

The silence was lovely. He unfolded his low-level Los Angeles sectional chart.

The 747 was descending over the water at a stately five hundred feet per minute. He had turned the plane back toward the city, dropped his flaps to dirty it up, and extended the landing gear. Its nose was up and its tail was well down. It was making only 160 knots true air speed. He peered ahead. The smog had cleared and the orange lights of the Los Angeles Basin stretched as far as he could see.

San Clemente Island, like a huge black log adrift, lay beneath his nose. Directly behind San Clemente, twenty miles toward the city, lay Catalina. Past Catalina, another twenty miles across San Pedro Channel, lay Los Angeles International.

Ordinarily, the landing lights of a long, thin stream of arriving aircraft would be trailing in to LAX, another chain departing—head-on—through the airspace he was in.

But there were no lights inching through the sky tonight.

Los Angeles Approach Control had cleared the basin, and shut the door on LAX as well.

He could see the garish floodlights on the dance pavilion in Avalon on Catalina already, twenty miles ahead. The cliffs of Palos Verdes, some forty miles away, were still a part of the jumbled coastline backlit by the Greater Los Angeles glow.

He glanced at his chart. On it, he had pinpointed Stanley Block's mansion on the Palos Verdes cliffs, sixty-two feet above the surf, at the end of Sundown Lane.

He had punched in all the way points on the INS. Now, hands carefully off the controls, he half-rose in his seat, watching San Clemente's Pyramid Head—latitude 33°03'1" North, longitude 118°43'3" West—as it slipped beneath the nose.

He had set the INS to cross it at exactly 5,000 feet, and this was his final check.

"Now!" he grunted, punching the clock on the instrument panel. He looked at the radio altimeter.

It read 5,010 feet: they had crossed ten feet too high.

Ten feet would hardly matter to Palos Verdes, when a quarter of a million pounds of jet-A fuel started the biggest barbecue on the cliffs since Nagasaki.

But he reset the inertial navigation system anyway. Airline flying was precision, and you might as well be right.

CHAPTER 38

Monty Starbuck, trying to force another flimsy deck plank into place, finally snapped it. Angrily, he rolled his wheelchair away from the workbench and stared out his workshop window.

He could not concentrate. He scooted to his workbench phone and called Flight Ops.

Against a background of radio calls, Trout seemed almost hysterical. "He's made a one-eighty. He's *east*bound, now, Monty, descending over water, southwest of Catalina—"

"*Catalina?*"

"—And he's down to four thousand feet! Inbound toward LAX!"

"Or *she*," murmured Starbuck. "There's a woman in that cockpit, too."

"Whatever." Trout was breathing hard. "I hope it *is* a hijacking, or they'll throw the whole damn company in jail! Monty, they're descending *downwind*! Wrong way up a one-way street!"

Starbuck hung up and rolled to the window. He lived only three blocks from the cliffs. Through the trees, in the faint moonlight, he could glimpse the silver water and the shadow of Catalina on the horizon, beyond the Block estate.

He spun his wheelchair from the window, sped to his workbench, and snatched up the phone. Block's red number was plastered on the wall above the drill press. He punched it in. The phone rang endlessly and finally he hung up.

They were probably upstairs in bed. He phoned Block's regular number. Busy: the daughter.

He started for the door, stopped, whirled, whipped back to his workbench, and called Block's regular number one more time. This time it was no longer busy. He let it ring until the terror gripped him; then he laid the phone on the workbench, sped from his workshop, and raced down the hall to the stairwell.

"Madge!" he screamed downstairs. "Get your car out front! We're going!"

"Why? When? Where?"

"Away from Palos Verdes! Now, let's go!"

He shot into his elevator and jabbed the button. Three blocks—*short* blocks—was too damn close already.

He hoped that he was wrong, but there was just no time to see.

Stanley Block, Junior, had been sleeping fitfully. He had awakened on the first ring, lunged for the phone, but missed. He tried again at the second ring and knocked over his bedside clock.

What time was it?

"Jesus!"

By the third ring, he had turned on the bedside light. He found the telephone and jammed it to his ear. "Hello?"

He heard nothing on the phone but the distant sound of a slamming door, then silence, though the line was open.

Now he was truly awake. "Bastard!"

"Who was it, Stan?" his wife muttered.

"The same asshole, probably. So he's got *this* number, too!"

"I showed you what to do," she murmured. " 'Night."

She was right. He unplugged the jack. Now he was restless. And horny. But she'd dropped off again already, or pretended to.

He got up and went to the bathroom. Then he stood at the open doors to the bedroom deck. The night was balmy and calm. He could hear the horses stamping in their stable and Sylvester pacing in his cage. He stepped outside and leaned on the railing.

The surf boomed below. He smelled night-blooming jasmine, and manure. The guard dog in the tack house began to bark.

There were no lights climbing out of LAX. He wondered why.

Cal McCann felt at ease in the captain's seat. If Junior hadn't fired him, by now he'd have been flying from the left-hand side for years.

Six miles ahead, Catalina Island spread before him, with Little Harbor snuggling under sawtooth ridges on its seaward side,

Home, sweet home . . .

The cove had been an Indian village, then a bootlegger's refuge. Now it was a smugglers' haven. In his dope-running days, he had flown in hash from Ensenada, air-dropped it here near Stolak's abalone boat, and flat-hatted, clean as a vestal virgin, back to San Diego for his Customs check.

The 747, flying on its autopilot, would pass over Little Harbor at precisely three thousand feet, and then sweep on past Mount Orizaba, across San Pedro Channel, descending toward the orange glow of Los Angeles spreading east.

He glanced at the clock on the panel. He had three minutes to get ready. He punched the stopwatch on his wrist, and slid from the captain's seat.

Looking down at Anne, he noticed that she had slumped sideways. He straightened her and sidled past Fremont's body. Katz was sprawled on the deck under the flight engineer's panel, the dart in his neck all askew.

He placed a foot on his chest and studied the panel above him. He jabbed the cabin depressurization buttons, and felt his ears pop.

He peered at his watch. Two minutes forty-three seconds to go . . .

He shrugged off his sport jacket and tossed it on the deck. He moved to the rear jump seat, where Mao sat stoically.

"Sorry, man." He unzipped the nylon zipper the sailmaker had sewed down its belly, from its chin to its furry crotch. From the panda, he pulled out the square-cut precision chute that he had used in skydiving.

In the sail loft, he had doctored it to get it through the airport's metal detector, removing its metal clips and snaps and refastening its risers with webbing on the sail loft's sewing machine. For the wire rip cord and its heavy steel handle he had substituted a strand of weed-eater nylon and a loop of duct tape.

Knowing he would be leaving the plane at 160 knots, he had rolled the nose of the chute when he repacked it, and doubled its rubber bands, to ease the shock when it opened.

Then he had gone to work on his harness, cutting the leg loops to remove the buckles, resewing the webbing, replacing his orange chest strap with white, so that it would not show through his shirt.

He had ended with a James Bond form-fitting torso harness. Getting in or out of it required contortions, but it had not a single piece of metal on it. He had worn it under his clothes quite comfortably all day long.

Now, standing over the captain's body, he unbuttoned his shirt, exposing the riser loops he had sewn in his chest straps. He'd replaced the snaps with Velcro strips. He attached the chute, smoothed down the Velcro, tested it with heavy jerks. All secure . . .

He glanced at his wrist. One minute thirty-seven, thirty-six, thirty-five . . .

He moved to the cockpit escape door in the fuselage behind the flight engineer's station. He grasped the red latch in both hands and exerted clockwise pressure. When he felt the latch move he eased off. At 160 knots, all hell would break loose from the slipstream, so he would wait as long as he could.

One minute twenty-eight seconds to go. He took a firmer grip on the latch.

One minute twenty-three, twenty-two, twenty-one . . .

The nervous blonde stared up at Henlein. "What's that island out the window? And why did my ears just pop?"

"I'm checking, ma'am. I'll let you know."

He seated Laurie in the window seat of the forward business-class row. "I'll get your ice cream, OK, sweets?"

Ian Corello sat down next to her. "I think something's really wrong," she told him.

They were the first words Henlein had heard her speak to the Irishman. Corello smiled: "Alternators? That's no problem, Laurie. They're like the one in your mother's Mazda, only bigger. You don't need them to fly."

Henlein brought each a dish of ice cream, stepped to the flight-deck entrance, and hesitated.

To enter the cockpit against orders, during a final approach, could cost him his job, but it had to be done.

He took a deep breath, inserted his key, and pulled open the door.

McCann, in the emergency door's recess aft of the flight engineer's station, saw the steward's silhouette as he closed the cockpit entrance. So he chopped at Henlein's neck as the steward stumbled over the flight engineer's body. Henlein dropped like a sack. McCann kicked him, automatically and swiftly, in the head.

While he writhed, McCann glanced at his watch. Twelve seconds until he opened the door, then one more minute to the island . . .

He took the red latch on the door and turned it gently until the seals popped, then set himself, yanked it fully open, and swung it aft into its stops.

When the hurricane slipstream struck it almost knocked him down. Moist night air screamed through the flight deck. The cockpit door ripped from its hinges and crashed against the business-class toilet bulkhead. An oxygen mask tore loose and slashed his face. Flight charts, Jeppesen approach plates, the captain's tunic on its hangar, Mao's empty fur, flew aft and out of the cockpit.

The captain's visored cap whipped past him through the cabin door. He heard passengers screaming and a cry of pain.

He peered out into the gale. The whole black night lay beneath him. In the moonlight he could see the wing, aft and far below, and the gaping intake of the starboard inboard engine. The whirling teeth of the turbine glittered in the moonlight. That air scoop, he must clear, and then the horizontal stabilizer . . .

He sensed motion behind him and whirled. The steward, blood pouring from an ear, was on his feet. McCann caught the glitter of a fire axe and felt a glancing blow on his ribs.

Awkwardly, Henlein swung the axe again, eyes bulging in fear. McCann grabbed its handle, yanked the steward toward him, stepped aside, and hurled him screaming into the void, axe and all. Frozen in a flash from the anticollision strobe, McCann saw him flailing at the air. Then the number three engine gobbled him with a *thunk* and a rending crash.

There was a blinding flare on the wing root as the turbo-blades gagged on bones and the fire axe and seized up with a screech.

The aircraft yawed as the right wing dropped. Then the autopilot, sensing the imbalance, leveled the wings.

The plane would continue on its sloping path, across the island and San Pedro Channel, to the cliffs of Palos Verdes on the mainland.

Fifty . . . forty-nine . . . forty-eight . . .

He faced the night, tensed to jump, a hand on each edge of the door. He sneaked a glance at his watch. Thirty-eight seconds. He began to chant: "Thirty-seven thousand, thirty-six thousand, thirty-five . . ."

He heard a wail of agony from the cabin: "Mommy!"

He froze at the voice. *Laurie?*

Impossible!

He had lost his cadence. He checked his watch. Thirty-one seconds. He resumed the chant: "Thirty thousand, twenty-nine thousand, twenty-eight thousand . . ."

"*Momm . . . ie . . .*"

This time the voice was right behind him. He turned his head.

Laurie, crawling into the flight deck, was breasting the gale. She stared up at him for an instant, wide-eyed, without a sign of recognition. Then she scuttled forward, between Katz's body and Fremont's, and lunged for her mother in the copilot's seat. "Mommy!"

On a flight to *Ireland*? What was she doing here? His first thought was to take her with him.

No: at 160 knots, the opening shock would break her in two, even if he could hang on.

There was nothing to do but land the plane at LAX, escape with Laurie in the confusion, and return for Block another day.

He lurched toward the left-hand seat, chute and all. He was clambering over Fremont's body when he caught a stunning blow on the back of his neck. He lost his balance and crashed against the pedestal. He whirled and dropped into a combat crouch, hands ready like blades, to chop or slice or blind.

The man towered, tall and rangy, against the glow from the cabin door.

Laurie screamed. The plane lurched gently, sending the big man off balance. McCann sprung, hands low and balled together, slamming them upward in an arc that started from the deck.

He caught his victim squarely in the testicles. The tall man grunted and staggered backward. His glasses clattered to the deck. McCann was on him instantly, hands at his throat, squeezing, crowding him toward the door.

The tall man arched and broke his grip. McCann found his wrists clasped tightly. The pressure was crushing his bones. He was slammed against the flight engineer's panel, then against the jumpseat.

Strong . . . Clumsy-strong . . . Farmer? Or a steelworker? Jesus . . .

He somehow ripped his hands loose, jabbed the naked blue eyes with stiffened fingers, and kneed the big man in his groin. The man roared a Gaelic oath and doubled over.

McCann was charging him when the huge fist, coming from nowhere, slammed his chute. The impact was so brutal that McCann felt it in the pit of his stomach.

Off-balance, spinning, he snatched for the side of the door, felt its icy edge, and missed his grip. He heard Laurie shriek and was suddenly hurtling backward into the night.

His ankle slammed the top of the dead engine. Lighted cabin windows flashed by. His head bumped the horizontal stabilizer, dazing him. He glimpsed the tail towering above him, and then he was whirling, flailing in the wake. He caught a whiff of hot metal, burning flesh, and blood from Number Three.

Instinctively, he arched his back and flung out his arms to either side, braking, belly down, stabilized and slowing. He found himself counting: *arch one, arch two, arch three* . . .

At the count of ten he estimated that he had slowed to a hundred knots. He yanked the rip cord.

The chute fluttered out, streamed above him in the moonlight, and jerked him to a stop.

His senses cleared. To the east, the 747's taillight skimmed Mount Orizaba and descended toward the coastal glow. In a moment it was out of sight, with Laurie, behind the island's spine.

"Pumpkin!" he howled after it, under the drifting stars.

He scanned the island. Fifteen hundred feet below, a half mile ahead, in Little Harbor, he spotted Stolak's abalone boat in the moonlight, still waiting for his drop.

As he watched, he heard her anchor windlass screech, then the grinding of her starter and the *puka-puka-puka* of her ancient Cummins diesel. Her running lights stayed off, but she was getting under way.

Stolak must have mistaken the roar of the 747 for a low-flying Coast Guard plane, and decided to haul ass.

Mind blank, McCann tugged a steering line, adjusted for a feeble crosswind, and swung gently in the moonlight, gliding toward the boat.

He could drop into a ten-foot bull's-eye four times out of five.

He didn't care if he lived or died, but there was no way he would miss.

CHAPTER 39

Anne felt Laurie's breath upon her neck. "Mommy, Mommy, Mommy . . ."

She heard Jackie Foley's voice, panicky and questioning, but could not make out the words. Then someone slammed shut the emergency door, and the flight deck grew quiet.

Faintly, she heard Ian's gentle brogue: "Go back to the cabin and buckle up, Laurie! Miss, take her back, please. Now!"

Then he was shaking her, hard. Clutching her neck, she opened her eyes. He was a huge, dark shape. She was in a cockpit, a 747 . . .

Her eyes fell on the panel before her, a puzzle of glowing dials and blinking lights. ENG OIL PRES, HYD SYS PRES, ALTITUDE ALERT, INST WARNING—PRESS TO RESET . . . Uncomprehending, she simply stared. BELOW G/S . . . INST WARN . . .

She had no idea what any of them meant. Who had the controls? The left-hand seat was vacant.

"Anne! Anne! *Darlin'!*"

She looked up. Ian's face drifted into focus. One of his eyes was a gory mess, and blood streamed down his cheeks. He was gripping her shoulder. "Got the door closed," he said hoarsely. "Think you've an engine on fire."

"Fire?" Her eyes roved the overhead panel, an occult hodge-podge of dials, switches, and amber eyes, taunting her in the dark. A bright red light was pulsing. She tried to focus on it. FIRE 3 PULL . . .

She recalled another cockpit, somewhere, and another fire. Gary! Where was *Gary*?

"Lass, we're going down!"

Her arms were paralyzed. Her eyes dropped to the altimeter. Two hundred feet? And descending? She struggled to sit erect, peering into the night. Ahead, she saw a path of moonlight on the water, and a surfline, under cliffs. She understood nothing.

"Anne!"

She found herself retching, strangling. The cockpit went gray.

He shook her again, even harder. "*Anne!*"

She came to and grabbed for the controls. Her arms were wooden, the yoke rock-steady, unyielding. Autopilot on? She found the button on her yoke and punched it off.

Where was Gary? What had happened to Ian's eye, and why was he up here?

The plane slewed wildly. She groped for the rudder pedals with her feet, heavy as lead.

Her eyes slid across the panel. Dimly she remembered a fire light. She flicked her eyes upward. A red light winked. FIRE 3 PULL.

She throttled back Number Three Engine, flipped the start switch off, then reached up and yanked the Number Three fire handle, cutting off fuel and hydraulics to the engine. She dumped its CO_2 bottle, but the blinking light continued. She had failed.

The plane began to wallow. *Add power* . . . She slid the remaining throttles forward. The plane slewed wildly. She fought to keep her wings level.

One hundred-fifty feet, and still descending.

"You ditching it, Anne?" Ian asked quietly.

"*Ditching* it?" She peered ahead. The radiance told her they were approaching a city. Not Vegas, or Shannon, so where were they? Over ocean? Los Angeles?

She saw cliffs a mile ahead. She tried to trade what speed she had for altitude, milking every foot, but still they sank. She fire-walled the throttles, jamming them to their forward stops. A hundred feet, ninety, eighty . . .

She reached up to the overhead panel and flicked on her landing lights, to better see the bluffs. The cliffs leapt into bright 3-D, hardly half a mile ahead.

Palos Verdes? How had they got to *Palos Verdes*?

The world grew gray again. She was slipping under, going, going, going . . .

"Anne!" Ian shouted. "Stay with us, lass!"

Her eyes snapped open. The world jumped into sudden focus, in reds and greens and yellows.

She saw three green lights on her panel: the landing gear was down, flaps too!

On three engines?

No wonder she couldn't climb!

Stanley Block stood transfixed by the sound of surf below his bedroom porch. Twenty miles across the San Pedro

Channel, Catalina slumbered by moonlight, but there was no sleep for him here.

A horse whinnied from his stable. The guard dog was barking in frenzy and had the panther rumbling, and now he had the horses restless too.

Suddenly the panther roared.

A zoo, a goddamn zoo! Tomorrow he'd move to the desert until the labor talks were done.

All at once he saw an aircraft's running lights, red and green, skimming in across the channel, very low. A fighter plane, checking something in the water?

Now he could hear the thunder of its engines rise above the surf. Not a fighter, an airliner! For a crazy instant he thought that the pilot had gone insane, was bound for him alone.

Then its landing lights came on, throwing porch, stable, trees into blazing black-and-white. The roar of its engines squeezed his guts.

He bolted back to the bedroom. "Dotty! Get out!"

The house was trembling on its foundations. A downstairs window rattled. He shook his wife and her bedside lamp fell with a crash. She shrieked and scrambled from the bed, teeth shining in the awful glare.

Passing his daughter's room, he roared: "Marjorie! Out!" There was no answer. He darted in, found her huddled under her blankets, hauled her out, all anger and balled fists. He shoved her toward the staircase.

Anne fumbled for the landing-gear handle. Dead ahead in her landing lights loomed a stark-white cliff, a mansion with a stone chimney above its red-tiled roof, out-buildings, Bougainvillea. She had seen it somewhere, once . . .

Block's!

She yanked up the landing gear. A hundred feet aft of her seat and thirty feet below her, the sixteen massive main wheels began to rise, with a groaning vibration she could feel through the controls.

Time slowed. They were going to hit the house. There was nothing she could do, but she found herself tugging at the gear handle, as if to hurry the gear.

When she felt a distant concussion, a little aft and far below, she knew that the nosewheels had struck the chimney.

Stanley Block dove for the sheepskin rug in front of his enormous fireplace. His wife and their daughter were crouched inside.

He heard a crash upstairs, and the wail of grinding metal. The home shuddered. Soot belched from the chimney, turning his wife and daughter into coughing, blackened apparitions cowering on the hearth.

A two-hundred-pound nosewheel, torn off, hurtled fifteen feet above their heads, removing an interior wall, his den, a three-foot-thick plaster exterior wall, and the guard shack at his gate. The other nosewheel detached the stable's roof, showering the Arabian geldings with Palos Verdes tile, killing the guard dog, but somehow sparing Juan, his stable hand.

Block had no inkling of this damage, nor that his mansion was now a bungalow, for he had turned feral, burrowing under the rug like a panicked fox.

Dotty was right: here by the fireplace, you could still smell Morningstar's blood.

The plane slithered to the right as Anne fought to control the yaw. She felt a final jolt from back aft; nose up, tail down, they had clipped the mansion's chimney and its gatehouse.

Now that her nosewheels were gone and the sixteen main mounts retracted, she was holding her altitude, skimming homes and tree tops, but slewing always to the right, lurching toward two-story buildings in Palos Verdes Village.

Panicked, she yanked up the nose.

The stall warning sounded and the stick-shaker began to jerk at her yoke. She rolled in trim tab: too much, she was stalling!

A gentle hand on the controls, Danny had said. Carefully, she eased some trim tab off, regained her airspeed. She had her leg jammed full length against the left rudder pedal, and her left thigh was tiring fast. She fought to keep the nose up. They were skimming the two-story buildings now, brushing a tall eucalyptus.

Ian still clung, standing, to the arm of her chair. When they crashed, he would become a projectile. She jerked her head toward the captain's seat. "Get *in* there and buckle up!"

She realized all at once that he was blinded. "Your eyes! What happened?"

"Not to worry, he's gone." He felt his way into the captain's seat and groped for the seat belt. The plane was slewing again.

"Gone?"

"Out the door."

"It was McCann," she said.

"My God!"

"Now, help me," she grunted. "Left rudder!"

In the dim light she sensed that he was feeling for the pedal with his foot.

"Both feet," Anne yelled. "I'm cramping! Left pedal. *Both* your *feet*!"

They were suddenly past the peninsula of Palos Verdes, sliding over Torrance. A power pole flashed below.

She grabbed for the audio panel. Three clicks, and she was on the emergency frequency.

"This is PacLant Four-zero-eight on one-twenty-one point five. Does anybody read me?"

CHAPTER 40

In moonlight at two hundred feet, gliding downward toward *Wet Dream*'s stern and overtaking her fast, McCann clearly saw Stolak put binoculars to his eyes. Their lenses flashed with silver as they zeroed on his chute.

McCann waved cheerily. He was almost home: Stolak, anticipating a dope drop, would be caught off-balance until he could dig the .45 from the life raft, blow out his brains, and head for Mexico.

"Hi, Top," he called down. "I had a little change in plans."

"You might say that, Lieutenant, yeah." The Top's voice drifted up clearly on the night air.

McCann had expected shock, and disbelief, but the Top was lounging carelessly, one hand on the scarred and battered wheel. Strange . . .

At thirty feet, McCann jerked his left steering line to line up with the wake. "The dope's on the next elevator," he called down. "Cargo chute, thirty keys, and coming down!"

At twenty feet, he shifted his weight in his harness, bent his knees. He would spill his air as he reached the stern, enveloping Stolak in silk, and snatch the automatic before he shed his harness. A piece of cake.

He stiffened in his chute. Stolak was reaching into his waistband, and McCann saw his own .45 in his hand. Stolak, eternally fussing with his boat and gear, had found the gun!

The automatic was suddenly on him, tracking. He saw everything in deadly clarity, black and white. He squirmed and twisted, swinging, to escape the deadly muzzle.

The gun went off twice. He felt the second round whisper past his ear.

"*Ain't* no cargo chute, Lieutenant," called Stolak from below. "You are all the dope there is."

"Top!" he shouted. "Look, I—"

"*Sayonara*, Lieutenant."

Another blast, and then another. His shoulder turned to flame. The next slug missed.

The gun roared again. He felt a locomotive blow to his stomach and fire through all his veins. The next round shattered his thigh.

The eighth round blasted into his chest as he hit the water, and the last sound he heard was *Wet Dream*'s screw, whining down the corridors of time.

Anne, fighting for air speed, climbed carefully toward the Seal Beach VOR, and tried her radio again: "Does anybody read me on one-twenty-one point five?"

A voice, edged with anger, crackled on the speaker: "Affirmative! This is Los Angeles Approach Control!"

She could see Los Angeles International, past Ian, out her left window. She assessed her situation. To belly-flop on the runway at LAX would probably tear her fuel-loaded wings from their roots and kill them all.

But the engine-fire light was still flickering. If she headed to sea and dumped her fuel, it would take another hour. If the engine flared again as they dumped, they'd go up in a sheet of flame.

"Approach Control, we had a hijacker. He's gone. I request a runway at LAX, wheels up."

"Have you dumped your fuel? Stand by!"

"I *can't* stand by, I've got a fire. I'm coming in."

"Negative!" There was a note of hysteria in the controller's voice. "Request denied! Dump and proceed to Edwards Air Force Base!"

She ignored the order: Edwards, near Palmdale, was too far.

There was no time for them to foam the runway, but there were other measures she could ask for: "I'd like local hospitals notified. I want all emergency equipment rolling." She put down her mike and picked up the cabin phone.

"Senior flight attendant," answered Jackie Foley.

"We're landing wheels up at L.A."

"I figured, boss."

"I want the cabin prepared for an emergency landing."

"I did that, when we hit whatever it was."

"When the aircraft stops, go into an evacuation drill *without* command!" They might both be dead, in the cockpit.

"OK."

"Now, take my daughter downstairs and sit her by the forward exit door. No matter *what* she says."

"I did. She's down there now, in a stewardess seat, strapped in and facing aft."

"She's *not* to try to wait for me."

"She'll be the first one down the chute, Woodhouse, I promise."

Anything else? Yes ...

"Good luck, Jackie, you're a pro."

"Good luck, Anne. You are too."

Her throat tightened. If she began to cry, she was lost.

"Anne!" Ian's voice was muffled. "If anyone *else* were flying this bloody bird, I'd be wishing I'd followed that murdering bastard out the door."

"You may wish you had, yet," she said tightly. "Ian, I'm scared."

"Not to worry, darlin', we'll be fine."

Kurt van Osten, in the Los Angeles Center in Palmdale, had been regularly relieved at his console an hour ago, but now he hovered behind the angry approach controller. He watched Flight 408's blip approaching the threshold of Los Angeles International on the controller's scope.

"You going to clear her to land?" he asked the approach controller suddenly.

"With fuel for Ireland? No! She'll blow up LAX."

"She won't make it to Edwards with a fire!" van Osten pointed out.

"But she forgot the buzz word, didn't she?" flared the approach controller. *"She never declared an emergency!"*

"So remind her!" Van Osten began to shake.

"Is this *your* goddamn scope, or mine?"

The approach controller was bigger than van Osten, who had killed giants and dragons on video but had never raised his hand against another human being.

But now, he moved swiftly. He ripped the headset off the other man and talked into the mike.

"Four-oh-eight! Are you declaring an emergency?"

"My God *yes*, it's an emergency," said the woman. "Look, I'm turning base. I request a long, straight-in final, and clearance to the tower!"

"Roger," said van Osten. "Cleared to runway two-four right, and you *are* cleared to the tower."

"Van Osten!" cried the controller. "I report this, you're *outta* here!"

Van Osten handed him back the mike-boom and walked away. He might be driving a diaper truck this time next week, but rules weren't everything.

She reached across the cockpit to Ian's shoulder straps and tested them for tightness. He was holding his hand over his eyes: blood was oozing through his fingers.

Dead ahead, under the enormous nose, past the sprawling city streets, fire trucks, cherry pickers, and ambulances raced from the terminal toward the lighted runway, red lights blinking.

She gave herself thirty degrees of flaps, and socked onto her final approach at a fast 155 knots, carrying excess airspeed for its lift.

She passed over the jammed, unheeding San Diego freeway, aiming at the touchdown marks a thousand feet from the near end of the runway.

The plane felt sluggish and very tired. She wrestled with panic. She had never landed a plane so heavy: maybe nobody had. And on its belly?

The fire warning light began to flicker again. Not now, please God, not now . . .

She tore her eyes from the touchdown marks to snatch a glance at her altimeter.

Sixty feet off the ground, fifty-five . . . She eased off

her power, gently, and heard the jets wind down. She was floating, now, with ground effect.

She had to get down, down, down . . . She reached out and popped her speed brakes—just a hair—to open the spoilers on the wing.

Thirty feet . . . twenty-five . . . no wheels and so no contact yet . . . twenty . . .

There was a sudden, awful roar from somewhere behind her, down below, and then she was riding on her inboard engines, sliding, scraping, grinding them to dust . . .

"Ian! Off that pedal!" She fought the rudders to stay on the center line. The roar of tortured metal was unceasing, they were hardly slowing down.

If she tried reverse thrust, she'd tear off her wings. As her speed slowed, her rudder lost bite, and she had to fishtail more and more to control the sliding plane. Her thighs began to cramp.

She glanced at the airspeed: Ninety knots . . . eighty . . . seventy—hell, she drove this fast on the freeway—sixty-five, sixty . . .

But speed was control, and at fifty knots, she lost it all. She could only sit and watch, gripping the yoke as the monster, unleashed, left the runway and headed for a fire truck.

The left wing root struck the cab of the truck. The aircraft pirouetted in a giant, stately arc, whipping her against her window. With a last, evil swing, the fuselage slid backward through a chain-link fence and into a parked L-1011 with the Delta logo on its tail.

In the cockpit, there was a moment of silence. She heard running footsteps behind the cabin door. The smell of fuel was everywhere, and burning metal. The fire-warning light continued to wink.

Swiftly, she reached up, flipped the red safety cover on the evacuation panel, and flicked the switch. The "evacuate" horn began to warble throughout the plane: *baa . . . baa . . . baa . . .*

She switched her phone to PA: "Evacuate the aircraft."

She retracted the speed-brakes—passengers scrambling out through over-wing exits could trip on them and fall fifteen feet to the tarmac. She pulled the remaining fire-handles and fired the extinguishers. Then she hustled Ian past Gary's body, and Katz's, on the flight-deck.

She smelled smoke in the upper cabin. Business class seemed deserted, a shambles of blankets, pillows, newspapers, but she still must check it out. She heard shouts outside, and footsteps on the wing. She left Ian at the head of the staircase and raced down the aisle. OK. Toilets? Empty.

She steered Ian down the spiral staircase, made him sit in the forward emergency door, and shoved him down the chute: they would catch him at the bottom. Then she ran aft, checking every seat.

A siren wailed outside. The smoke was thicker now. She checked the cabin-crew bunkroom, the toilets, and found them clear. By the time she had finished, her eyes stung and her chest burned and the cabin was full of acrid, blinding smoke.

She groped for the rearmost exit door, sat down, and slid down the after chute, expecting helping hands at the bottom. Instead, she found herself sprawling alone on the concrete in a two-inch pool of jet fuel, coughing in the fumes. The flight attendants tending the bottom of the chute had already left.

Suppose they'd left up forward, too? Ian couldn't even see!

The tarmac glittered with fuel. Clouds of black, oily smoke were drifting back from the number three engine. She could not see the wings, but the nose of Delta's L-1011 lay crumpled on the macadam like a giant aluminum beer can.

There was no one anywhere, although she could hear shouts from firemen somewhere forward. A hook and ladder crept from the smoke, gushing foam along the fuselage. An asbestos-suited fireman on the rear step shouted down at her: "Cabins clear?"

"Everybody's out." She pointed forward: "A tall man? Blinded? He can't see!"

"Nobody! Just get away from the goddamn airplane, lady, now!" He jerked his thumb toward the glow from the emergency vehicles on the taxiway. "Get out! There's nobody up there!"

Spewing foam, the truck rounded the tail and she lost sight of him in the smoke.

She couldn't take his word for it. She sloshed forward through hot jet-A; it filled her shoes and burned her calves.

She could see flames, now, reaching over the fuselage from the right wing.

"Ian!"

Nothing.

"Ian! Are you still here?"

She thought she heard a shout.

"Ian?" she screamed. "I'm here!"

She froze, listening. Nothing . . .

Then she heard his voice: "Anne?"

Like a wraith he appeared from the billowing clouds, covering his eyes with one hand, groping with the other.

She was leading him in a shuffling dogtrot toward the amber light on an ambulance when PacLant 408 blew up with a roar, taking the rest of the L-1011 with it and breaking every window in Delta's hangar.

The concussion hurled them to the ground. He held her close and covered her with his body while the debris rained down, and neither of them even got a scratch.

CHAPTER 41

Anne sat alone in liquid Irish sunlight on the grass by the water, her back braced against the trunk of a sweeping Dutch elm.

Ian's family home lay on the curving banks of the Liffey, near Lucan, five miles from Dublin. Over the generations, it had grown from a single farmhouse with a thatched roof into a tiny squiredom.

The thatched cottage was still there, with a centuries-old stone landing on the river, a boat shed for his racing scull, a rose garden, a stone barn, and a lawn like a putting green sweeping down to the emerald waters.

The rough-hewn lintel over the old cottage's door was so low that even Anne had to duck when she entered. Last night they had let Laurie sleep there, in a wooden bunk under the eaves, all by herself.

But a larger, liveable home lay between the farmhouse and the barn—now used as a garage—built by his great-grandfather in the first days of the Irish Free State.

Ian, whose parents had died in the '70s, rented the place to a German couple for the summer, while he lived in his Dublin flat. His tenants had just left.

"I wanted you to see it, both of you," he'd said last night, after she'd tucked Laurie into the age-old cot. "A sanctuary, in the Land of Time Enough."

She needed no haven now, at least from McCann. Two weeks ago, boaters had found his body, free of his chute, on the rocky seaward shore of Catalina. Someone had shot him: no one knew why.

It was worse than anyone had known. Ruble, before he died, had somehow discovered that McCann had tried to kill her—and poor Gary—on Christmas Eve: sabotage, was the verdict, and Danny Cable was home free.

"A sanctuary, from *what*?" she'd asked Ian. "He was worse than we thought, but he's gone."

"From the North Atlantic run, perhaps? From jet lag? Bill collectors? Sure, Anne, you bloody *need* a place to rest. It's here," he'd said, "in forty shades of green."

Now the tree above her rustled gently, preening itself in the sunlight. Cottonball clouds raced east. She heard Ian's voice singing, and the creak of oarlocks.

She looked toward the bend in the river. Ian and Laurie were skimming toward her in the little varnished dinghy that he tied to the dock.

When they had left, he was kneeling before Laurie, guiding her hands on the oars. Now he was draped in the stern and she was rowing in long, smooth strokes, as if she'd been born on a Viking galley.

She rested on her oars and turned. Her voice piped across the water. "Mom! We saw a *leprechaun*!"

"I don't believe it!"

Ian wore a piratical red eyepatch on his left eye. He'd spent a week in the infirmary, and awaited an artificial eyeball: Irish health services were slow. But his right eye was quite all right.

Anne walked down to the quay, in time to fend them off and secure their line.

"We saw one," Laurie insisted. "We really did."

"Lives around the bend in a hollow tree," Ian nodded. "Rings the bells of Lucan Church." He glanced at the sun. "He'll be ringing them any moment, now."

As if he were a wizard, bells began to chime from the steeple at Lucan, visible in the distance above the nodding trees.

"How did he get up there so fast?" scoffed Laurie.

"He flies."

"Come on!" said Laurie. "How'd you *know* they'd ring?"

"We know, we're a magic race."

"Yes," said Anne. "You are."

Carefully, he slid the oars from the oarlocks, and shipped them by the gunwales. He smiled at Laurie and looked up at her. "And the two of you? Mere mortals? Do you think you'd like to *join* us, now?"

Anne stared at him. He meant it. "PacLant—"

"Is a bloody rotten airline. You're a heroine of the skies. AerLingus and BOAC have left-hand seats too, you know. And you'd be living here in Lucan, on the Liffey, with the little chap around the bend."

Laurie's gold-flecked eyes were on her, waiting. She tried to read them, but could not.

"Laurie?"

The eyes were unwavering: She would get no help from those eyes, nor the bells: bells had chimed in Vegas, too.

"Anne?" he urged her softly, from the boat.

She took a deep breath. "Yes, we'd like to join you. We'd like that very much."

Laurie twisted suddenly and dived into the water, knifing back across the river toward the bend.

"Oh, Ian," she murmured. "I knew it! Too damn *soon!*"

"Sure, and I think you're wrong," he muttered. "Wait!"

Midstream, Laurie stopped. Treading water, she raised her head and sent a yell of triumph echoing from the banks. She churned around the curve of the river and was gone.

"She'll scare him fair away, she will," said Ian, climbing from the dinghy.

The bells of Lucan trailed them to the house.

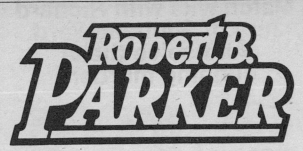